CHAPTER ONE

'I remember it as clear as if it was today. I was just a little girl back then, not old like I am now. I hadn't even become a beautiful young woman at that point. I was just a young girl of only six and a half. We lived in one of the new houses near the town hall away from the seafront you see. We had the quarry nearby which meant it was a bit cheaper for my dad who had moved us there for his work. He was a strong man, a strong and loving man. Or at least that is what I remember. My other memories of him have become softer with time, I wasn't much past thirteen when he was killed. But this day stays with me as if it had only happened this morning. I was barely coming of age when he left my mother and me to fend for ourselves. Not that it was his fault.

Anyway I remember it as I had been sent down to the bakers to buy bread for our picnic tea and the town was bustling. I mean it was a big month anyway that summer. You see the King was coming to officially start the work on the library a few weeks later and it was really pushing life into the little place. We called the town our little secret, hidden away from the rest of the world. That is why it would lend itself to being a haven in the wars that would follow. Anyway I remember almost falling over myself seeing big expensive the cars coming through the town and I knew then it was a special day. I got the loaf and walked back to our home. Walking up the steps to the door straight off the road I remember the warmth as the sun shone through into the kitchen whilst my mother boiled the eggs on the stove ready to make picnic sandwiches for later. We would then go to the beach for tea as my dad liked to do every Wed-

3

nesday evening to celebrate getting through the middle of the week, sometimes even in the winter. But today was about to get very different indeed.

My father burst into the front door leaving it open behind him and scampered into the kitchen. I remember him calling my name out loud. *Gladys* he shouted. *Gladys!* He told me to get my sun hat and meet him at the door immediately. He was as excited as I had ever seen him. Quickly I ran up the wooden stairs and grabbed my hat before meeting him at the door as my mother made her way from the kitchen. Grabbing my hand he pulled me almost off my feet and back down the stone steps onto the street. Quickly we made our way to the promenade through the streets following others who seemed as excited as my father. As we walked he praised the weather and the miracle that was the natural world. I was pulled along with my poor mother following behind trying to make herself look present-able. I didn't know what I was about to see. He hadn't told me. I am not sure if it was just due to him being so excited or if he wanted to keep it a surprise but certainly in the five months we had lived in the town I had not seen anything so unexpected in my life.

We arrived on the promenade overlooking the bay and the sun was beaming down welcoming us to the sea front. There were more folk than ever before all trying to make their way to the beach. I was so busy looking at all the people and back to check on my poor mother that I didn't see them at first. As we got to the crowd I looked up at people who were pointing and chattering but I could not see as I peered up to witness my father shrilling with pleasure. I asked him what it was as he turned to lift me. Squinting in the sun I was unsure at first but then I heard the magnificence of its trumpet when it called out with such glee, a feeling my dad was reflecting back at it. I stared in disbelief as I saw something I had only read about in books and had only seen before in a poster for the circus. Frolicking in the sea as happy as any bathers were the most beautiful crea-tures I had ever seen to that day and have ever seen since. As if they belonged there with the bathers was a herd of elephants. I had never seen such a thing and was so happy I clapped with pleasure as my father held me above his shoulders before moving us forward through the crowd. My poor mother was left up at the promenade as father took me down to the water's edge so we could stand with others looking in amazement and awe.

They were so large and powerful but played like children splashing and laughing as they enjoyed the cool of the water on the hot summer's day. The crowd indulged in the free treat for a long while as the press collected photographs of the elephants. They were from Bostock and Wombell's Menagerie who were touring the Welsh coastal towns making the most of the wealthy holiday makers from the big cities of England and from the mining towns of Wales. Some men couldn't help but swim up to them and try to jump on their backs. Luckily they were tame but a few men fell into the water triggering laughter from the crowd. I can still feel the breeze on my face and the spray in the air as if I was only six years old again. That was the most happy memory I have from my childhood. That day put the town on the map and I stood with my dad as the elephants came out of the water showing their full size. I fell in love that day'.

CHAPTER TWO

David Jones sat in the back of the black taxi cab anxiously looking at his watch whilst listening to his girlfriend's phone ring out as the car pulled into their long narrow road. Jigging his legs with the pressure of needing to catch the train on the hour he sat looking from his cab at the road works that would slow his progress. Running his hands up and down his thick brown hair which hid his stressful career better than his neatly groomed beard that showed the tell tale signs of aging, he made a decision. Leaning forward he tapped on the window to speak to the driver.

'Listen up mate, let me out here. By the time you get up to the house I will be coming back out of the front door with the paperwork I need'. The driver turned as he continued with only thin wisps of his accent remaining. 'If my girlfriend has realised I left my papers she probably will have them ready for me, okay'?

With a nod from the front of the car David jumped out onto the pavement. He marched down the street with pride and expectation of himself as he looked at the fine frontages which his splendid road in Chislehurst had to offer. He had done well for a boy from Wales, he had made it. Most people he grew up with had not even ventured from their hometown and they were doing well for a couple living in London for only a few years. They were successful and renting a semi-detached three bedroom house with a driveway on a road with trees lining it. In the capital this was as much confirmation of that as he needed. Thinking of his bank balance which was almost at the point of being able to put a deposit down to buy one of these houses when one appeared on the market made him smile further. Striding forward in his long black overcoat which he had put on dubious of the Welsh weather he should be heading into, he felt felt strong in his shirt and tie. He could have got changed before leaving but his designer clothes would show his brothers how well he was doing. Turning into his drive way he shrugged off the smart sports car that was blocking the exit as he didn't need the car and most likely it was just an inconsiderate neighbour. Pushing the key into the door he quickly turned the latch and heard music upstairs explaining why Kelly hadn't answered her phone which he soon found in the living room. *She would be doing her workout in the gym upstairs before she headed to work* he thought smiling as he saw her phone and quickly made his way through to the conservatory where he picked up his paper work. Quickly sticking it into his leather satchel he headed towards the door and looked out to see the taxi still had not made its way up the road. He quickly turned slipping his shoes off before making his way up the plush thick cream carpets lined stairs. Even in his need to hurry he realised she would not be pleased at him for treading mud onto them. As he climbed the stairs he heard her laughter making him smile. He loved her laugh. Pushing the bedroom door open to the sound of music he was confused to see the bed was not made and several clothes were scattered around, some of which he didn't recognise as his own. Walking passed the bottom of their bed he passed the speakers which had two half full wine glasses with his favourite Merlot bottle next to them. Pushing the en-suite door open his eyes met first with the naked stranger in the shower who held Kelly in his arms. As the man's face changed it took a few seconds of confusion before she stopped giggling and turned looking in shock back at David.

Feeling numb David watched silently as she slid the shower door open before covering her toned and tanned body with a towel and grabbing another to wrap her long blonde hair in. Not watching her David just stared feeling completely inferior at the naked man who had a much more muscular physique than

7

him but less hair, on his head at least. The two men both seemed embarrassed and unsure of whom was in the wrong.

'David, I thought you would be at the station by now'?A shaky Kelly softly said coming forward to hold his hand whilst looking upwards lovingly at him from her petite frame.

'I forgot the papers'. David answered calmly not looking at her, knowing it would crush him. Choosing the lesser of two evils he continued to stare at the man who was so much more physically superior to him. 'Did you meet him at the gym'?

'David, listen to me. You shouldn't have seen this'. Her guilt ridden voice almost made him want to tell her it was his fault and apologise for intruding. 'It's not what you think'.

'He is a specimen, I see what you see in him'.

'David, look at me'. Kelly stroked David's face moving his gaze down towards her eyes where he looked at her beautiful face now enhanced by the water glimmering off her skin. 'I love you, this was just a thing thats all'.

David's face started to crack under the pressure he was now feeling inside as he looked down at the neckline he loved so much avoiding her eyes which somehow made him feel guilty. Suddenly distracted by the sound of the taxi's horn from outside he made a snap decision.

'I am on the meter, I had better go now'. Calmly he stepped back looking forward at the naked man who was now standing half in the cubicle and half out waiting to see what would happen. 'Nice to meet you'. David turned as Kelly clung to his hand. Pulling away he felt his heart tear in two but he could not look at her again. Walking passed the speakers he pushed the wine bottle over getting some cheap gratification that the deep red liquid was seeping onto the carpet. Grabbing his bag as he stepped out onto the street where the wind was picking up he felt the coldness of the sweat now covering his body as he climbed into the taxi.

Charlotte Davies kissed her lips forward as she applied her dark red lipstick which enhanced her strong brown eyes and finely defined eyebrows. Standing inspecting herself in her blue dress she shifted her body stance to double check her features were as clearly on display as possible, tugging down on her dress to ensure her cleavage was easily visible for any red blooded male to see. Deciding to free her dark brown hair she pulled out the clip and shook her head giving her a more playful look. Making her way down the corridor of the bungalow she sneaked passed the living room where she could hear her Nanna giving him a history lesson as she ventured into the kitchen. Placing the bread into the oven she turned in the limited space to put the coffee on and took some mugs out of the traditional oak Welsh dresser. Standing she looked out onto the yard nervously as she waited for the inevitable to happen.

Within minutes Trevor Thomas came bumbling into the room as she had anticipated. Giving it a few moments she gave his eyes long enough to wonder down her backless slimline dress. Turning slowly using her best smile to cover the disgust at the desperate bloated sweaty man she saw in front of her. With hardly a hair left on his head she found it hard to believe he was less than ten years her senior. She tried to stop her mind floating back to their night together. She only had herself to blame using him to find out what it was like. For her a voyage of underwhelming discovery, but for him a few minutes that would set his heart alight. Back then she found him annoying but now she was approaching thirty she found it quite repulsive that he was the only eligible bachelor left in the village. It was times like this that she wished she would have left ten years ago when she had the chance, but as her friends moved on she stayed faithful to her Nanna and wanted to ensure she was looked after in her own home. Looking at the floor she registered his less than polished shoes before moving up the cheap nylon trousers and the multi-pack mass produced thin white shirt which allowed her to see the dark areas of his nipples clear to anyone who had the misfortune of standing too close. It wasn't his large stature that repulsed her so much rather than his inflated ego which she could see shining out of his bulging sweaty dark ringed eyes.

'Charlotte'! He cheered with his arms parting in a movement of anticipation.

'Trevor'! She responded in her best attempt at hiding the nauseous uprisings as she looked at the sweat patches under his arms. Reaching forward spreading her arms she moved towards him as he launched himself into her like a little child. Feeling awkward with the the small five foot man now resting his head on her chest she pulled back but just felt the pull of his sweaty paws on the open back of her dress. After a few more moments of uncomfortable hugging Charlotte pushed backwards smiling pitifully as he looked up at her lovingly.

'Coffee Trevor'? She asked with smile.

'Oh no I shouldn't really. You see I am on a diet. Getting back to my fitter days when I was in the rugby team you see', he smiled impressed with his own expected body improvement.

'Right then, well I suppose I won't keep you then'. Charlotte moved to the kitchen door to open it in the hope he would call the visit finished but knew his decision was about to completely flip.

'Well now. I suppose if you want some company. It is only the gentleman thing to do having a coffee with you as you asked so kindly', he nervously backtracked pulling out the chair next to him for Charlotte to sit on.

Charlotte poured a coffee for him and made herself a glass of water before sitting in the chair opposite from him across the small dining room table, ignoring his seating suggestion. Taking a long sip of water she was aware of him watching her every movement. Deliberately she delayed saying anything waiting for him to lose his nerve.

'Gladys, she can tell a story or two can't she? She still has got an imagination alright'.

'What do you mean'? Charlotte looked strongly at him.

'Well she still tells the stories we were told by her as kids. She thinks she was in Aberystwyth back in 1911. That would make her over one hundred years old'.

'Yes, one hundred and twelve to be precise'.

'What? Are you actually saying that is the true story behind all of this'?

'Well her memory isn't what it once was but she clearly has it edged into her head and how else could you explain this place'?

'Well it is a shame that these financial issues have come up then isn't it'?

'Yes she loves this place. It has been her home since long before I was born. She raised her own children here long before she adopted me'.

'Yes, you have never told me how she adopted you Charlotte. Do you remember coming here with them'? Trevor leaned forward with interest.

'No, look I think you probably should head off now Trevor'. Charlotte stood moving to the kitchen door avoiding his eye contact clear feeling uncomfortable by his question. 'It has been nice seeing you and I know you are taking Nanna to the doctors this Friday. I am really grateful, her chest and her arthritis seems to be getting a lot worst recently. She can't walk far no matter how much she may hide it. I can hear her pain in her breath. She hides it but I know she is suffering'.

'I am sorry Charlotte, I didn't mean for this to go badly'. Trevor sensed he hit a nerve realising in all the years he had known her she never mentioned her parents. Knowing he needed to pull it back, he refocused the conversation to something she needed his support in. 'I just thought we could talk about her position and your predicament'.

'Well you see I just don't understand what the problem is Trevor, she has lived here since 1911. The council have never been interested in the place before. Why now'?

'Well you see the council had the land on one hundred year lease. That expired years back and they were lenient. You know, I guess they didn't need the land but now they see an old lady who could do with being in a place she could be looked after and some pets who shouldn't be allowed to stop here'.

'But we cannot afford to move out Trevor, my wages at the pub barely cover the bills when we put it together with her pension and we still need to eat and feed them'.

'Look Charlotte, I love your Nanna very much but I feel this is not helping. The thing is this land could be built on and I am sure you could get a job somewhere else with an apartment very reasonably to live in'.

'She wont agree to that Trevor, you know that'. Charlotte looked intensely at him, giving him time for her wide eyes to trap him into her thought process. 'Is there not anything I could do to make you go to the council or that developer boss of yours and just give us some time? I would do *anything*'. Looking away coyly she felt the time freezing as she waited for his response. She hated herself for playing on his feelings. Feelings that were only one way but this was the only card she had left to play. Even for a man she didn't care for this felt so wrong. Just as she gave up she felt his hot sweaty hand rest on top of hers before looking up.

'Listen, why don't we go out for some food this weekend and we could talk about the situation some more and come to some sort of arrangement then'?

'Arrangement'? She couldn't help raise her eyebrows in question.

'Yes, I am sure between us we can agree over something. I will book us a table at Cloyster's for seven thirty'.

'Cloysters'? Sighed Charlotte. 'Do you not every wish you had left this place Trevor when you were younger? You know, traveled a bit and lived a little'.

Trevor laughed. 'On the contrary Charlotte. I have paid off my little house now and went away to the Costa Del Sol with my friends last year. I would say I have made it'. He laughed ending in a satisfaction fulled snigger sending shivers up Charlotte's back as he continued. 'And beside if I wasn't here then how would we be going out for dinner this Saturday night'?

'And this is enough for you is it? This small village where everyone knows everyone else's business. Don't you want to move away, get out of here and just be free'?

'No, I have got all I want here'. Smiled Trevor as again he placed his clammy hands over Charlotte's which she quickly retreated away.

'It's not enough for me', she sighed. 'Not any more'.

'But it must be enough Charlotte. You are a bright, attractive girl. If deep down you really wanted more you would have found it by now. Instead you have spent your life here with them'.

'I have thought about leaving, but I have to stay for Nanna'.

'That is just an excuse and you know it. She would have coped, she could get care, she has her biological family out there who could come back to help. You are still here because you did not want to leave really. If you did you would have left by now'.

'I need to do it don't I'? She found herself squeezing his hand now as a flutter of anxiety passed through her body.

'Nonsense Charlotte. You need to stop here with me. We would make a fantastic couple wouldn't we? Come on, I know you look at me and remember that night all those years ago'. He smiled making Charlotte feel more guilty about her false suggestions. 'What would you do anyway, where would you go? You can't just move somewhere without the appropriate financial planning'. Trevor smiled pushing up his fat eyebrows wrinkling the his forehead into three sweat fill gorges.

'I don't know I just want to be able to go to work and do a normal job where I can meet people and not have everyone know everything about you'.

'But in a big city you would just be a normal person Charlotte. In a few years nobody will even notice you as you get older and your looks fade. You will be lonely in a big town, people wont look out for you like I do. And besides, what job would you do really? You like it here living off the reserve and doing the occasional shift for cash in hand from the pub'.

'I don't know, I would love to work in a real bar or a coffee shop serving people and being in the center of their lives, where they meet and talk. Watching friends meeting for the first time in ages and sharing their stories. A place where people have time for themselves and for each other'. Charlotte smiled thinking of herself serving customers.

'You want to work in a cafe'? Trevor looked unimpressed back at her in an almost mocking fashion.

'I just want to work with people Trevor. More than the usual villagers who drink in the pub'.

'Why don't you work down at the Black Mine Cafe or Esther's Tea Room then'?

'Esther's Tea Room! I want to work somewhere pleasant. Not a trap for unfortunate hikers who think it might be quaint and then are too polite to think of an excuse and get out of there'.

'I think it it quaint'. Trevor smiled.

'Trevor! The doilies are yellow'. She snapped back in disbelief.

'They are rustic', he defended.

'They are stained and older than I am. It hasn't been cleaned properly since I was a child and they had a fire. Even the teapots are fire damaged'.

'See! There it is. The reason you cannot go and will not go anywhere'. He smiled knowingly as he stuffed some cake in his mouth.

'Why'? She placed her head in her hands showing her desperation.

'You know everything about this village and everyone in it. You are part of the furniture now. You belong here. Nowhere else would you know about Esther's burning down twenty years ago and the fire damaged teapots. You are a a small village girl quickly becoming a part of small village history. You belong here Charlotte and dare I say it'...

'What'? Charlotte lifted her head up and responded with growing frustration.

'You belong here with me'. Smiling from ear to ear at his newly found confidence from the financial predicament he knew she was in, he looked hopeful but purposefully at her.

'Have you not been listening. I need a change', Charlotte responded attempting to not follow his expectant attempt to have any false feeling of hope.

'I can give you that change, you can live with me in my house'. He said smiling and displaying the final bits of chocolate cake he had stuffed in his mouth.

The room went silent as Charlotte froze but acted coy in an attempt to buy her time and not to embarrass him from the awkwardness she had gotten them into with her suggestive tones. He did repulse her but grudgingly she felt a fondness to Trevor in that he was always keen to see her. But he was nothing but a narrow minded, self indulgent man who she shared no interest with and felt strained to stay polite to every time she met him. Her mind rushed through the predicament and how she could support her Nanna without being put in a very awkward position with him. As he looked over her stooping body across the table Trevor thought finally he had cracked the code to her vulnerability and she would have to accept he was the best man available. His thoughts were soon shattered by the door swinging open as Gladys walked into the room far more sprightly than he believed she could. Standing slightly obtuse she looked strong for a woman of her advanced years with only a walking stick to aid her. He knew it was a staged entry to show she was still capable of living without help but he didn't argue the point. Sitting at the chair he had moved to invite Charlotte, she pulled out a pack of cigarettes from her pinnie and quickly lit one up in front of him.

'Mrs Roderick! Do you not know how bad those thing are for your health? They can make your asthma even worse'. Looking at her he did not get the response he was expecting as after a brief look of anger towards him she simply smiled so he continued. 'They could kill you Mrs Roderick'.

'So could old age. And besides me tabs have never killed anyone'.

'Cigarettes are bad for you I am telling you'.

'Who says'? She effortlessly responded like a child winding up a teacher.

'Science'. He was flabbergasted as gestured his response to her using his hands to emphasise his point.

'Who is that'?

'The Government then', Trevor became increasingly flustered.

'They say cake and coffee is bad for you don't they'? Gladys questioned looking across the empty plate and cup he had just consumed.

'Yes but that is different'. He defended.

'How'?

'Cigarettes will kill you quicker'.

'Anything will kill me quicker, I am over 100 years old'.

'But they are dangerous'.

'No not me tabs'.

'Yes your cigarettes. Look at the packet, it says they may cause impotence and infertility'.

'Ooh I should still worry about that then'? She replied as Charlotte tried not to laugh.

'No they do other things too like heart disease, cancer and premature aging'.

'Oh dear'.

'You should stop smoking. You have smoked ever since I can remember'.

'But I like them', Gladys looked at the pack fondly like it was her medicine.

'You can live without them'.

'I have been smoking for 100 years I don't think I will stop now'. She shook her head.

'That's ridiculous, you would have been killed three times over by now'.

'The twelfth of November 1918'.

'What'? He looked at her with confusion but intrigue.

'When I had me first tab'. She nodded back at him.

'But you were just a child surely? How old are you'?

'I remember it because it was the day we found out the Great

War had ended. So my mother and me went to the beach and celebrated by sharing a pack of my dad's tabs'.

'Your mother gave you your first pack of cigarettes'?

'Yes. They were good for you in them days you see'. She explained the logic to him.

'Mrs Roderick, they were never good for you'.

'You tell me that when you get to one hundred years Trevor'.

'I have celebrated many events with a pack of me tabs. The birth of my children, the end of the second war'.

'You smoked when you had a child'?

'Yes, the midwife had to light it up for me though'.

'I had better go'. A flustered Trevor stood up looking towards Charlotte. 'You remember what I said though, I will see you Saturday night. I will let myself out'.

Charlotte watched him leave via the kitchen door before looking at Gladys who was content enjoying her cigarette. Hugging Gladys' shoulder Charlotte's eyes welled up.

'What are we going to do Nanna'?

'It will be alright my lovely'.

'How'? Charlotte sat beside her.

'They have been trying to get me out of here for years, nothing I haven't expected'.

'But I don't want you to lose your home with all its memories'.

'Charlotte, don't you realise my love. The memories are up here not in this building'. She lifted her finger to her head before looking at Charlotte and pointing at her head. 'You need to stop worrying about me and go and make some memories of your own'.

'I don't want you to lose your home'.

'It's not the home I care about. Its what happens to you and them'. Gladys arose from the chair using the kitchen table to steady herself as she put out her cigarette with a smile looking at Charlotte. 'I am over one hundred years old and I can look back at my life and know that apart from the occasional heartbreak that I have had an amazing life. I have had the love of parents, the love of two good men, four children, seven grandchildren and several great grandchildren. You came into my life like an angel keeping me young and giving me joy after my family had long moved on. I have lived my life looking after the most wonderful things in the most magical of settings. I can't have that long left'.

'Nanna, don't say that', whimpered Charlotte reaching out for her hand.

'I am not saying it to upset you my love but I am 40 years past my sell-by date. All the healthy living that the old *Fat Controller* just went on about is really to late for me to take on board. I have lived healthy for longer than most people will dare live. Apart from a few days or maybe a little more time of sadness I have been content and happy. I reckon I have had a life and a half of happiness my love'. Gladys stopped walking around the table to Charlotte who held her hand as she came down to hug her. 'If they slapped me in a home tomorrow I have so many memories that I wouldn't even need a window to look out of and I would still be happy', she whispered before continuing into Charlotte's ear. 'My only concern is when are you going to give someone a chance to make you happy? I know I joke about Trevor but if he is the one, I will support it'.

'Nanna, you know I regret that night. He isn't the one, he can't be. I am sure someone will appear at some point', Charlotte smiled.

'Who is going to show up here? In a village with one road in and so deep in this valley the sun only breaks the tops of the hills in the summer months? You are a beautiful intelligent young woman who has a heart of gold but who are you going to meet if you don't start accepting people'?

'Nanna, no! Don't be silly'.

'If you don't get out into the world you are going to run out of options and time. At some point Trevor will end up being the only option left and by then he will be ten years older and ten years fatter'.

'I am twenty nine not thirty nine, I still have time to meet someone'.

'How? You are not going to meet them here in this isolated little valley'.

'You met your first husband here'.

'That was 1937, this was a thriving slate mining outpost with the fools gold bringing them in. I had my choice of business men coming into make a cheap shilling. How are you going to meet somebody here? Catch a hiker who has got lost'?

'Well I am getting the train to Aberystwyth this afternoon, I might meet somebody there'.

'Yes and you are going to see that stuffy councilor boss of Trevor's and then hop on the last train back'.

'Well what else should I do'?

'I don't know my love, live a little maybe? You could stop the night there and see some night life or go the other way on the train to somewhere a bit more exotic'.

'Like where'?

'Wolverhampton, I went there once to see Neil Sedaka at the Civic Hall. It was really something I tell you'.

'I have told you before Nanna, I don't know anyone in Wolverhampton. It sounds like a crazy place full of higher class people who would turn their noses up at someone like me'.

'You don't know anybody in Aberystwyth either'.

'And that is why I will be coming home tonight'.

'You will never meet anyone that way my love'.

CHAPTER THREE

His heart pounded through his chest as he crawled along the the side of the wall. Like a spy in a film he needed to be invisible until he got to the refuge that was waiting for him. Nearly half a mile so far but now the final part of the journey would be the most risky. He was heading into the more populated and tourist filled part of the town. If he was seen it would cause at best panic and at worse serious legal ramifications. The dilemma was serious for he could either go through the castle ruins but then alongside the children's playground which if an incident occurred the follow up would be even more problematic and difficult to hide from the full force of the law. This would mean however he would be off the roads and would probably cut a significant distance off his journey. However, if we went up by the theater and behind the market he could potentially get through with less chance of being spotted but then the clock tower square was always busy. He would take the risk of the children's playground.

Ziggy Jones stood looking across his coffee shop proudly, enjoying the rich conversation he could see in front of him. As a pair of customers left he handed them their mobile phones back and smiled at the controversy it had caused when his partner suggested the confiscation of phones for a table and how much free press it got them in local and national media. An infringement of human rights was the initial out pouring by some with refusal to drink in the shop. It was a tough few days but with his support, Ziggy stuck to it and now he looked at the skillfully taken photograph that had been placed behind the counter. Showing the relaxed phone-free customers deep in conversation, laughing and relaxing in the warmth whilst outside the protesters were soaking wet in the rain on their phones trying to making a statement. In the time it took to develop, frame and place the black and white photograph on the wall they had soon got bored and moved onto the next moral battleground. If anything it was that one change which raised the level of clientele that frequented his little slice of slow pace and luxury. A matter which the papers soon identified as a healthier way of life and deemed the coffee shop an independently owned social rebuilding activity which they claimed as a critical part of destressing in modern world. All the media coverage help in putting the shop on the map and allowed him to even start selling quirky t-shirts that introverts who hated coffee even flocked to buy. He smiled as he unpacked his secondhand preloved books to fill his new *Mind Drifting Aids* cabinet which was free to use including classic literature, board games and modeling clay. The latter he was considering taking away for the late night opening hours at the weekend when the male students often spent time crafting skillful models which demonstrated only a wishful self advertisement of appendage size to females who passed by. With the money that the coffee shop and his partner's business upstairs was now bringing in he hoped that soon the furniture could be replaced to be less random and match although he did question the need for this himself. He loved the hum of the low volume civil chatter, the sharing of experiences, the recapturing of forgotten memories made by friends meeting up and choosing to do it over a freshly ground coffee which flavored the senses even before it met the lips, allowing the customer to enjoy its taste of freshness without them even having to drink it and interrupting their flow of conversation.

The sudden sound of electronic intrusion simulating the natural sounds of bubbles popping insulted him in the simultaneous moment of the harsh vibration which drilled on his temple cutting through his happiness like a circular saw cutting through metal. Turning in alarm he looked across his customers who mostly hadn't noticed and were still in conversation. This had happened a few times by a planted protester but not for a while. Where was the phone? Who was the culprit and how would he deal with this? For he had no authority, he couldn't really ban the right to communicate with others. It could have been a call for help or an emergency. If he had taken the phone maybe a man would not know his wife was in labour or an elderly lady would not know her husband had fallen back at home. All these reasons could be justified for not abiding by the rules of the shop he was certain. But then again no, it was his shop and they were not being forced to use it. If they wanted to use their phones and feed their electronic gratification they could go to one of the chain coffee shops and use the free charging devices supplied. They were not forced into coming to his shop and he couldn't have one selfish customer ruin it for all. He was going to stamp this out now.

Stepping forward he cleared his throat about to publicly announce that that person should leave the shop when he heard the sound again and turned to the counter where his staff member Lynne stood leaning down over the counter reading her phone which she had placed on a plate amplifying each vibration loudly. Looking across at her apparent lack of understanding at the concept of *no mobile phone usage* he stared hoping to get a moment of remorse from the *middle aged battle-ax* as one customer recently called her.

'Lynne, an important message is it'?

Looking up in annoyance that she was interrupted Lynne displayed her still shapely body for a woman of early forties helped by years of horse riding keeping her healthy and active around working for the coffee shop. With dagger eyes she stared a hole into him before responding. 'It's just our club leader telling me about the competition on Saturday'.

'Oh, well you shouldn't be on your phone when you are at

work Lynne'.

'Why not'?

'Lynne, I am not getting into another argument with you I am truly not. This is a phone free coffee shop and therefore the employees need to follow those rules'.

'Tara has a phone with her during her shift'.

'She works the late night shift, sometimes she is on her own when I pop out, you can hardly expect her to be here alone without a phone'.

'Sometimes I am on my own during the day. What if someone attacks me'?

'I doubt anyone would be brave enough to attack you Lynne. You would chew their ear off before they got chance, now put it away please', insisted Ziggy.

'Yes I suppose so, anyway I need Saturday off'.

'Lynne it is too late notice. How am I supposed to cover you'?

'I don't know, you said in the interview there was an importance in being flexible'.

'Yes I meant you being flexible in when you could work not being unreliable. If you want it off you will need to sort somebody to cover you, get it'?

Lynne was about to offer an answer when a customer appeared with her bill.

'What'? Snapped Lynne.

'Can I just get our phones back please'? The slightly confused customer looked back in an awkward response.

'You had better ask him', Lynne looked towards Ziggy.

'Lynne! I am sorry madame, let me get them for you'. Ziggy walked behind the counter and using the receipt identified the phones from their box handing them across before looking at Lynne. 'I am sorry my colleague hasn't quite got the method of the phone retrieval yet'.

'I got it, I just don't get why we do it', snapped Lynne back.

'Thank you, hard isn't it'? The female customer commented towards Ziggy.

'What's that'? Questioned Ziggy.

'Working with your spouse. I used to do it, spending all day together prevents you being able to diffuse the arguments'!

With shock on his face Ziggy tried to explain they were not married but the customer left convinced with a smile on her face as he turned back to look at Lynne.

'I don't believe you sometimes I really don't. I give you a job, train you up and give you the best pay I can afford and you are still horrible to the customers'.

'I am just myself to them'.

'That is the problem Lynne, if you are going to be yourself to them I suggest you find a more suitable job where your natural charisma can shine through. You know something like debt collector. I question my decision to hire you sometimes I really do'.

'You have got more problems than me right now'. Lynne responded with a sudden rarity of a blooming smile from ear to ear looking forward to the shop entrance.

In confusion Ziggy looked upwards and became horrified to see his younger brother Joseph Jones stood in the shop window completely naked apart from the slight modesty that his builders tool belt offered him. As the coffee shop went silent Lynne looked his muscular frame up and down admiring the man of similar age to her fully and picking up her phone to take a picture before she could be stopped. With a smile Joe looked at his brother who after several more moments of shock ushered him into the back corridor out of his customer's view.

'What the hell is going on Joe'? A flabbergasted Ziggy questioned in the narrow corridor.

'Yeah, I am sorry about this but I had nowhere else to go'.

'Nowhere else to go, how about home, the police station or the hospital? Anywhere but my full coffee shop'! Ziggy paused to look back down the corridor and motioned Lynne, who was continuing to study the builders belt from afar, back to work.

'I couldn't go home. What if Heather had seen me on my way there'?

'What if she sees you on the local paper wanted for public indecency? I mean what on Earth has happened? How did you get here'?

'Can I borrow some clothes first and then tell you, its a bit awkward this is with Lynne showing customers and all'. He looked up the corridor confirming his statement.

'Well I don't have much down here but I will take you up to Paul, I am sure he has some outfits that are suitable'.

'I can't go up there', stained Joe.

'Why not'? Questioned Ziggy.

'Because he is, you know'?

'What? Gay? Just in case you had forgotten so am I and he is my partner'! Growing angrier he lowered his voice as he offered an ultimatum. 'Either you can come upstairs with me now or you can go back out onto the street. What is it going to be'?

'It's not that he is gay', a sheepish response came back.

'Really'?

'No its the fact he is your partner that makes it difficult. Would you be happy in coming into Heather's if we get our act together'?

'The chances would be remote'.

'No I know you wouldn't end up in this situation'.

'No, I mean the chances of you getting your act together. Now make your mind up. Go upstairs or go back outside'.

CHAPTER FOUR

Watching the train depart David felt the isolation of this part of the world return to him. Dovey Junction was unlike any other station he had experienced on his travels. He was literally stood on a platform in the middle of nowhere. Alone as the train he was on pulled away west towards Pwllheli, at least the sun was shining to remind him of the stunning wetlands and coastal areas making up the Dyfi National Nature Reserve around him. Standing on the empty platform he was the only passenger on the train for Aberystwyth and would now have to wait the fifty minutes until the joining Shrewsbury to Aberystwyth train came through and he could finish the final part of his journey. As the train crossed the bridge and disappeared from view he became the most separated he had ever felt. Renting in London he was never alone, living the busy life of a young professional in the financial capital of Europe, he was used to hustle and bustle. His normal journey to work involved standing packed into a train on the tube everyday before sitting in a overly polished and cleverly illuminated glass high rise building which payed both in monthly wages and bonuses but also in status. Like a fish tank the further up you were the more important you had become. David had spent his time feeding off the scraps at the bottom and now was well on his way to getting the fresh food at the top of the building. He was successful but like fish in a tank he needed that building to keep his future safe. He had not slept a full night's sleep since starting his career path in the large firm he was currently at and he knew it made him miserable and short tempered but he had become obsessed with it like it was his lifeline. They were well off and had a huge amount of savings in the bank ready to buy the next time the housing market crashed. It was more than most would have and yet not enough to match the level they wanted. His journey today had represented the slow release from that fast pace life for the few days he was away as gradually the numbers on the train fell less and he became now the only isolated passenger sat waiting on the most picturesque but lonely spot on the planet. A few minutes of breathing the fresh air passed the time as he navigated around the platform which couldn't have been more than one hundred meters long and twenty meters wide with the rail track either side forking around him. But now his busy mind was getting bored and this was a problem. He realised if he couldn't distract himself then he would have to consider the events back home this morning and more to the point what he would do next. Looking towards the edge of the station platform he couldn't believe there was not even a road linking to it. He knew the nearest road was not far as it weaved around the train tracks all the way since Welshpool but that didn't mean there was any actual life nearby. There was one path which seemed to disappear uncertainly into the woodlands and that was the only way to and from the station. He was truly alone.

With that thought his mind started to move to his current status. What if something happened to him? What if the past few years of high pressure, high pace and high luxury living caused him to have a heart problem which the stress of the day was about to bring upon him? He had a dry throat and his arm was aching. Maybe he was seriously ill and about to collapse? He would be left undiscovered until the next train came by and then what if they didn't see him? What if he falls into the track and can't get up? What would he do? Realising his throat felt tight he undid the top button on his white shirt and loosened his tie. Trying to make himself get into a more calmer frame of mind he stood and focused on the trees in the distance. Looking at his watch he was horrified to see he had only been alone for nine minutes. Why was he even going back to Aberystwyth? He hadn't been back for over ten years and had not seen his brothers in over three years since he met them on a stag weekend. They were not close and really he didn't care what the outcome was of this meeting other than he had to have an input. So far it had cost him a days work and he had never felt so out of place as he did right now. He would have loved being in the quiet holding cell he currently found himself a decade or so earlier but after the hustle and bustle of the city for so long he was finding the quiet natural countryside deafening. His head bounced backwards and forwards between work and Kelly, between work to Kelly and that man, from work to Kelly and what he was going to do, from work to where he would live. This wasn't part of the life plan, having to start again. Feeling his head getting dizzier he lent against the bench lowering himself into a seating position similar to that of a young child. He raised his knees around his head as he gripped at his hair before crying out loud.

He was broken.

'Hello, are you okay'? The distant call of a female voice came from up the path he was inspecting only minutes before. Looking up through his teary eyes he couldn't see anyone and looked back down assuming he had misheard an angel like answer to his unintended cry for help. Looking back at his feet he felt empty but again a single word calling across the tracks seemed to shatter years of false city confidence he had.

'Hello'? Looking up this time he saw the woman looking across the track concerned about his wellbeing.

'Oh shit', he whispered to himself realising she must have heard him and now he was feeling ashamed and embarrassed by his previous outburst. With an automatic displacement behaviour trying to get out of having to speak to her he stood and walked around the small shelter looking out towards the river in the distance and trying to convince himself that he was once again alone which he now believed to be the better option. Aware of the slow movement at a distance of someone looking unsure but concerned at him, he wiped the tears from his face and continued to look forward. Feeling a game of patience at play he did not respond and felt her moving to the other side of the structure allowing him to relax somewhat and slowly look to his right where he was relieved she was no longer stood. Now they could spend the next thirty minutes ignoring each other at either end of the shelter until the train came like normal city folk would. Turning he moved to go back to his suitcase.

'Hello, are you trying to ignore me'? The friendly young Welsh lady's voice was now next to him.

He was surprised to see the naturally beautiful girl in front of him which momentarily took his thought process away. With the sun glimmering down onto her pale skin she seemed to glow heavenly in front of him as she brought her hand up to comb her long dark brown hair from her eyes. Smiling nervously at him like she now realised she had made a mistake in approaching him and she bit her bottom lip as the two stood face to face before she turned slowly thinking it was best that she left him alone.

'Sorry for bothering you', she said before turning and heading around to the other side of the shelter.

Calling himself an idiot under his breath David looked upwards at the sky before quickly moving the opposite way around the shelter almost knocking her off her feet.

'I'm the one that should be sorry', he rushed to apologise as she jumped back slightly with a startle. 'I wasn't expecting anybody else to just appear'.

'And that is why you were shouting'? She cautiously questioned him.

'Yes, not one of my finest moments and not the best way to introduce myself to follow', an embarrassed David looked down.

A few more awkward moments followed as she assessed him carefully deciding if he was a safe person to talk to or if she should keep her hand on the pepper spray cannister in her handbag. As he looked upwards she thought he looked innocent and decided he was too good looking to be bumbling through a sentence and be sinister. He was not confident and he looked embarrassed.

'I'm Charlotte, Charlotte Davies'. She smiled widening her eyes with her soft cheeks as she extended her hand for him to shake.

'I'm David. It's nice to meet you'.

'I take it you are not having a very good day from all that noise you were making and the blood shot eyes and all'?

'No you could say that. It has been bad from start to finish so far and to top it all off I got the wrong train and I ended up here in the middle of nowhere'.

'Well its not really the middle of nowhere now is it'? She quickly responded with a strengthened Welsh accent.'I mean there are places around here but you need to know the area. You are not from around these parts though I am guessing'?

'No, well yes, I mean sort of'?

'Sort of? Well no wonder you don't know where you are'.

'Well no, I grew up in Aberystwyth but have been in London for a long time now. What about you? Where did you even appear from'?

'Aberdyfith'.

'No sorry never heard off it. Do you mean Aberdovey?'.

'No that is over Ynyslas way on the coast, I think I would know if I mean Aberdovey'. She looked at him as if he was a tourist. 'No Aberdyfith, its about five miles from here by road'.

'How big is it'?

'Oh yes its quite big, there is a street with a tea shop, an accountants and a cafe. There was a school but I think I am the youngest in the village now so it was shut down over ten years ago. How big is London'?

'A little bigger I think'.

'I know that, I may live in a small town but I study using the internet'.

'Sorry, you have never been to London'?

'No I have never left Wales truth be told'.

'What'? David laughed as he said it realising he had now offended the pretty girl he had become so keen to speak to.

'Sorry, just surprised me that's all'.

'I am thinking about going on a trip though. My Nanna told me about the City of Wolverhampton. It sounds quite spectacular'.

'Yes, I suppose it does'. David tried to hide his confusion at her lack of exploration in life.

The two continued to chat about their homes and Aberystwyth in a relaxed manner together on the bench which soon carried into the train which within a few minutes arrived in Borth. Sitting next to each other they continued to talk and felt very at ease in doing so.

'So David, you have told me everything so far apart from the reason you were upset and the reason you are going to Aber'?

'Well lets see'. Pausing David considered how he could breach the situation of Kelly this morning with a complete stranger and decided to go for the easier route instead. 'I am going to see my two brothers Joseph and Ziggy'.

'Ziggy, is that a nickname'?

'No he was born in 1973, one year after David Bowie released the album. She didn't want to call her first son after our dad, so David Bowie will be forever remembered in our family through Ziggy'.

'But you are called David'?

'Yes well I guess by son number three she got fed up of arguing or there were no good music albums that year, and named me after our dad who happened also to be called David. Anyway I am off to see them for the first time in a long time. I haven't been back here since mom died. We are not the closest family. Well they are I guess but I am sort of the youngest brother. The mistake truth be told. Mom and dad were fine with two but then five years on I happened'.

'Did your parents not treat you well'?

'Yeah they did'.

'Then they loved you', she abruptly turned looking across the fields.

'Are you alright'? Sensing he had hit a nerve, David questioned his new found traveling partner feeling he had upset her.

'I was left, in the exact same spot where we met when I was seven on the Dyfi or Dovey Junction platform as you call it. My parents who brought me up in Aberystwyth packed to take me on holiday in the car at night time. They drove all the way to Dovey Junction and walked me down the same path I used earlier and told me to wait why they went back to the car and just left me'. With a quiver in her voice Charlotte looked out of the window again to avoid him seeing the tears she was holding back unsuccessfully.

'Jesus, I am so sorry, that is terrible'. David led a tissue from his bag which she dabbed her eyes with. 'What happened to you'?

'Well I stood waiting as it got darker and then a train arrived. Getting off that train was Gladys and Simon Roderick. They took me home with them and after my parents were unable to be found they adopted me'. Breathing inward with a sigh she wiped the tears from her face. 'I mean what sort of parents do that to a seven year old? Just leaving me there in the dark, they could have abandoned me anywhere but they chose the most remote place possible and just drove away. I could have gotten into an accident and not have been found for days, if at all. I wouldn't have survived an Autumn night out there that young'.

'I don't know what to say, I feel terrible for you'.

'Don't, I have had a good upbringing. I lived a magical childhood thanks to my new parents. Yes they were older than most so they made me treat them like grandparents. Hence I call her Nanna, but they helped me get through it and I helped them in their reserve'.

'Reserve'?

'Yes they home orphaned animals, I suppose I was no different'.

'You are far more precious'.

'If you only knew'. She smiled before continuing. 'When I was fourteen Simon got poorly and within a year it was just Nanna and me. He was younger than she was so when he went I had to start supporting her in looking after the animals. Gradually, all my friends went to colleges and universities before meeting their husbands and moving away. All the time I looked after the reserve and that became my adult life. Don't get me wrong I don't regret it. She looked after me and so I must now look after her but then when you realise you have spent nearly three decades of your life looking at the world from a valley, you have hardly seen the sky. My friends have had love, heartbreak, jobs and children. I haven't done anything other than tend to animals and look after our home. I haven't even been to Wolverhampton'.

'Erm, right yes. Well you must have been other places before though'?

'I have never been anywhere other than Aberystwyth to Aberdyfith'.

'Well look I am sure you will do, you could drive to Wolverhampton and back in a day if you wanted or you could do the same on the train'.

'I know it's not real David but tell me you will take me to see London and the sights. Tell me you will take me to the big posh cities like Wolverhampton'.

'Yes I will take you there, we can go to wherever you want'. As he looked out of the window he realised their journey was at an end as they pulled into the final stop on the train line and his heart sunk a little. He was intrigued with Charlotte. How could a girl who had spent the last twenty years living in a tiny village isolated and alone be so comfortable talking to a complete stranger?

The two got off the train and walked down the platform towards the town. As they got to the end of the pathway David felt the want to not walk away from Charlotte but his head was telling him at home he had Kelly who he would have to speak to soon. As they reached the road outside of the station they came to a stop and looked at each other.

'Well Mr David Jones, it has been lovely meeting you. I hope whatever the reason for your visit it is a nice one and that whatever it is that you have spent the last hour not telling me about that got you upset earlier sorts itself out'.

'Thanks, you know I have really enjoyed the last hour of the day. I hope your council meeting goes well and that you get your trip to Wolverhampton someday soon'.

'Okay, bye then'. Charlotte smiled looking at him with the same smile that stole his voice an hour earlier before raising her hand slightly and turning slowly walking away.

'Number'? David called out causing a confused Charlotte to turn around and walk back to him. 'I mean number'. Charlotte again looked confused as internally David cursed his own incompetent ability to deal with any female he liked in the smallest way. 'No sorry that was just repeating myself. I mean number, if I could have your number then maybe when your done we could meet up and talk some more maybe'?

'Number'?

'Yes mobile number, sorry I just like talking to you and enjoyed it, reading too much into it I know but I am just intrigued by, sorry'.

'I can't, I am sorry'.

'No of course my fault, sorry'. David felt his cheeks bloom as blood filled them showing his embarrassment.

'No I don't have a mobile phone that's all. I would love to have a drink and a chat with you'. She smiled causing a wave of excitation through his body that he had forgotten he could feel. 'How about? My train is due to leave at five tonight. If I meet you back here then I can catch the next train three hours later if you like? If you don't come I will assume your business is sorted'.

'I will be here'. He couldn't hide the smile as he nodded.

'Well maybe you need to just consider contacting whoever got you so upset earlier before you make that commitment. I will be here from about quarter to five'. Charlotte moved forward and hugged him, he felt a warmth that he wanted to cling to and a sweet smell of her hair as she moved away. Smiling the two waved and she turned walking down the street in the opposite direction to which he was heading. As she reached the corner and disappeared along the side of the chip shop she glanced back as he raised his arm to say goodbye.

CHAPTER FIVE

Walking down the high street David was amazed by the changes that had happened in the past decade or so. He felt the usual hustle and bustle of people everywhere but this was not the town he had last seen. Much more chain linked shops and food outlets had now replaced the independent stores which seemed to have a strong hold on the town last time he had visited for his mother's funeral. Walking past the clock tower he saw the coffee shop on the corner and smiled. He was impressed by the signage which looked classy and sophisticated even if it was for a shop called '*Ziggy's*'. He stood for a few moments taking the scene in knowing he felt relaxed and at home which he was not expecting. He anticipated that feeling would be shattered once he and his brothers got down to business. He smiled to himself thinking the idea of this meeting happening in a public place would probably be a safer option as blows could not be fired if there were others around them. He was under no illusion that just because his brothers were now in their forties that they would be any calmer and get along any better. In-fact it was he who had to sometimes gel them together following disagreements, his mother always said they were born too close together to get along.

Heading in through the main doors he approached the stern looking lady at the counter who looked suspiciously at him before he spoke.

'Hello, I'm looking for Ziggy'? he asked in a polite manner as she looked him up and down whilst chewing.

'Sorry, never heard of a Ziggy', she said as she turned to work on the coffee maker.

'You work in Ziggy's Coffee Shop don't you'?

'Do you want a coffee'?

'Well I am not sure yet', a confused and shocked David responded.

'Decide and then come back to me'.

'David'! Ziggy appeared behind her from the corridor to the back of the shop smiling and immediately walked around to give his younger brother a welcoming hug. 'How long have you been here'?

'Just long enough to meet this nice young lady. Strange because she has apparently never met you before'. David looked across to her.

'Lynne, are you being difficult? Why didn't you tell me my brother was here'?

'He looks like a solicitor, they always deliver bad news'. Lynne looked unapologetically and then walked away to go and collect some finished cups and mugs.

'Is she always that friendly'? David questioned watching as she barged around the tables.

'You caught her on a good day, she normally bites strangers', Ziggy responded with a huge grin as he continued to hug his brother with one arm much to the surprise of David.

'Why on Earth do you employ her then'?

'Well I ask myself that regularly but she is a pretty good guard dog and she is reliable. She also makes the best coffee's this side of Wales, even you would like them. Damn its good to see you. How was your trip? How is work? And that beautiful girlfriend of yours'?

'Hey is Joseph meeting us here'? David changed the subject moving around towards the service bar.

'He is already here'. Changing his face from a slight perplexity to a smile. 'Just look for the pilot in the corner'.

David turned and saw in the corner of the room a man dressed in what appeared to be a pilot's uniform. Approaching he saw the quality of the shirt was minimal suggesting it was a fancy dress costume of some sort.

'Joseph'?

Joe turned to see his brother for the first time in years and with a big smile on his face he stood and embraced him. Unsure and slightly uncomfortable with the apparent fondness to the heart which his absence had caused David stood waiting for it to end feeling the hand of Ziggy on his back.

'Take a seat David, let me guess a hot chocolate you Neanderthal'?

'You know me'. Sitting opposite Joe, David smiled at his brother who had a sandwich in front of him as Ziggy returned sitting next to David.

'Wow'! Burst Ziggy. 'When was the last time we all sat in Aberystwyth together? Must have been at mom's funeral. It's been far to long'.

'Its good to see you David. How are things back in the big city'? Joe quizzed him.

'Don't worry about me. Are you not going to explain why you are sat in a pilot's outfit'? David quickly responded avoiding the question again.

'I can answer that one for him' laughed Ziggy. 'He is wearing one of Paul's fancy dress outfits he keeps for the prom photobooth. I had to lend him it because an hour ago he arrived wearing nothing but a tool belt'.

'What? You were naked'?

'Yes he was, I think it's time you explained why though'! Ziggy looked at Joseph expectantly.

'I was doing a job down near the castle at a bed and breakfast. Just sanding down the windows and painting them fresh. Well there was this young girl I don't know probably a bit younger than David'.

'Nothing changes. Its always a girl, isn't it'? David smiled shaking his head.

'Well anyway, she started flirting with me and one thing led to another but the thing was she wasn't a guest but the owner's daughter'.

'So he caught you at it with his daughter'? Laughed Ziggy.

'Not quite, I hid for half an hour behind the fridge and then snuck out. She was still relatively dressed so she pulled her clothes back on and acted innocently'.

'Where were you'? David interrupted hungry for more details.

'In the kitchen of the bed and breakfast'.

'So where are your clothes'? David grilled him further.

'Stuffed behind the fridge in the kitchen, with my wallet and van keys'.

'Well what are you going to do'? The lack of responsibility by his older brother shocked David to the core.

'We need to go and get them back'.

'Jesus Joseph, no wonder Heather doesn't want anything to do with you. You are a forty two year old man and you are running around like a teenager', David turned the humour into a more serious affair.

'Come on then David, tell me about how wonderful your life is down their in the big city'? Ziggy stepped in sensing the mood change.

'No don't worry about me'.

'Now, now David but I do worry. Especially when your mobile phone said you have 17 missed calls from that beautiful lady of yours. What is going on'? Ziggy questioned.

'I caught her with another man before I left this morning'. David's response was monotone as he looked down at the table.

'That's awful, I am sorry to hear that. No one should ever catch someone they love in bed with somebody else' Ziggy looked at Joe as he said it.

'Well I caught her in the shower so at least she was being hygienic I suppose'.

'So what are you going to do now, you have told her it is over I presume'? Ziggy questioned him hopefully.

'I don't know, I just don't know'.

'You need to leave her'. Joe boldly stated.

'Its not that easy a decision to make'.

'Of course it is. She was having sex in the shower with another man. Whatever she says and does to fix it means nothing. The first time she got it on with that guy is the last time your relationship meant anything. Take it from me mate, it is done'.

'I know, I get it. But this time yesterday I was still happily in a relationship with her, it has all just happened really quickly, I need time to process it'.

'Process what? She was with another man. It is over'.

'But we live together. What do I do now'?

'Well from my point of view brother, you kick her out. She is the one who is cheating on you'.

'I don't know, I could have been there more. I work a lot'.

'It doesn't matter. You must have enough to get another place to rent. Just do it'.

'I have been saving up to get a mortgage deposit for a house for us to live in and get married'. David sighed putting his head into his hands.

'Then you have got the resources and funds to do it. You need to walk away' Ziggy confirmed supporting Joe's answer to the problem. 'Look, it is Wednesday, you have a few days with us now to sort out dad's mess and then maybe stay till Monday instead of going back Friday. Use the seaside to clear your head and think things through'.

'But my work'.

'Maybe she isn't the only thing you need a break from? The big city will keep going without you I am sure. Sounds like you need to step away from it for a while and press the pause button on life'.

'Or maybe I shouldn't have come at all this weekend. But then I wouldn't have just met the girl I just did on the train', smiled David.

'Oh hold on a minute, did you see that Ziggy? I think that was the first genuine smile we have seen since he got here. Girl on the train, go on tell us more'.

'There is nothing to tell really I just felt at ease talking with her'.

'Is she hot'? Joe looked at him expectant for detail.

'Yes she is very nice'.

'Then my God man, you have been given a lifeline here. Forget Kelly ever existed and move on'. Joe instructed as if he had not just had the previous conversation with David. 'Do you have her number'?

'We said we would meet later on'.

'Well then I would say you are already on the road to recovery my good man', jollied Joe.

'Shall we head over to the site'? Ziggy interrupted the others pointing at his watch.

'Yes, is he meeting us there'? David questioned finishing his drink.

The three got up as Ziggy nodded in confirmation. Heading out of the coffee shop the three men seemed the closest of any brothers. An image that would appease any parent hoping that the sibling bond would last a lifetime long after they were left to cope for themselves.

CHAPTER SIX

The tall man stood impeccably dressed in a dark navy blue designer fitted pin striped suit with his briefcase resting on the floor. Waiting in the middle of the field he seemed completely oblivious to the youngsters trying to play football around him on the neatly trimmed grass. His mind was busy behind his thick glasses calculating the potential earnings of a development here and how they could make it the most desirable hotel in the town. They would maximise the available space by using underfloor car parking which would also be a first in the town. In the warm afternoon sun his spiked grey hair glistened in the breeze either showing the impacts of a high pressure lifestyle aging a young man prematurely or the thick hair of an elder gentleman who would be always looking younger as if his sins were hidden like those of *Dorian Gray.* Looking across the field the brothers saw him standing out like a fox in a hen house the moment they came around the corner.

'That has got to be Splythe'? David asked the others.

'Yes that is the right honorable Herman Splythe M.P. Councilor, business man and all round opportunist. Key Development Consultant of Merriman Initiatives Wales', Ziggy confirmed.

'More like conman, rip off artist and second hand car salesman if you ask me'. Joe added.

'He can't be doing bad for himself, not in that suit. Anyway shall we go and meet him'? David led the way.

The brothers headed across the field walking calmly towards the man who turned slowly to face them like a slick protagonist in a Hollywood film.

'The Jones brothers, you are a sight for sore eyes. I didn't know how much of this fresh air I could take. A threesome for the first time also, that means we are doing some business then'? He stopped with a confident smile looking directly at David.

'David Jones, pleased to meet you, sorry it took so long to get me here. You are a bit isolated from the rest of the country'.

'I couldn't agree more David but that may well be the best trip you have ever made'.

'Nice suit, looks like a Barren's of London'? David complimented him openly to the bemusement of his siblings.

'Good eye for a suit Mr Jones, I didn't realise your brother was going to be so smart and sophisticated gents'. Splythe turned to Ziggy and Joseph unintentionally insulting their lack of perceived style. 'Lets hope this will make things a bit quicker'.

'We wont be rushing into anything Mr Splythe. You realise that don't you'? Joe rebutted at him.

'You are a smart family unit gentlemen, I have the utter most respect for that. But I think by the time we are finished today that you will be ready to agree on some numbers. You are my most important meeting of the day, God only knows I have spent the rest of my day in pointless no go meetings'.

'We will see, my brothers need to be happy for anything to be considered', confirmed Ziggy before continuing. 'Where are we meeting'?

'Well gentlemen I thought I would start here and then we are going to our office on the front. We are having catering brought in'.

'Sounds nice'. David nodded at him approvingly.

Herman Splythe stood and started displaying a passion and confidence in his sales pitch that he presented to them in an overly animated way. The three brothers stood back slightly uncomfortable as the man continued as if preforming to thirty prospective clients rather than three Welsh brothers who had differing interests in the reason they were there.

'Gentlemen I give to thee the site of Aberystwyth's most exclusive hospitality location. Look at this space which you are the owners of. People sitting on your property enjoying the sunshine as if they have a right to be on the land which your family has owned for so long it has simply been forgotten. What we are standing on gentleman is the biggest undeveloped piece of land in the town. Apart from the university owned playing field there is no flat open plots of land left to be developed in the main town. The opportunities for this piece of grass are endless and easy to do. We are planning on developing a three floor luxury hotel with facilities which would challenge any of the more luxury country retreats in the area and be a world class site over-viewing the beautiful views of the Cardigan Bay. We have carefully laid the plans out so that there would not only be hotel rooms but also conference suites to challenge any other, a health club, spa and restaurant open by membership to the local public including a roof top terrace and bar which could if we get the licensing permission become an exclusive bar for the local nightlife. All of this here, where these people simply are sitting littering the land for free. Think about it gentleman, you could help bring the tired Victorian esplanade back to the twenty first century. You could bring this seaside town rich in history and beauty into the eyes of modern society and stop it being a forgotten jewel lost by years of neglect. How does that sound to you three? Doesn't it sound wonderful? How about it gents? How does it sound'?

'Rehearsed' an unimpressed Ziggy walked away looking at the ground.

The offices of Merriman Initiatives were impressive. It stood out from all the other sea front buildings as being completely revamped and freshened up completely with the expense that only a highly financial organisation could afford. The boardroom office was designed across the front middle floor of the building. In what would have been at least two previous rooms knocked through in the Victorian building it now enjoyed four large sea view windows overlooking the promenade and the beach. The room had a fresh modern feel to it with a large glass table in the center towards the front where the brothers sat awaiting their host to return from ordering the food. The floor had been replaced by rich wooden flooring and the art on the wall demonstrated some impressive architecture that was clearly linked to the international company which Splythe represented.

'What would this building have been fifteen years ago'? David asked the others as he looked down onto the rocky beach across the road through the open window.

'I think it was just a private building or student accommodation possibly. I can't say it ever stood out', Joe answered with clear thought running through his head.

'They have certainly done it up nicely, made a really impressive job in my opinion'. David said looking around them.

'I am not sold myself. I mean people used to live in these buildings, seems a shame its been all knocked through and turned into offices now to me'. Ziggy looked around unimpressed.

'I agree with what you're saying if they are forcing people to move out but I think this place was derelict or at least on the way to it' Joe suggested.

'So they have invested and given it a new lease of life then? Doesn't seem so bad when you think it makes the seafront look more business like and more attractive to investment. It shows what could be done with some fresh financial backing'.

'Yes but does this town really need to be transformed into hub of investment'? Ziggy sighed.

'Well apart from the Sustainable Development site and agricultural industrial investment there is very little else going on here is there'? David commented expertly.

'But what is the problem with this just being a student run and tourism run town. The Welsh Assembly is here and there has been some new investments. We could lose the heart of the place if it gets too developed'. Ziggy was interrupted as Herman

Splythe entered the room.

'Gentlemen, sorry to keep you waiting I had to take a call from Manchester updating them on our country spa we are looking at developing. Anyway the food will be with us shortly but in the meantime I thought I could show you the artist impressions of the development to start off with'. Splythe tapped a password into his computer as a projector turned onto the white wall at one end of the room. Opening a folder on the desktop he clicked on *Aber1* and the first photographs of the site appeared.

'Okay, gents here is the site as it currently stands, empty. Approximately 150m in length and 120 meters width. This as you can see is the view from the seafront towards the field where it is hidden from view largely by the castle walls. We are proposing that the hotel will have an entrance at the other end of the building so not to use valuable viewing space of the sea and historic Old College for the reception area. This will be low key but will make up for it by using the incline from the coast to allow the ground floor rooms to have raised level and thus secure balcony areas each with its own hot tub. High enough from neighboring paths to stop people seeing in or getting in but low enough to give fantastic views. Rooms will fill the main floor on the middle level allowing fantastic views of the Castle grounds, the sea front, the Old College and St Michael's Church. On the top floor their will be rooms around the side of the floor allowing sea views above the castle ruins and at the front of the building a magnificent wedding suite and conference room with balcony leading up to the roof terrace and restaurant. Parking I here you say, how will this work with such limited car spaces nearby? Well simple, we are going to build underneath and this will have more than enough spaces for the hotel guests and clients that it will not cause congestion in the town'.

'It just doesn't seem big enough, you know the land and all'. Ziggy questioned in a genuine interest.

'The hotel will have up to sixty rooms dependent on final facilities decided all of which will be to the highest standards. I know as an empty space if I hadn't have done this before I would be questioning the area myself but experts have come in and planned this I assure you'.

'How are you going to stop a car park less than twenty meters from the Atlantic storms getting flooded'? Questioned Joe.

'Clever drainage, it is all going to be planned and besides these are problems you do not need to worry yourselves over'.

'No I am just interested from a construction point of view, that's all' Joe answered.

'Well I will find out and tell you. I forget you are a builder Joseph. In fact I am sure that if you help the company out here, there is a lot of scope for your company getting potential contracts with us. In fact we would be looking for someone with local knowledge to lead the construction teams on all local projects'.

'So this is just one of Merriman Initiatives projects around here is it'? Ziggy questioned.

'Indeed Ziggy. Merriman Initiatives see Aberystwyth as a potential hub of development for central Wales. You see this part of the country has been ignored as the south developed but now investors are looking for a less industrial area to win business and commerce over. We see Aberystwyth as a jewel in the crown of our company'.

'And what is it that your company does exactly? Build hotels'? Joe asked sarcastically.

'No Joseph, hotels are an essential part in triggering new growth and investment in areas. You see unless you can make investors stay here then they will not invest. We develop and lead initiatives for everything from business centers to industrial units for engineering to power station investment. Hotels and health spa's are where our name stands out to most but behind most regeneration projects now Merriman Initiatives is normally present. You see you need to look at the greater picture here gents. This is the very first stage in developing our Welsh headquarters. With you agreeing to this it will enable us to bring new business in that will benefit everyone from the town. New jobs, new transport links and new investment. This town could be transformed in a decade to a modern day Welsh Capital of Business Innovation. You three could start this all off'.

'Jobs for who though? Not for the people who live here all year round. For some students yes but what about the local people who live here? What about the small independent guest house owners that need the tourism to keep their bills paid in the cold winter months'? A concerned Ziggy stared at him intently.

'Firstly, there will always be room for your coffee shop I am sure, people like independent companies like that. The same goes for hotel owners and bed and breakfast owners. People like supporting local business. Yes they may need to step up their facilities in some cases but to be honest we have all stayed in a drab guest house who doesn't deserve our money. This will help the small guest houses raise their standards'.

'Yeah but it wont be like that will it? This will drive different people here at best and at worst will steal the custom of the local bed and breakfast chains for some faceless business. How is that going to support local business'? Ziggy now seemed to have a point to prove.

'I assure you the company is very dedicated to improving the local area when we invest. Think about it like this. What is that ground being used for now? Family picnics during the day which people can still have on the beach if the development goes ahead. At night time it is a site for drug addicts'.

'I have never seen anyone taking drugs there'. Joe interrupted.

'Look all I am saying gentlemen is the answer to all societies ills are not due to this development going ahead or not. It has been in your family for three generations now and this may be the last time it is able to be developed on'.

'Yes, how has the red tape disappeared all of a sudden'? David questioned. 'When dad tried to sell this land for housing developers twenty years back it was blocked by the council stating it had a dual purpose as common ground. How can you build if the public have a right to use the ground'?

'Your dad was trying to sell the land for houses which was not the original purpose of the buying agreement that your grandfather made from the council. The planning permission granted which was locked in said that any construction needed to have either educational or public benefit. House building was not foreseen to cover those areas'.

'I'm sorry that makes this all a little more suspect. You are telling me that building a high price hotel will have enough public benefit to give this the green light'? David continued.

'The council and the Welsh Government see the need to bring in new investment opportunities to the town and surrounding areas which will boost business and tourism and thus be of public benefit. They have given the green light for numerous developments we have carefully planned in the county to attract further investment'.

'Bit strange though isn't it Mr Splythe'? Ziggy interrupted.

'I am sorry Zigland I am not sure what you mean'?

'Well its just that you happen to become elected on the Welsh Parliament and now you have convinced the council that the red tape of bureaucracy can disappear for enough time to build the sites needed for the company you represent'?

'Simply well planned politics gentlemen, that is all. The red tape has been lifted to prevent the historical insignificance of this town stopping it from having a future. Now it will be up to you to decide whether we use your site and you benefit or we find somewhere else to do it. I am sure if we can't focus on Aberystwyth then the company will move along the coast and look at other potential sites. I have enclosed the offer in this envelope for you with details on the legal process. I am not going to insult your intelligence by offering it you with a decision here and now. I want you all to consider it. I want you to decide without the pressure of here and now. I need to know by Saturday however as I have pressure on me to make this happen. Have a long look at the offer gentlemen I think you will find it most generous'.

CHAPTER SEVEN

The three brothers sat in the quiet coffee shop with Joe and David looking down at the offer silently whilst Ziggy flicked through a folder of documents about the land purchase his dad had passed onto them.

'I think the best part of this whole day has been that we have been offered all this and have to make a massive decision like this whilst you are sat in a pilot fancy dress outfit' chuckled David. 'Look, that is a lot of money being offered for a piece of land which we have never had anything from. It was a mistake that has survived generations still with no benefit to us. Dad knew it when he tried to flog it twenty years ago but couldn't. Would he have been successful it would have been a housing estate now so why are you worried about the ifs and buts of it'.

'So you think we should just sign it then'? Asked Joe.

'Yes for God's sake. What have we got to lose? That is a lot of money even split three ways. Chances are it still wont get developed on even if we sell it'.

'It says here if we find a purpose for it we can build any type of non brick construction there for the lifetime of that purpose as long as we invest a percentage of our profits into the local community'.

'And what the hell are we going to do with it? Open a burger wagon or something'? David argued sarcastically.

'I don't know David'! Snapped Ziggy slapping his hand onto the table. 'I just feel that we are letting three generations of our family history go for some easy money we don't really need. We could do something with that land that makes it more beneficial to us and to the town'.

'Like what? Listen to yourself Ziggy. I am not investing money into that strip of land. If you didn't contact me about it I wouldn't have even remembered it existed. What do you wanna do with it? Open a wooden hut coffee shop on there? Joe can't build anything on there as he doesn't have the planning permission, even if he did we would be gambling our futures just doing it. Look as far as I am concerned we would be crazy to turn this down. You two can do what you want but as far as my involvement, here you go I am done'. David pulled a pen from his jacket pocket as the other two say watching him print and sign his name before dating it'.

'What the hell man? That is it'! Joe angrily shoved him clenching his fists as David moved back away from him..

'I am done, I am done with this town, this family, this day'! David quickly got up and walked out of the coffee shop.

'You had better have a room in a hotel tonight because you are not welcome in my house'! Shouted Joe after him as he left.

Not quite sure why his rage had surfaced so readily over this issue David paced to the sea front and continued to walk along the long promenade. Past the glorious Old College building and around the outside ruins of the castle. Minutes later he reached the harbour and continued walking along the wooden harbour wall until he reached the metal railing. Looking down at the water, he had more than a strip of land which he had almost forgotten about on his mind. He played back in his head recent relationship highlights with Kelly and tried to consider how long she had been in bed with another man. Thinking about his work and the long hours he spent in the office she could have been doing this for a long time. She could for all he had known spent the occasional weekend away with her friends in this man's arms.

Staring down at the waves for some time he was unaware that his brother had followed him until he broke his thoughts.

'I always thought it is funny how we are the most advanced animal on the planet and yet we are the only animal that can be so distracted by the waves moving forwards and backwards to the point where we find it relaxes us'. Ziggy waited but with no response as David continued to look out to sea and so he joined him at the metal railing. 'What was all that about? The David I know wouldn't have signed that deal without knowing every tiny detail about what was going to happen with it afterward. You got really hot there, really quickly. It's got nothing to do with the land though has it? This is about you and whats going on with your life'?

'It's such a mess Ziggy', a calm but almost distant David spoke looking out towards the horizon.

'Look I get it. You are in love with her but Joe is right. You cannot sit and hope things will fix themselves'.

'It's not just that. It is everything'.

'Come on, talk to me buddy. I can't help you if you don't talk to me'.

'Its just today, when I was waiting on the platform at Dovey Junction it all came crashing in on me. I knew I wasn't feeling good about work and life but I was just going with it. You know just sort of riding the tide of the daily grind. Working 12 hours a day, spending hours on the tube, eating fast, clearly not spending enough time at home. The pressures of it never stop, you work hard to make a good first impression but then you set the bar right to the highest level and they expect that level constantly. I feel like coming out here took me out of the tide for the first time in a decade and I feel like if I jump back in I am going to drown trying to keep swimming'.

'Then maybe this trip is exactly what you needed to do, get away from the fast moving life and spend some time just to yourself'.

'I spent five hours alone with myself and it led to a mini breakdown on the platform'.

'Well maybe you needed that moment of realisation to show you that you are not happy and something needs to change.

Everybody needs to standstill once in a while to look at their life',

'It was the standing still that did it. You know I have spent so long looking forward that when I was left on my own on that platform it was literally the first time in over a decade since my life was not going anywhere. I was trapped literally without anything to keep my mind occupied and with the vision of Kelly and that man I literally have lost all my long term plans and goals. I was going nowhere and for that moment there was nothing to distract me. I hate my job, I go in everyday and its always just to get to the next payslip so I can be another step closer to my massive mortgage I am saving to get trapped into. But now I don't even have that dream, I don't even want to go home'.

'That's why you were so desperate to sign the contract then? So you felt like you were moving forward with something'?

'Maybe, I don't know'.David shook his head clearly holding tears back from his brother.

'I think you need to make a few more decisions in the next few days before you decide whether you really want to sign that contract. Firstly, you need to decide if can you trust Kelly again? Do you have a future? Does she really want a future with you? I don't know her well enough and neither does Joe to tell you that. Only you really know whether you can make it still work, but you can't hold onto a false hope of achieving a dream that doesn't really exist. Do you want to go back and work like you have for the last five years or is it time to look at doing something different'?

'How do you do that, how do you just start doing something different and living a different life'?

'Well firstly you have got to make that decision you want to make a change. Figuring out how is the next part and thats when you will start moving forward again'.

'How do I even talk to Kelly'? David's body was filled with dread at the thought of hearing her voice.

'It seems to me that you are getting worked up about talking to her when she is the one who should be worried about explaining herself to you'. Ziggy responded in a logic which David couldn't argue with as his brother led the way.

Walking back towards the town the two returned to the topic of the land.

'You think that there is something below board going on with Herman Splythe then'? David asked Ziggy.

'Come on, all this benefit for the local community and society rubbish. They really don't care about anyone here do they? But then again they are offering us a lot of money. It could pay off the mortgage on the coffee shop and make life a lot more comfortable'.

'Well look I am happy to go either way with it. I am not here enough to really notice whether we own the land or not but that could really set me up back home'.

'So London will still be home then'? Ziggy stopped walking with his question.

'I don't know. I don't seem to belong anywhere right now'.

'You do my brother but you need to decide where that is. You know what you need to do in order to make that decision don't you'?

'What'? David looked at Ziggy unsure.

'Call her'.

CHAPTER EIGHT

'He has been gone a while, how long did he say he was going to be'? Paul asked Ziggy as he sat going through his books on the table.

'Well he just said that he was going to take a walk up Constitution Hill and back down to clear his head. He was upset after speaking with Kelly. He just needs to take some time to digest it all I think'.

'It's over then'? Paul continued intrigued by the recent events.

'I think so, he seemed to have told her it was over himself, before she said it to him. I don't know what his plan is now. What the living arrangements will be'.

'He isn't going to come back here'?

'No his life is in London'.

'Thank God for that, I don't think I could take three of you brothers together', he smiled looking up at Ziggy who sat next to him and held his hand pressing it against his cheek.

'Bloody pain in the backside. I don't see him for years and then the moment I do he is already causing me worry and stress. I think he brought it on the train with him'.

'Well at least he doesn't arrive naked', Paul smiled.

'That is true. I wonder how Joe is getting on trying to get his clothes back'. Ziggy laughed.

'Hey here he is'. Paul stood demonstrating his tall stature to David who came back to the restaurant and across to greet them. 'Good to see you again David'. The two hugged as David sat down across the table from Paul and Ziggy.

'Feeling better'? Ziggy questioned him.

'Yes thanks, I think I just needed to talk to her', David nodded as if to reassure himself.

'How was it'? Paul questioned softly.

'She cried, I listened, she cried some more and then I realised she was the one who cheated on me so I told her I was moving on with my life and I would sort out things as soon as I could'.

'Good man'. Smiled Ziggy. 'And it's not like he hasn't already started moving on'.

'Oh yes why is that'? Questioned Paul.

'He met a nice girl on the train didn't you brother'?

'Shit! What time is it? God damn it I left my phone in the box'. Quickly David shot up and went to the counter. 'Lynne I need my phone quickly'.

'Hold on can't you see I am busy'. Lynne looked up from her crossword in anger.

'Just tell me the time', David demanded.

'Ten to five, why'? Looking up Lynne saw David running out of the coffee shop and sprinting down the street. 'Rude bastard'!

David knew if he had a clear run he could make the station in ten minutes. He saw an vision Charlotte in his head and now he was desperate to get there in time. He needed to see her again, she was the only positive thing he could see in his life moving forward. Running down the main street of the town he felt confident until he took a short cut down the side street. Immediately he was upon the car and he couldn't stop as he heard the brakes. Rolling across the bonnet he saw the world spin around him and hit the floor hard ripping his shirt and cutting his arm. As the driver got out of the car she was confused to see the man she hit running away down the road and shouted some abuse which David barely heard as he continued in desperation. With the station in view his arm was throbbing now but he had his destination in site as he saw people coming out of the station. With hope that the train had just arrived but not yet departed he pushed onto the platform with his head and arm pounding in agony. Bursting onto the platform to see the train heading out he had one last sprint left in him. If only he could get her to see him she might be able to get the next train back. Running as quickly as possible he took several steps before his legs final gave way. Collapsing onto the floor he blacked out momentarily before coming to just to see the train roll out of his view into the distance. Lying face down on the platform with his body seething in pain he tried not to vomit as people gathered around him.

'Next train is in three hours son', the elderly platform attendant told him.

'I can't wait that long, I need to get to Dovey Junction', David whimpered in a low voice to himself.

'Well you could get the bus in half an hour or I suppose a taxi if it's urgent'.

'A taxi, a taxi'! David stood thanking the confused man gripping at his arm as he ran down the platform out onto the front of the station. Running around the side of the building to the taxi waiting area he was in luck at such a busy time of the day to find one taxi waiting. Running across the road toward it he reached for his wallet as he approached.

'Taxi'! Shouted Lynne as she approached from the other side.

'No'! David shouted at her as he crashed across the front of the car. 'How did you get from the cafe so quickly'? David questioned her but decided it didn't matter. 'Lynne I need this car, I need to get to Dovey Junction'.

'And I need to get home, I have dogs to walk'.

'Lynne, I have lost everything today, I can't lose her'.

'Who'? She looked at him perturbed.

'The girl I met on the train this morning'?

'Oh my God, you are worse than your other brother you are'. Lynne got in the taxi and shut the door talking to the driver.

'No, I need this car'! David stood in front of the car blocking it as it started moving. He could see Lynne shouting and the driver hit who the horn several times before slamming the car in reverse and then powering around him. With his last chance escaping David collapsed to the tarmac with his head in his hands realising that every moment passing was his last chance to catch up with her. Today had now been the worst day he could remember.

David at first didn't hear the sound of the reversing car behind him but quickly recognised the bitter growling of Lynne's husky voice.

'You can drop me off on the way and you are paying, get in the back', she cried at him.

'Lynne, I love you' he smiled as he jumped to his feet.

'Hurry up will you! Bloody stupid men'.

Jumping in the car, he lay on the back seat as she continued to talk.

'This woman better be worth it. How much do you have on you'?

'What'?

'Money, how much money do you have'?

'I don't know one hundred'.

'Allan we need to get to Dovey Junction in twenty minutes, there is one hundred pounds in it for you if you can do it'!

David felt the car pull him backwards as the driver pushed the small engine to its accelerating limits as Lynne shouted at him to put his seatbelt on. Sitting up he saw the driver run a red light and continue to speed up the hill past the university.

'Penglais in two minutes, not bad'. Lynne commented to the driver before turning to speak to David. 'So let me get this straight Romeo. You met this girl on the train this morning and now you are literally chasing the train to beat her home'?

'He is romantic' Allan butted in whilst keeping his eye firmly on the road he was now speeding down leaving Aberystwyth.

'He is either that or a stalker. Do you not think this girl is going to be a bit freaked out when you appear at the station? Its a bit over the top isn't it? And to be honest boy, you look terrible. Your arm is bleeding and your shirt is ripped'.

'I have got to try, I don't want her to think I didn't care'.

'Well you clearly care about catching up with her. This is

going to be slim though David. Allan is risking his license here. It only takes twenty minutes on train. There is a chance we aren't going to catch up. Your only chance is if there is a lot of people getting on or off at Borth'. Lynne stopped looking at David whose face dropped again. 'My God you got it bad for her haven't you? Man I am to good for my own good. Alan don't drop me off until we pass back through, we can't afford to lose the time'.

'Thank you'.

'Shut up, bloody stupid man', she growled at him looking angrily via the rear-view mirror.

The red taxi cab continued through the villages and along the windy Welsh A road through woodland and countryside as the David got more and more impatient. Arriving at the road by the Dovey Junction sign where there was a few car spaces they pulled over and David jumped out of the car running down the path leaving the taxi behind him. Running down the very path he first saw Charlotte just hours before he was relieved to see the train wasn't there yet. Running onto the track he stood and looked in the direction of Borth expectantly but then he saw the train information screen which stated the next train would arrive from Aberystwyth at 20:58. He had missed the train and hadn't seen her heading home either. Standing in pain and out of breath he now sunk to sitting on the platform in the same place he did only hours earlier. The sun still high in the sky but with less power, he felt a cold chill. Sitting on the concrete considering what he had been through in the space of one day. He had finished a relationship, realised he hated his job and subsequent whole lifestyle and that he no longer belonged anywhere. Yet the thing that held him together was the smile of a complete stranger and now he had lost his chances of seeing that even one more time. Staring forward he looked into the bleak countryside feeling he knew more what Charlotte must have felt being abandoned with nowhere to go in her childhood. He had nothing now, no one and nowhere he felt he could go to. He replayed the day in his head, trying to think how he lost track of time. He blamed his brother for suggesting he called Kelly back in

London. He played the conversation over in his head and slowly stood up thinking about the long wait he now had.

Suddenly, the thought of Ziggy telling him that making the decision for change was the hardest part came into his head. He stood and looked at the map in the weather shelter before turning and looking down the path that he first saw her answer his cry for help this morning. He spoke to himself, verbalising his thoughts as if to double assess their value as he looked closely at the map.

'You either sit here and go back to Aberystwyth in a few hours achieving nothing. Or you go and find Aberdyfith and see if you can find her. Either way the worse that can happen is you feel as terrible as you do now'.

A decision made, a forward movement in his mind. David set of with some pace back up the path hoping but accepting that the taxi would no longer be waiting for him. Getting to the main road he figured it must be north as he hadn't seen any signs so started walking along the road and continued for over a mile before a tired looking outdated road sign pointed him up a narrow side road which steeply inclined upwards into the wooded hillside. Feeling encouraged that he was getting closer he pushed himself up the hill walking at the edge of the road which hugged a mountain stream. Every turn around a corner he assumed would be the final turning but eventually he saw a sign stating two more miles as he passed over the top of the hill and started heading downward finally seeing signs of buildings in the distance. Coming at the tiny habitat from above he stood looking at the town he had never even imagined was there before thinking about how he would find her. Hugged between two mountains the village was bigger than he expected but unless he knocked on every door he would struggle to find her. Heading down into the village he realised he hadn't thought the plan through but had no other option if he was every to see her again.

CHAPTER NINE

The small village was exactly how she described it but even more remote feeling. The narrow road he had been walking down didn't lead into the town but just passed straight by with a road turning off it into the main street. Thinking *why this town would ever be created in the first place* he continued walking towards the first buildings which were traditional Welsh stone with slate roofing. Looking ahead down the road of what could only be twenty buildings he first came across a cafe which was closed and upon further inspection he saw a tea room across the street which was also dark and closed. The only chance he had was also on the opposite side of the road to the cafe which was a small country pub. He looked at it for a little while feeling it didn't look too friendly and was confused as to how it could stay in business along with everything else in the tiny hidden empty village. *The Tusk Trail,* which was printed in dark green itallics on a equally dark red background, seemed a very strange name for the village pub. An establishment he assumed would be used mainly by the people of the area. Approaching, he could hear laughter and sound from within and felt a bit more reassured that if he asked for how to contact Charlotte that somebody would help him. Walking toward the door he stopped and turned looking back towards the village wondering if it would be easier to go from door to door. Entering through the heavy dark green painted wooden doors he was pleasantly surprised by the homely feel of the small lounge area he walked into. Looking around he could see a pool table and darts board in the far corner with a trophy cabinet suggesting they were a successful league team. The bar was a heavily polished dark wood above a brick wall curved around the L shape room. He waited as the bar man was busy changing the television channel for one of the clientele. In the pub there was three different groups of people and an elderly lady who was watching the television. David scanned the room hopeful but Charlotte was not in there. Sitting on a worn pale blue fabric covered stool at the bar he watched the room continue without noticing him and relaxed a little as the barman made he way around to him.

'Yes good sir, and what can I get for you on this lovely evening'? The white haired slightly overweight man said as he lowered his head to get back under the drink glass shelves above the bar.

'Erm yes, can I get a red wine please'. David asked.

'Yep certainly'.

'Have you got a merlot'?

'Nope we have got Welsh red wine'.

'What is that'?

'It is wine that is from Wales and is red'. The man explained slowly as if David was a child.

'What does it taste like'?

'Red wine'.

'Okay, that sounds lovely'.

The bar man turned and grabbed a bottle of wine with a plastic stopper in it. Brushing the dust off the neck of the wine. He poured a very generous glass out and turned giving it to David before taking the money from him. 'What are you doing in these parts then'?

'What do you mean'?

'Well its a rarity that at six in the evening we get anybody in here not from the village on a weekday. Sure we get walkers and tourists at the weekend but look around. We got the people from the cafe over there, the local accountants there, some local pensioners there and we got her there. She comes in everyday to watch her soaps over a pot of tea and then heads back home. Probably costs me more in electricity than she makes me in money. Just stumble across us did you'?

'No not quite'. David coughed after taking back some of the charcoal like tasting red wine for the first time. 'I am looking for somebody actually, I missed an appointment with her earlier and she lives in the village. I am just not sure where exactly'.

'Oh right who might that be then'? The barman became a bit more weary of the outsider now as he dried a glass with a tea towel in his hands.

'A girl called Charlotte, in her late twenties, long brown hair, brown eyes. Lives with her Nanna'? David looked on hopeful as the barman paused and looked upward as if contemplating.

'No sorry I haven't heard of her, must have the wrong village. I know everyone here and a young girl with long brown hair doesn't sound like anyone here'. As they spoke David moved slightly to let somebody pass him on their way back from the toilet. 'Trevor, this man here is looking for a Charlotte with long brown hair and brown eyes. I told him I don't know anybody with that name in our village, do I'?

'No I think you must have the wrong village there Mr'? The short overweight balding man in a cheap suit came closer inspecting David closely.

'Jones, David Jones'.

'Why are you looking for this girl'? Trevor tried to ask him with a more serious demeanor.

'I missed her earlier in Aberystwyth, I just don't want her to', David paused feeling he wasn't being told the truth and not wanting to reveal his need to see her again before he continued, 'I just needed to finish out our conversation'.

'So you are from big old Aberystwyth are you, what do you do over there'?

'No, no I am here just for a few days, I live in London now. I am just sorting some business out'.

'Well I am afraid you have the wrong village young sir. You should drink up and go back to check your details, probably best'. Trevor continued back to his seat where he continued to watch David as discreetly as possible.

'Sorry son'. The barman said almost apologetically.

'Well I suppose I will have one more, the next train isn't for another hour' David said before collecting his drink and sitting at a table near the door. He wasn't convinced by the barman and Trevor's performance and he hoped if he stayed a little longer they would be proved wrong if she came in for a drink. For the next half an hour he made his drink last until he admitted defeat and accepted sitting waiting for her to randomly appear in the pub was a waste of his time. It was nearly time for the next train towards Aberystwyth and it was too late to start going door to door. He could always come back tomorrow although he knew it was unlikely that he would. He to was starting to feel a little obsessed and felt he would come across creepy. Standing he looked around catching the eye of Trevor again before taking his glass to the bar. Waving at the barman who again was at the television he walked out of the room just hearing the barman say goodnight to the old lady who was called Gladys as the door closed. Immediately, he remembered the train conversation and felt the likelihood of there being multiple really elderly people with that name in the village was remote. Unsure of how to respond he walked away from the pub and crossed the road towards the cafe where he stood waiting with his phone as if sending a message, not that there was any signal in this remote location. Feeling really unsure of himself now he was aware that following an elderly woman home would make him seem very strange and that it was potentially difficult to explain to the police if she got scared. He also felt the need for one last attempt so he considered the best approach would be not to follow her but to watch from the end of the road and then follow her to the house or as close to it as he could work out she went to without raising her suspicions. The elderly lady walked at quite a pace on her two walking sticks but did not seem to go into any of the houses. Instead she appeared to disappear down a track at the end of the village into a woodland. Giving it a few minutes David slowly followed feeling more and more like he was doing something extremely wrong and then as he passed the buildings and got to the end of the track he saw that there was a tired stone wall marking the edge of the property a few meters behind the overgrown bushes. The track went about fifty meters into the woodland area where it cleared slightly to a small bungalow cottage which looked dilapidated at best. White originally but now more grey in colour, the lights were already on inside as the summer evening was dimmed due to the trees blocking the sunlight and putting the cottage in a dark shadow.

Walking down the track he questioned his actions and momentarily stopped reconsidering what he was doing. Feeling like he had put to much emphasis into his hope that she actually did want to see him again he was not feeling his previous determination. Why would she be interested in seeing him again? She surely was just being polite. He could have been anybody on that train and she would have spoken to them. It was just a nice girl being friendly and he had read to much into it. Turning he started walking up the path away from the house. Leaving the village down the main street he passed the public house where Trevor and the barman watched him leave whilst having a cigarette outside. The walk back to the station took him 25 minutes which he had very little thought running through his head. As he sat on the bench again at the platform he started evaluating his day in a business meeting like manner. His relationship back in London was over but in the last few hours he was more concerned about a complete stranger than Kelly. He put logic in and summarised that this was his coping mechanism. She was there at the right time and place and it would have been really uncomfortable if he had knocked on the door. His brother was right, he needed to think how he was going to move forward now and he would use his time in Aberystwyth to make that decision whilst supporting his brothers decision about the sale of the land. Sitting on the train he did a very good sales pitch to himself and believed his own reasoning until he left the station in a fresh rain shower that was filling the drains as he walked along the quiet streets. Looking at his phone he saw multiple regular missed calls from Ziggy. Undoubtedly trying to get an update after Lynne would have contacted him. Standing in the spot he last saw her, his heart sank and now his barriers were dropped. Suddenly he felt like he had lost two people that day, one who he thought he loved and one he wanted to believed he could love. His life was a lie like most of the business deals he made. Walking back towards the coffee shop in the diminishing daylight enhanced by the heavy rain-clouds, he added to the water collecting in the guttering with his tears. Alone and broken again.

CHAPTER TEN

January 4th 2014:

Ziggy was exhausted but finally things were getting to where he needed them. 2014 was going to be a much better year than the last one and a few months into his new business opening he felt more positive than ever about that aspect of his life. Sitting in his closed coffee shop he watched the rain lashing down at the windows as he calculated the days takings. He assumed with the students away that Christmas would be hard but his takings were actually quite strong in the run up to New Year, however the weather if nothing else had stopped many people coming out. He swept the floor whilst listening to the local radio talking about the on going storm which was reaching its climax as they spoke. Looking out onto the street he was shocked to the foam from the sea breaking on the shingle beach was floating all the way up the street. He had never seen that much before and he was feeling somewhat smug that he hadn't purchased a seafront shop as a result. Finishing his work he locked up for the night and set up his make shift bed in the store room using the handy shower cubicle in the back room to wash before he ate a microwave meal and settled down for the night. Reading in a dark store cupboard wasn't such a bad way to spend the night for him. Even back at the house with Liz he rarely watched television but he was able to escape with a book. When their marriage had fell apart the previous summer he was still in the process of signing for the shop and she agreed that if he would just walk away and leave her and his young son Noah alone that she would not argue her part ownership of the business.

He was tired and he agreed to being able to move on with minimal hassle. He had not seen Noah now for four months. He had missed his 7th birthday and his Christmas although he dropped a present outside their house both days. Knowing she felt he had embarrassed her he did not stick around to see him as he did not wish to put his young child who could not understand at his age through the emotional trauma the encounter would cause. Turning off his lamp he settled down for the night. The benefit of a store cupboard was it had no windows and therefore the sound of the rain and wind running up and down the streets had no impact on him and soon he was asleep which was the one place he felt he could truly be himself.

Suddenly the sound of breaking glass disturbed him as he sat up with a startle. Quickly pulling on his trousers he investigated to see an empty shop. Turning he headed upstairs to the photography studio he rented out to a gentleman called Paul. Unlocking the door he entered to find a roof tile had come through the window in the strong winds. Looking at his watch it was only 11pm and so he called both his brother Joe who would be able to board the window safely until he could get some glass the next day and also he contacted Paul as some of his work had got dampened by the rain water now blowing into the room. Within an hour Joe had got to them and blocked up the window before being called out to other numerous emergency jobs. As Paul was getting ready to leave they had a visit from the local police who asked them if they could open up for some international students staying over the Christmas break whose sea front residence had been flooded. It would only be a short while until the officer was able to secure a place for them to stay. Without a moments hesitation Paul went behind the bar and helped Ziggy serve the temporarily homeless students hot drinks and light snacks. Paul was impressed with Ziggy for not even questioning the financial cost of it and the two worked well as a team.

By one in the morning the police had worked with the university to find suitable emergency accommodation for the students away from the sea front. As they tidied up they both agreed that they would open later than normal in the morning as the custom would be low with the storm still battering the coastline. Paul also informed Ziggy that there was a spare bed for him in his flat that he would make it up for him as he wasn't letting him sleep in store room any longer. Going back to the flat Ziggy was impressed by how well made it was inside. The flat was part of a 19th century four floor building which looked small from the font but due to its length it made it spacious dwellings. Being on the top floor meant whilst on this evening the wind howled around them it had an attic conversion giving Paul an en-suite master room and a regular rooms below. After clearing the spare bed Paul joined Ziggy on the sofa with two glasses and a bottle of red wine.

'I don't know about you but I could do with a drink', he said as he opened the wine not waiting for it to breath and pouring a large glass for them both.

'I agree. What a night'. Confirmed Ziggy. 'Nice place you have here. I bet the sun terrace is nice out the back. You know in different weather conditions obviously'.

'Yes it is, you can see into the harbour when you sit out there. You will have to take my word for it though'. The two sat quietly for a minute or so before Paul continued. 'How long have you been living in the closet'?

'Wow'! Sniggered Ziggy. 'That is one double barreled question if I have ever heard one. In what way do you mean'?

'I mean living in that store room'.

'Since September. When Liz and me finally agreed it was over I agreed to walk away and she would have the house, I would have the business and it would be cleanly separated. She wanted Noah to have stability but nothing else from me. In return I agreed not to confuse him and just have to stay away'.

'Confuse him'?

'Yes, this way he doesn't have to deal with the fact that daddy is now gay and Liz doesn't have to feel ashamed with friends. It is easier if I am the bastard that just walked out on his family'.

'Easier for who? Liz? It's a big thing and awkward I get it but couples fail more than succeed these days for all sorts of reasons that are far less acceptable than being honest with yourself'.

'You think'? Ziggy stared into his glass as if looking for answers in his drink.

'Yes! Okay you probably have hurt her. But you didn't do this to hurt her on purpose did you? You didn't say I know I will go gay now and hell with consequences. Oh yes and to make life just a little bit more fun I will start sleeping in a store cupboard. No, you didn't because you wouldn't set out to hurt anybody'.

'No but I did hurt her and my son'. The regret became edged over Ziggy's face aging him instantly.

'No you are hurting your son'.

'What do you mean'?

'I get it. It's a bit of a difficult situation to explain but who is it protecting Noah or Liz? He is a young boy who will get upset and then like all young lads realise he really loves his dad. Who by the way hasn't actually changed and he will accept your honesty in yourself. You aren't going to rub it in his face, you aren't going to take someone round that he must also call daddy. He has to know you are just going to be there as a normal dad. His mom is the one who may need to get over that'.

'I don't know if I can cope with that just yet'.

'Well have some more wine and I am sure we can talk you into it'. Smiling he poured another glass for Ziggy.

'You are too good to me'. Ziggy looked at him longer than intended.

'You are too hard on yourself and too stubborn to ask for help. You knew I had a flat and have lived on my own since before we met, why didn't you ask to stop over or if I could help you out'? Turning to face Ziggy, Paul insisted on an answer.

'I guess I just didn't want to complicate things'.

'Sometimes the best things start out complicated'. Paul looked at Ziggy and took his glass from him. Hearing only the sound of Ziggy's breathing rate picking up he knew the feeling was shared between them. Lifting his hand he stroked the side of Ziggy's face and slowly leaned forward kissing him softly on the lips. Stopping and looking at each other, Ziggy displayed a reciprocal smile before pulling Paul towards him. They now kissed intensely and Ziggy pulled at Paul wanting more.

'I haven't, with another man I mean'. Ziggy whispered receiving a reassuring nod from Paul who pulled him from the sofa with clear intentions.

That night the two became lovers. As the rest of the town slept Ziggy was awoken and honest fully for the first time. He felt love for Paul and not that he would admit it for many months to come, Paul felt complete in return.

CHAPTER ELEVEN

The coffee shop was lit largely by candle light in the evenings to add to the special ambiance. All of the electric lights were low wattage and just added to the background glow of serenity as Ziggy intended. Each table had its own lamp shaped to effectively light the table but not around it for those wishing to read. Tonight was quiet and on other evenings like this Ziggy may have closed but a few were in and he liked that people socially gathered at his shop rather than in the bars and clubs. He saw it as doing his bit for society. He may have aided caffeine addiction but whilst people were in his establishment they were not drinking alcohol or smoking the local varieties of specialist drugs he had gotten involved in during his youth. Sitting at the bar opposite Ziggy was Paul, his partner of over four years and the man he loved. He had his head down in his paper diary that was more of a disorganised scrap book which only he could manage a business from. For a man that was so linked in with photographic technology and had a huge resume on his website it always amazed Ziggy how he had his system of making detailed notes of his event coverage in his books before putting the information onto his wall planner by hand upstairs. The man who employed two full time photographers for studio and event work refused to join the modern world for planning and organising his business. Looking at the small group of students chatting Ziggy smiled as he watched them deep in discussion probably about the latest American political agenda or some part of life they were way too young to fully comprehend yet. He loved the young enthusiasm of students who had not been tainted by life's ultimate disappointment. He looked on hopeful for them to block that part of the world out and ensure they would live to their potential and make a positive difference. His own son would be twelve now and must be getting opinionated. He hadn't seen him in nearly five years. He longed for him but he couldn't go against the wishes of the boy's mother. She had the power to take everything away from him. Looking back at Paul he smiled at the man who supported him through the difficult times that followed the separation and slowed their relationship. Apart from missing his son, Ziggy was happy. Content in work, content with his man and content with his alloted niche. Looking across the shop he worried about his brother and the lost look and thought process he had shown today but believed the visit would help him.

The door of the coffee shop opened as a rain battered David walked in to the welcome of Ziggy's smile. David looked like a weathered statue of his younger self with signs of tiredness and self doubt cracking his relatively young good looks. Turning he slowly took his coat off revealing the pain his body was in and hung it on the hanger before placing both arms on the service bar next to where Paul was working. Turning to face him Paul smiled at him with a huge grin on his face as if he knew of some success that David was unaware of but David's face told the true story.

'Tough few hours brother? Why don't you go and sit over in the corner and I will bring you over a large hot chocolate'? Whispered Ziggy in a secretive manner confusing David as Paul looked on.

'No, I think I will just go back to my hotel room and have a long soak in the bath if it is all the same with you. I have a cut on my arm and I am bruised all over. Can I grab my bags please Ziggy'?

'It's fine by us mate but I think it might be a bit rude'. Ziggy smiled.

'Who to'?

'To that very nice young lady who had been sat reading patiently in the corner over there since about six this evening'.

Ziggy raised his eyebrows and pointed in the direction of the girl sitting curled up on the bench deeply reading a book as David's eyes lit up in more a sign of relief than excitement. 'Said she was late and missed her train, for some reason she wanted to see you. I tried to ring you but there was no answer. I managed to keep her here saying I would drive her home if you didn't get back by nine thirty. I didn't think she would stay to be honest so I said I would put her drinks on your tab and she could borrow a book to read. Surprising really, she seemed really keen to wait for you. I am quite impressed by her'.

'Why'? David smiled with almost tears coming from his eyes.

'She chose to read Cranford by Gaskell. Very powerful. Anyway, shall I bring you some more drinks across or shall I tell her you have gone home'? He smiled waiting for the returning smile which David cracked after panicking momentarily with his rising heartbeat as Paul spoke quietly to him.

'She wouldn't be here, waiting for you if she didn't want to see you again. Go and be you. Not that annoying businessman that your brothers had to deal with earlier but you, nothing but you'.

David walked around the group of students and stood looking down at her curled around the book. The vision of her waiting for him lit his heart like an uncontrollable fire which equally dried out his mouth and cleared his mind of any logic. Eventually he could only think of one thing to say which told him how sweet she must be.

'You have four sugars in a hot chocolate'?

Turning to see him she smiled immediately as he sat across from her unsure of himself in a way she found refreshingly reassuring.

'I was tired, I thought it would wake me up slightly', she responded.

'He serves strong coffee you know'?

'Your brother, yes he is really nice and so is the other man'. Charlotte looked across as Paul and Ziggy tried to busy themselves as if they were straining to listen into the conversation.

'No I told him I don't like coffee and needed some sugar. I haven't eaten yet so was feeling a bit weak to be honest. They gave me some cake as well. Apparently, you are buying? I hope you don't mind'? She scurried through each point feeling unsure of herself as he smiled. 'I am sorry I was late to the station but I left my bag at the council house and had to run back before they shut. I missed the train and so I thought I would come here as you said your brother had a coffee shop. I didn't know if you would mind. Its a bit weird I know but I didn't want to miss spending some more time with you'.

'It's the best part of my day'. David blushed as the two smiled at each other awkwardly before they were interrupted by Ziggy.

'The girl hasn't eaten this evening. I think the best you can do is some food David. You can borrow my car if you want to get back home after, he can give you a lift'. Smiling with a mischievous look on his face Ziggy placed his keys down before practically skipping off leaving David to follow up on his offer.

'Would you like to? I mean if you don't have to get back? It would be nice and the least I can do for you waiting for me'. He waited as his heart almost tripled in beats.

'I would like that very much. I spoke to my Nanna a while back on the shop phone. I told her I would be late back so she wont be waiting up'.

The two soon left the coffee shop using one of Ziggy's customary umbrellas to cover from the rain and headed towards a local restaurant. Having talked about their options, David soon found out that Charlotte had never eaten Indian food before as she found the choice intimidating so he suggested they go to the *Shilam*. Entering out of the rain her senses were hit by a banquet of rich cooking spices diffusing from the kitchen much to her delight. Watching David as he asked for a table she was impressed with his maturity and knowledge of the world. Whilst he spoke with the waiter at their table she was able to study him more. She felt attracted to him but was not able to decide why. Looking at him she could see he was tired and had a stressful life with less colour in his skin than others his age and that his eyes told of a hard few years but his kindness could be seen through all that and when he looked at her his hopeful youth seemed to shine through. She felt a want to understand this man and felt he was genuine about being interested in her. Talking her through some of the food in the menu he ordered a mix of foods for them both and watched as she devoured her poppadom.

'So how was your day? You seem a lot more relaxed than when I first met you'? She asked whilst pouring what she felt was a magical luminous green sauce onto her poppadom.

'Yeah, it has been interesting but positive I think' David responded not wanting to ruin the evening by mentioning the fact he was that very morning living with another woman in a long term relationship.

'Okay, we are still not at that point then? How did your business meeting go with your brothers'?

'I am not sure to be honest'. Again in a single sentence answer.

'Are you going to actually talk to me this evening'? Charlotte suddenly seemed upset with him.

'Sorry'? He questioned.

'I have waited hours for you. Stupidly maybe, but something made me do it. Do you realise how difficult that is for me? I have lived in a tiny village for most of my life and this is the first time in years I am not there as it is getting dark. I am taking a chance to get to know you and you are telling me nothing'.

'I'm sorry. It's just'. He paused.

'What'? She seemed agitated by whatever excuse he was about to give.

'I went to find you as well'.

'What do you mean'? She said trying not to release an uncontrollable smile with her mouth full of tangy mango chutney.

'Well after getting to the station late I took a taxi to Dovey Junction trying to catch you. I missed the train arriving there so walked to your village'.

'No, I don't believe you'. Charlotte couldn't hide her smile any longer from him.

'The Tusk Trail is it? I went in there and asked how I could find you but the barman said he had never heard of you'.

'That will be Erik. He told you they didn't know me'?

'Yeah him and another guy called Trevor'.

'I do shifts there on weekends sometimes to help out. I can't believe they told you they didn't know me'.

'I don't think they liked me being there to be honest'.

'Oh my. How sweet of them. Trying to protect me from the stranger'. She shook her head in disbelief. 'Well I guess that is why Nanna said there was a strange business man looking for me'.

'That was her wasn't it watching the television'? David asked excited that he could confirm his theory.

'Yes she watches her soaps in there every night, we don't have a television in the cottage. We can't receive a signal you see. I can't believe you went after me'. Charlotte squeezed his hand lovingly across the table triggering the release of waves of adrenaline through his body.

'I didn't want you to think I hadn't shown up'. David looked at the table unable to be push the confidence to look her in the eyes.

'But you went all the way to my village'?

'You are the best thing that happened to me today. I didn't want to lose you as well'.

'Then you have got to be honest with me about what is going on with you. I can't help you if you wont tell me what it is that made you look like you did this morning on that platform'.

'I don't want to scare you away before I even get to know you'.

'Not being honest is what is scaring me', she leaned inward signaling him to tell her his story.

'Okay',David paused. 'I have just come out of a long term relationship. I guess I should tell you that. And I mean just literally this morning when I caught my girlfriend in the shower with another man. It had shocked me but as I sat on the train I wasn't surprised about it. Playing different things in my head I can see we had drifted apart but I was working hard saving for our house deposit which is a big amount in London. I think I became so obsessed with getting that and doing well at work that maybe I stopped living for the moment. She probably got bored of the late nights alone I guess. I have become obsessed with work. It pays really well but I am there fourteen hours a day and it is so highly pressured that people not too much older than me regularly get seriously ill from it. You get on a cycle of the same pattern though and yet you can't see it. You have a repeating daily routine, you get up and skip breakfast to get their early, eat on the go and then work late before being too tired to cook properly when you get home. That becomes a pattern for five days and then you spend the weekend recovering so you are about ready to start again when Monday comes around. It becomes a weekly pattern and then monthly. You become obsessed and don't even take your holiday as you don't want to miss a beat. Standing on that junction today alone was the first time I was faced with nothing to do and occupy my mind in years. Mixing that with what I saw this morning I was filled with dread. Not of what had happened but not knowing where I was going'.

'What is her name'? Charlotte questioned almost in pain.

'Kelly'.

'Have you spoken to her'?

'Yes she cried but agreed it was over eventually. I am happy I called her, Ziggy made me do it'.

'So why are you here in Aber? Were you just running away from it'?

'No, this was a planned trip. My brothers and me own a strip of land. We inherited it from our dad who inherited it from our grandfather. We have tried to sell it before back to the council but every time there has been some legal loophole stopping us. They haven't been able to build on it as my grandfather promised it would be used to benefit the town'.

'That's good of him'.

'I am not so sure of that from what dad told us'.

'Go on, why not'? The smile returned slightly to her face as the story intrigued her.

'Well my grandfather, William Jones moved here in 1925

working with Great Western Railway to develop the station. He built the original grand terminus building we are now sat in. Apparently all of this was at that time a train station before the number of platforms was dropped down to two. Anyway he worked on the construction of the business but then fell in love with the town as so many people do. A few years later after the building was completed and the rail line work was completed he got a job with the university. He did very well for an unedu-cated man and managed to raise some serious finances. We are not sure how to be honest but what he made early in life he certainly lost through gambling later in life. Anyway he put a successful bid for land from the council when the economy of the town slipped. He was convinced that the university which was then housed almost completely in the Old College would need to expand so he bought the nearest piece of land he could afford feeling it was only logical they would expand to build the campus up by the sea. That was in the mid 1930's and he lived in a nice house near the castle. He was a player and used his confidence and good looks to charm my grandmother I have no doubt. She was younger than he was and they were married in 1939 as the war broke out. He served and when he got back soon after my dad was born. The land he brought was an invest-ment in his eyes thinking the university would be desperate to buy it off him and this would be in the public benefit which is why he accepted the terms of buying the land. Problem was in the 1950's as he was getting towards wanting to sell the land, the university moved up the hill away from the seafront and became the Penglais Campus. My grandfather died and my dad inherited the land. Dad tried to convince the university to use the land for something but there was always more problems in building on the land. It was designated common land in an his-toric sense so as I said unless it had public benefit construction was prohibited. At one point dad almost got a housing company to buy it off him but they decided the legal issues would be too great so when dad died we inherited it from him'.

'Wow, and now you are finally going to sell it'? Charlotte

asked with further interest.

'Well we are working with a man from a development agency and a hotel chain who are interested in developing it'.

'But how can they build a hotel on it if your dad couldn't build houses'?

'Well this is what I thought but apparently according to the agent dealing with us there is a short time frame where the council are lowering the red tape to help reinvestment in the town and they have agreed if we sell the land now for this hotel to go ahead'.

'You don't seem so sure'?

'Well I was earlier but now I am wavering. I just think whilst nobody would ever celebrate the land it is an open stretch of grass where the public can enjoy the views. We have never had the money from it before, do we really need it that badly? It just seems a bit suspicious to me that the council are just going to let it go after all this time and I don't think it will help the local independent hotels if another big name opens in the town. Having said that Herman said it could bring further investment into the town'.

'Hang on a minute, Herman? Do you mean Herman Splythe'? Charlotte's eyes opened wide.

'Yes he represents the buyers. Why do you know him'?

'Yes he was the councilor I had my meeting with today. He must have seen you afterward'.

'Why were you meeting with him'?

'I don't want to go into it, but I wouldn't trust that man as far as I could throw him'.

'Well hold on a minute, you said I had to tell you everything so does that not mean you should tell me everything'?

'No because I am not ready to tell you everything' she smiled.

'Well, when you are I am ready for you to do so'.

The two continued to eat and conversation went backwards and forward about their childhoods. All the time David feeling she was hiding something about herself from him. But the two both enjoyed each others company and the meal came to an end sooner than either wanted. Walking along the sea front in the warm July night air the two passed the Victorian Pier and Charlotte grabbed David by his hand pulling him down onto the beach.

'Did you ever see the photo of the elephants on the beach taken just over there'? She questioned him pointing twenty or so meters into the sea.

'Yes I think anyone that knows this town had seen that'.

'Can we go to your hotel room? I want to tell you a story', she smiled as he nodded slightly shocked by the rapid development of events.

Quickly the two walked to his seafront hotel where they went to his room. She sat in a chair in the bay window as he made them tea from the miniature kettle that was so traditional of rooms in seaside hotels. Sitting on the bed he took his shoes off as she started telling him a story which dated back over a century.

'My Nanna was on the beach, the day of the elephant's visit'.

'Really'? Interrupted David. 'How is that possible wasn't it over one hundred years ago'?

'Yes, she was a small girl then, Nanna is over one hundred years old'.

'My God, she didn't look bad for a girl that old, you could make a fortune if you bottled her secret'.

'Yes a lot of people say that. She has really slowed down recently though. Her body is in a lot of pain'. Charlotte paused before moving on with her story. 'Anyway my Nanna's parents moved to Aberystwyth that very year in fact. They rented a nice house near the old quarry that they've now put those luxury flats on. They say the land wouldn't be stable enough for a large development so the flats being spread out meant they could charge high prices and actually get something on the land without subsidence. My Nanna lived in a house you can still see there today. They moved here when her father got a job leading part of the team which were going to build the National Library of Wales. She used to tell me the story of the elephants visit all the time when I was younger. I didn't realise it was so long before I was born. Anyway it was 1911 and the town of Aberystwyth was a prosperous seaside resort for the rich and wealthy of Wales and England. My Nanna tells me about how she met people from London, Manchester and even Wolverhampton in her summers here as a young girl. It wasn't like today with children. They were allowed out in them days and it was safe to be out. That summer she tells me the town was on tender hooks awaiting the visit of King George who would be laying the foundation stone of the National Library in the same month the elephants unexpected visit occurred in fact. She is forever telling new people she meets about the elephants in the sea and if you look very carefully at that picture you can actually see her father standing on the beach. The elephant visit was not a planned thing and in fact it was really just a publicity stunt by a visiting circus called Bostock and Wombell's. They traveled the U.K with these animals and then went to Europe or that was the plan. Well the story goes the weather that July was extremely hot and the one morning the keeper decided to take the elephants for a cool dip in the waters off Aberystwyth Promenade. That is when Nanna's father who was walking through the town spotted the elephants. Now in those days elephants were a really big thing and he ran home to get Nanna and her mother. They all rushed to the seafront and saw the elephants that magical morning which became a part of the town's celebrated history'.

'That is amazing that she was there but I don't understand why are you telling me this'? Questioned David as he lay against the headboard as Charlotte moved across sitting on the spare side of the bed next to him.

'According to my Nanna the elephant keeper wasn't finished then and this is where historical events do go a bit hazy. My Nanna claims and, there is to be honest very little evidence to back this up, that there was a terrible accident which she witnessed an hour or so after that photo on the beach was taken'.

'What sort of accident'? David was genuinely intrigued having never heard of the story before.

'Well Nanna would tell you that whilst her father had to go off to work, her mother was as even more enamored with the elephants than he was and the two followed them as they were taken along the seafront towards Constitution Hill. The keeper wanted the press to take photos with the elephants on the top of the hill which was a very regarded tourist destination. Well the elephants got more stressed as the crowds grew and as they went up the hill the pathway crossed the funicular railway which was water operated at the time. It was really a miracle of design with one cart going up the very steep incline as one came down but due to how its water operated system it was very loud. Anyway Nanna says that the descending cart scared one of the elephants and it smashed through the picket fencing colliding with the cart going up the hill knocking it off the track and on it's side. My Nanna and her mother saw it all and apparently and at least two people died at the scene. One being a local baker and some say the other was a visiting royal dignitary from another country. She thinks some others later died also but definitely there were more injured'.

'I have never heard that before'. David said leaning forward with interest.

'No well, that is the thing you see. It is largely a forgotten event now because according to Nanna, her parents and everybody else in the town were sworn to secrecy about it and told to pretend it never happened as it would have put the planned visit of King George V only ten days later in jeopardy and could have damaged the whole reputation of the town. Instead the funicular rail was repaired quickly and the press did not report the incident at all, only the initial visit of the elephants in the bay waters which is still remembered today. Within a generation it has been almost completely lost as if it never happened. Behind the scenes though there were serious problems which needed to be sorted and quickly before the King's entourage arrived. The circus moved on immediately but left the elephants behind not wanting the disaster to be linked financially to them if the council followed it up. The elephants were abandoned in a field tied to a post and somehow it landed on Nanna's father to sort out the removal of them. At the time freight trains were more common and used to deliver goods by rail as the roads were so difficult and with only a few days until the King arrived the mayor ordered the removal of the elephants immediately. Nanna's mother who had shown such a love for the animals and had spent time visiting them for the previous few days was employed to remove the elephants from the town and take care of them until they could be dealt with properly following the visit of the King. Anyway they managed to get them on a freight train and decided to use the Dovey Junction Terminal to take them into the woodland and keep them on an old abandoned farm which still had a good cottage attached. So on the twenty third of July only two days before the King's visit they took them across to the small village of Aberdyfith and kept them in a barn. Nanna's mother stayed with them for days as the King's visit kept her father busy. After organising the removal of the two elephants they had to clean up the trail of elephant dung left behind to make the town sparkling for the King.

'So what happened next'?

'Well the King's visit was a success and he officially laid the first foundation stone for the National Library of Wales. Nanna met the King that day as her father helped him lay the foundation down due to his role on the construction of it. The next day the mayor had to make a decision about the fate of the elephants. Whilst he probably wanted them shot and forgotten about, apparently there was enough public following of the story to prevent that. So he visited the farm in Aberdyfith and decided if Nanna's parents were happy to look after them that he would legally sign over a one hundred year lease on the land to them to look after the elephants. I don't know why one hundred years I guess he thought they must live that long or something'.

'So he let them just have the land for free'?

'As far as the Mayor was concerned it got rid of his problem and let him keep face with the public at the same time. He went back to Aberystwyth having solved the problem making others in office pleased with him and the focus of getting the library completed could continue. Well for a while the elephants were quite a big tourist attraction and just an added place you could visit on the way to or from Aberystwyth on the train but things would soon change'. Charlotte paused as David finished their drinks and she took a sip from the small cup before placing it on the bedside cabinet. 'In 1914 World War One started and had large ramifications on the town and also on Nanna's new found home in the village. The town was hit by financial hardship as was the rest of the country. The National Library was put on hold as money was put into the war effort. With the pressures of this and the expectations upon him, Nanna's father was signed up and left in 1915 to represent his country. He never came back. The money they originally had to advertise their reserve from the council stopped and income pretty much became the soldier wage during the war. Then later village handouts kept Nanna and her mother there'.

'So how long did the elephants last'?

'Strange thing about the two wars according to Nanna was that it caused a lot of circus companies to go out of business. When councils around the country suddenly had to deal with abandoned elephants they were told to send them to to Aberdyfith. Soon the numbers went up to a point where they had over ten elephants who ranged from new born to over fifty years old. Some arrived more tame than others but her mother would calm them and somehow kept their health good by exercising them through the endless valleys and woodlands, taking them to wash in the river Dyfi and down to the isolated beaches during the summer. In the winter keeping them locked inside during the cold wet months insulated in barns packed with hay'.

'So how long did this all last'?

'They had over ten elephants and happy elephants inevitably have children leading to a new generation'.

'Hang on you are telling me that they bred elephants in that little tiny village in the middle of nowhere'?

'Nanna said the elephants were highly stressed when living in the circus and this loss of stress made them quite amorous let's say. As her mother got older Nanna took over and continued to run the business which whilst the village was still a slate mine town there were plenty of visitors. Nanna met her first husband Alexander Smith and married in 1931 in her twenties. She was quite old back then to still be single. Makes me feel like a lost cause. They fell pregnant within a year and had some children before he went to fight in the second World War. He also lost his life meaning that nanna had to fend for herself with young children just like her mother did only 30 years earlier. Again with the war being on, more abandoned elephants were delivered. Following the war she met Simon and got married to become Gladys Roderick in 1953 before having more children. Well times had changed and as she got older her children left and by the time they found me on the platform twenty years ago they were living alone. They were already in their 80's but she was going strong and Simon was still strong enough to do many of the farm chores. He died about five years after they found me but by then I was able to help her out. Since then I have done the harder jobs as we don't have the money to employ anyone now. The whole place is forgotten really'.

'Are you telling me that you have elephants still there today'? David could not believe the insinuation.

'Yes we have three, two females and one male they must be about 40 years old now so they are now. Not young anymore but they are all very healthy'.

'But how is that still allowed today'?

'It wouldn't be if the we started up today but it was deemed a supported venture back then and has survived ever since'.

'But how do you survive'?

'We have Nanna's pension and her savings. Her children and grandchildren send money to support as well'.

'But you have stopped to look after her all these years preventing yourself from leaving the village and living your own life. Shouldn't her biological children have helped to'?

'She looked after me when my biological parents walked away. She could have walked away as well but she didn't so I am not going walk away now. Besides that, some of her children are gone now, they died of old age'.

'But you need to worry about yourself. Look at you, you are a stunningly beautiful intelligent woman who is living almost in hiding. Your life is going to pass you by and all you will do is stop in that place. I think you are an amazing person but what happens when she does go in the future. You will be left there alone'.

'Well unfortunately I don't think that choice will be left to me'.

'Why'? David quized her with interest.

'That meeting with the council today was to discuss the future of the farm. You see the one hundred year lease signed to Nanna's mother and that was transfered to her but has expired and now there are several years of unpaid land fees. They want to sell the land to some company that Herman Splythe represents'.

'What? Why would Merriman Initiatives be interested in your cottage'? David sat up in shock.

'I don't know but they have been putting the pressure on more and more recently. Nanna would be forced to go into a home. I am not sure what they would do about the elephants'.

'What about you'?

'I don't really matter do I? Not to a company that big, I am just collateral damage. I guess I would just get put in some bedsit until I can find some place to work'.

'I won't let you end up like that, let me help you'. David took Charlotte's hand as she rested her forehead against his neck and chest.

'You don't owe me anything', she whispered softly.

'I owe you from this morning and I want to be there for you'.

'But you don't even know me', Charlotte pulled away and

looked at him with slightly watery eyes.

'No but I would like to'

'I would like you to' she smiled at him and raised her face towards him where slowly the two came together and kissed for the first time with a soft passionate and lingering embrace. Lowering onto the bed they continued the moment, kissing as their hands explored with slow advancement.

For Charlotte she felt a want to trust this man and be his at that moment but felt he could be responding to his broken relationship. Continuing to get more excited she could feel his emotions stirring and didn't want to upset him by stopping. For David, he felt the tiredness of the day override him, ending it in the most perfect way.

CHAPTER TWELVE

December 19th 2015:

Heather Jones sat in the dark living room not paying attention to her television which was providing the only illumination and could have been on mute for all she knew. Her head was empty of hope and her heart hurt following her loss. Now all alone she had no idea where her husband Joe was as it got later each night until he rolled in not able to face her and talk to her as she needed him to. He had ensured that she was suffering her loss truly alone. For the first few weeks he was okay in the hospital but as he went out of auto-pilot mode and he could no longer treat it as an illness that would pass he withdrew from her. She watched as he faded backward to avoid accepting that their unborn was gone each day as he became more separate and distanced himself. She didn't blame him. She knew he wouldn't cope and worried about him as she lay in the hospital bed facing the unimaginable truth. She felt to blame as his emotions rotted in his mind leaving only a wrinkled stress calved shell of his former self which was unable to communicate with his wife of three years. At first he avoided her in their small home which they had done up together as a team but now each meeting was like two strangers. He kept the nursery shut unable to deal with the empty cot and room he had lovingly painted. Soon he found even the house too painful and seemed to avoid it at all times. Leaving early and getting home drunk when the bars closed if at all, he slept in his clothes on the sofa and left as soon as he could. Weekends were the worst when they were trapped together until he would mutter a weak excuse to get out of the house. An excuse she would sit and wait for without fighting. She didn't have the strength any longer. She knew they were not going to survive this but each night she waited hoping he would come back and just hold her. She didn't need words of comfort, she just needed him there.

This Saturday had been a particularly bad morning when she tried to move them forward. She got herself up early and had cooked them a breakfast with all the trimmings. The last time that she had done that was on the first of January that year. Since then times went from happy to the happiest and then to the heart break they faced in the early Autumn. She called him from his bed which was the sofa and he sat in silence as she tried to talk about what they would do on Christmas Day. But he was not there. He stared down at the table and when she cracked and sobbed in front of him he simply stood walking away and out of the house. She had lay on the sofa for most of the day not able to open her curtains. She was trapped and alone. She needed him but he needed an out.

Sitting on the bench in the bus stop across from his house Joe sat waiting for the television to switch off in the drizzle of the cold winter's night. He had drunk so much he felt like he had all the answers and yet he didn't have the strength to deal with them. He loved her but he could not make it right. He knew he needed to go into that house and be there for her but he couldn't look at her anymore. He was a failure and in her weakest moment he was not there. He had not been there for her or for his clients and now he was paying more into the bar tab than his mortgage which would soon become another thing she would have to deal with. He loved her, he really did. That is why he was sat in the rain sobbing. If he didn't he would have been in a different part of the country now but he just couldn't show it. Momentarily he was distracted as his phone buzzed. Looking at the incoming call he rejected the call from Ziggy and stood. Crossing the road wearily he slid the key into the lock and turned it pushing the door directly into his living room where she sat. Still in her night gown from this morning, it was clear he had done this to her and he broke. Quickly he rushed passed and went to the kitchen where he clasped at the sink with his hand struggling to breath. Feeling her warm hand on his arm he turned unable to look at her and banged his hand down smashing the glasses on the draining board. Holding his cut hand against him he pulled away as she tried to check on it a few moments later. Walking to the door she desperately put herself in front of him.

'We need to talk Joe. We can't keep doing this'. She pleaded through floods of erratic tears at him.

'I am sorry, I just can't face it'. He reached past her shoulder to unlock the door and walked away onto street. Leaving her behind he walked into the darkness not able to look back.

CHAPTER THIRTEEN

Ziggy wiped the table following the early morning rush of students getting their caffeine fix for a discounted price and another stamp on the loyalty card. Turning he rejoiced in the fact that Charlotte and David entered hand in hand looking very much together.

'Well it looks like you two had a wonderful evening'. Smiling as they embarrassingly acknowledged him they quickly sat down at the nearest table. Ziggy went to the counter where his brother joined him moments later as Joe entered the shop preventing the two from being able to start the conversation that Ziggy wanted.

'Good morning gentlemen. I trust you both had a fine evening'. Joe stopped as he spotted the smallest glance from Ziggy to David. 'Hang on one minute. What was that look for? I sense something has happened and by the look on your face Zigster it is a good thing'?

'I think it truly was my brother'. Whispered Ziggy. 'Let us just say David here had a particular lovely night last night'.

'What? David you little Casanova you. Who is she, what happened'?

'Can you be a little bit more discrete please'?

'Is that her? Sat in the corner over there? She looks far too attractive to be interested in you. I am going to have to go and say hello'.

'No wait'. David watched as Joe jumped in front of Charlotte who was staring into space making her land back in reality with a bump. From the counter they watched him shake her hand and start talking enthusiastically with her. Within a few moments she laughed and turned with a loving smile towards David.

'I think I preferred it when he was embarrassed wearing a pilot outfit', David sighed.

'He is harmless, you know he won't do any damage don't you'?

'Yes I know'. David nodded.

'You look happy David. I got to say you are a quick mover but if its just a quick fling that you needed then it looks like it did you the world of good'.

'A quick fling'? David gave an unimpressed look towards his brother.

'Oh wait. You really do have it bad for her don't you? Bedding her the first night may not have told her that though you know'.

'I fell asleep'.

'What'? Ziggy laughed.

'We sat and talked for hours but by this point my day had been a very long and stressful one. We were getting intimate and the next thing I knew I woke up in the morning light and she was having a shower in the en-suite'.

'Well she must really like you then'.

'Why'? David did not follow his brothers thought process.

'If you fell asleep on someone who didn't like you they wouldn't have walked in here with you hand in hand all smitten with you. There is some unfinished business in her mind though, don't you forget it'.

'I can't think about anything else now thanks to you'.

'Just be careful brother. She is lovely, you both look so happy. But in a few days time you are going to be going back to London and she will be stopping here'.

'I know. Look anyway before I take her home I need to do something. I need to go and speak to Mr Splythe from Merriman Initiatives again'.

'I haven't decided if I am going to sign yet David, and I don't think Joe is keen on the idea to be honest. We have got until the weekend, don't you think you are rushing it a bit'? Whispered Ziggy to ensure Joe didn't hear.

'No, it's not that'. David turned his back away from Charlotte and Joe's table. 'Charlotte is involved with them as well'.

'What'?

'Her home is at risk from them and I want to see if there is any-thing I can do to help her'.

'Are you sure she is being legitimate with you'?

'Yes. Look I need to go and see him. Can you go and talk to Charlotte for me? She can tell you the story behind this and maybe you two can come up with some ideas of how to help her'?

'Of course I will but how do you think you will get a meeting with Splythe with no notice'?

'Simple. I am going to go down to his office and ask to see him. You don't turn someone away who you are waiting to sign a contract that will start a multi million pound complex devel-opment do you'?

'No I suppose not'.

Herman Splythe sat in his office reading the broad sheets feel-ing satisfied that his objectives for the month were all coming together. Listening to the sound of the waves crashing on the beach through his large open window he had to admit that he was enjoying this assignment more than he thought he would. He originally felt the two year transfer to Wales was a demotion but he was happy to swallow his pride for the paycheck. Now as the project developed he found himself actually excited by the potential developments he was coordinating and believed they could get the strong hold on the town that was needed to carry out the larger innovation plans. This was a new beginning for the company which he was leading from the small suitable office allowing him to keep face with the locals he was initially working with. Indeed the headquarters would need to move to the hotel facility once that was built to start phase two. The meeting with shareholders and investors today would be fine as long as they could see progress and thus they had hired out the Old College in order to make a grand impression. Sitting drinking his protein shake he smiled over the plans and walked over to the table which had a map of the town and local area. Standing above it he looked at the sites and smiled down upon the place as he felt he was now making considerable strides forward.

Suddenly distracted by his office phone ringing he walked over and pressed the speaker button.

'Mr Splythe, there is a David Jones here. He doesn't have an appointment but he says he would like to talk to you a bit more about the contract you gave him yesterday'. The voice of his secretary downstairs informed him.

'Okay, that is fine. Send him up Donna'.

'Yes Sir'.

Folding away the map on the board room table Splythe quickly sat back in his chair to direct his guest away from the table and to his desk when he entered. Within a few moments a knock at the door followed and he called David into the room.

'David. Please do take a seat'. Splythe stood giving a confident handshake before sitting back down behind his desk. 'Some Nepalese coffee? I wasn't expecting to see you so soon. What do I owe for this pleasure? Have you got me a signed contract'?

'I am afraid not yet Mr Splythe. I have signed it but my brothers want to wait a few days not to make a knee jerk reaction'.

'Fair enough, they know the deadline. Are you confident they will sign it'?

'I am sure I can sway them if needed'.

'Well I would be grateful. It is a very good offer David. So what is it I can do for you'?

'I was impressed the other day at the designs for the hotel but I got the feeling this is part of something bigger. You see I work for a development agency in London and I know we never just look at the one site. You must have other plans to develop a bigger network or you wouldn't be setting up office here'.

'Very astute of you David but I assure you that this will not impact the sale of your land so I am not sure what you want me to tell you'.

'I am considering moving back out of London. I have never been that fond of the place and was looking at other cities but then I found myself in your office here yesterday and I have got to say Mr Splythe I was excited by the idea of redeveloping this place. Its long overdue and I would love to be a part of it'.

'Are you asking for a job David'? Splythe allowed a smile to leak from the side of his mouth.

'I would be very interested in looking into an opportunity with you if you see any potential in me. I have got a good resume'. David found himself selling his credentials.

'I am aware of that', Splythe nodded.

'Sorry'? David was taken aback by his response.

'Well, I made a few phone calls yesterday about you following our meeting. You come highly recommended I have got to say'.

'I would love to learn a little more about your plans and look at how I could help. I think with my local knowledge from growing up here I could be a strategic use for you'.

'We are looking at significant development here David. Not just the hotel. It will ruffle some feathers at times. Are you going to be able to deal with that'?

'Look, I think the bigger picture is important here. This town is tired and still trying to be a local town in an international marketplace. People will not always see the bigger picture and why would they? I saw those plans you had the other day. I can see you are planning to expand into the local church yard and possibly the children's play area. People are not going to like that at first but it has to happen'.

'I am impressed you were looking so closely David. This is a tricky game though. I need to know only the right people are interested on coming on board'.

'Here is the contract'. David pulled the paper from his jacket pocket and put it on the desk in front of Herman. 'It's not signed yet by my brothers but I have already agreed. I will get them to sign it by the weekend. Surely that demonstrates my convictions for this'?

'Alright you have convinced me. But getting that contract signed is critical David. Now you presumably would have to work a months notice'?

'Yes but I have a few weeks holiday due so maybe could move sooner. I will need somewhere to stay'.

'We could sort out accommodation if the investors agree. Let me show you this map'. Herman stood and David followed him to the table as he opened the map up. 'I cannot go into full detail with you myself but this is the first eight sites we are looking at developing. Your land is the first here, but you can see we are also looking at developing several sites around the town for commercial use in redeveloping buildings'.

'What about this one'? David pointed at the site identified around Dovey junction. 'Seems a long way out'?

'Oh that. Just a little site near Dovey Junction. Yes erm a health spa that's all at the minute'. Herman seemed to be quickly trying to cover his own tracks.

'Building around there seems a bit strange, wouldn't a site nearer the town work better'?

'Site is already available, council owned. Used as an elephant reserve currently if you believe such a thing'. Splythe chuckled at the ridiculous nature of the land's current usage.

'Really'? David covered the flustering feeling inside.

'I know, but anyway should be simple enough. The occupants are a batty old woman and her eccentric granddaughter. They haven't been out the village in years. The best bit is we don't even have to find alternative accommodation for them. Don't get me wrong we probably will but that offer will make the move so much quicker'.

'What about the elephants'?

'Who knows? I guess we might sell them off to a zoo or get them put down if not. Not really our concern'.

'Won't look to good to the public though'.

'Very true but thankfully I have resourced the main decision making to a half wit from the village who is obsessed by the granddaughter. He is busy trying to convince her she needs to put the old lady in a home. He has known them for ages and I think he has some romantic feeling for her. If it ends badly, he will have egg on his face over this not us'.

'What about this one here'? David pointed to a site south of the town. 'Why is it a different colour'?

'That David is the Welsh Fertiliser research facility. We are going to invest with them to increase some output to try and move their experimental work forward'.

'The others must be existing buildings that you are renovating'?

'Yes absolutely'. Splythe nodded.

'So apart from our strip of land and the elephant place I don't see much controversy with those plans'.

'Well this is only stage one David'.

'So what does stage two or three entail'.

'Well stage two is more higher level than I feel I can go through with you at the moment to be honest'. Herman paused and sat on the table edge before looking excited at David. 'I tell you what. This evening I am doing a presentation to the board of investors in the Old College. Why don't you let me talk to our investors about how we could use you and then if they are happy to have you at the event I will contact you'.

'That sounds great'. David felt excited even though he knew this venture could affect those around him.

'David, you must understand that we are at a very early stage in our progress of this development. You need to be very tight lipped about this. We are payed well here but it doesn't always pay to let others know everything that is planned'.

'I get it'.

David left the office following this meeting and was confused about what he was looking at. What on Earth would stage two be that was so big and would be so controversial? He needed to get to that meeting later but now would have to consider what to do about Charlotte and her family home.

CHAPTER FOURTEEN

David felt uneasy about everything as he collected Charlotte and used Ziggy's car to take her back to her home. As the two approached the village he had avoided conversation to any depth about the meeting with Herman Splythe and she could sense he wasn't being completely forthcoming about the situation. For two new potential lovers the conversation dried up as the first trial of their relationship was emerging. As they came into the village David was not sure how to tackle the fact that he knew Trevor Thomas was being manipulated by Herman. He couldn't fit all the pieces together and he knew he would have to be honest. Pulling up he turned the car off and sat for a moment as Charlotte got out. Assuming he was behind her she started walking before turning to see him staring into space momentarily. Realising she was waiting for him he then quickly followed.

'Do you want to go'? Charlotte asked clearly becoming upset.

'No, why do you want me to'? A concerned David answered back.

'You haven't said a word for most of the journey. If you want to forget this you just need to tell me'.

'No, no. I really don't'. David grabbed her elbows with each of his hands.

'Then talk to me David. What happened at the meeting? You went to help me out but now you seem to be hiding information from me'.

'I am sorry, I am just processing it all. I just don't know if I can help you with this and I don't want to let you down'.

'You will only let me down if you don't talk to me'.

'Okay, lets go inside and have a chat'.

The two headed into the cottage and David was struck by how old fashioned it was in the hallway. Brown wood chip wallpaper and dark red carpet made him feel like he had traveled back in time as Charlotte called for her Nanna. With no answer she assumed Gladys had gone to the tea rooms to see her friends and they headed to the kitchen. Turning the kettle on she asked him to take a seat still clearly not happy with how he had handled the information so far. David, feeling the pressure was worried and knew he could lose her before this potential relationship even started unless he was honest.

'I am so sorry Charlotte. I just don't want to mess this up and feel I am now so involved it will affect us'. He couldn't look at her and put his head in his hands with frustration until he felt Charlotte put her hand over his and squeeze it. Looking up at her, allowed her to see his worry as his eyes were teary. In a strange way this reassured her as she sat next to him, now holding both of his hands.

'You have just walked into this. I will not blame you for anything. If I end up with nothing it will be okay as long as you are honest. I just don't like lies'. She softly reassured him. 'Please tell me everything, it doesn't matter how bad it is. You can't protect anyone by telling them lies, please'.

'They are developing a couple of sites for definite. From what he told me they are planning on developing this place into a health spa. He said that the land is owned by the council and not your Nanna. They will look at rehousing you if needed but relatively it will be cost effective method for them. He seemed pretty confident about things. They have been using someone I think without him fully realising to try and lift you out of the property and avoiding them getting their hands dirty'.

'Who'?

'Trevor Thomas'.

'Unbelievable, he has been telling me moving Nanna into a home would potentially be the best thing for her. That no good scumbag'! Charlotte stood up and moved toward the door as if she was going to seek him out about what she saw as a betrayal.

'Wait'! David stood pulling at her arm to stop her leaving. 'I really do not think he knows he exactly who he is working for. I think he is trying to soften the blow for you, I think he might have feelings for you? From what I can tell on the map it is not just this piece of land but much of the village. Surely that would affect him as well'?

'What about the elephants'? Charlotte sat back down now with her head in her hands.

'He said they would look at selling them on or if not they may be put down'. The hesitation in his voice showed her just what he read that information as.

Hating seeing her so upset David tried to pull her into his arms but she pushed him away and mumbled an excuse to him as she left the room. Weighing up the situation he decided giving her some time to calm down would be the best option and so he waited for several minutes before following her. Walking down the corridor he knocked on the only closed door in the building and after no answer he pushed the door slightly open to see her lying with her back to the door on a single bed in again another old fashioned room. Entering the room he moved towards the stool in front of her dressing table and sat down now facing her as she looked at him.

'I am sorry, I just needed a minute' she whispered.

'Don't be'.

'Making a good start to this relationship aren't I? I am going to scare you off back to London before we even go on a second date at this rate'.

'No you won't. Look, I get this is not nice but'. David stopped.

'What is it'? Charlotte slowly sat up. 'Go on just say it'.

'I get this is your home and its been that way for the majority of your life but change can sometimes be a good thing. Would moving to Aberystwyth be such a terrible thing? You could get a job and make friends, get some qualifications. I am not in a place to judge but what happens when'…

'I know you are making sense, Nanna said it to me as well. I need to get out there and do more for myself before its too late.

She said she wouldn't mind a home'. She paused as David passed her a tissue from her dressing table and sat next to her on the edge of the bed. 'I just think it is wrong that's all. Two generations have lived here looking after this area and the elephants. It think it should be more important than that. You can't just pretend they are not here anymore'.

'No you can't, but someone in authority can take the responsibility for that. Who is going to look after you if you don't do it yourself? This is an amazing part of history but you seemed have become trapped by it. Instead of being out there in the real world breaking hearts and making a difference you have been here looking after an old lady and her history. Maybe it's time to consider moving on'?

'I need you to see them, you might understand a bit more then'.

'I am just worried about you that's all'.

'I know, can you make me a drink and I will just sort my makeup. My eyeliner has run I look like Alice Cooper'. Charlotte lent forward kissing David with salty tears before hugging him.

David quickly left the room and headed to the kitchen where he was greeted.

'Sit down'. The calm but stern voice of Gladys Roderick commanded as he entered the room.

'Hi, I am David I am Charlotte's friend'.

'Sit down young man I want to talk to you'.

'Yes, erm no problem'. David was now panicking as he was unsure how to react to the intense old lady sat staring a hole right through him. 'I said I would do Charlotte a drink. Would you like a drink? Tea maybe'?

'I have made us some coffee, good black Welsh Coffee. Sit down'.

David sat down opposite Gladys as she poured the coffee from the decanter into his mug filling it to levels that made him feel a little less at ease knowing he couldn't refuse.

'So who are you and why are you sniffing around my Charlotte'?

'Well we met on the train and we agreed to meet up. She is really nice'.

'I know that, I am her Nanna. It is you I am concerned about. How nice are you'?

'Well I don't really'.

'Sniffing around the village looking for her yesterday and then making her stop with you last night. I know how you men work, sex, sex, sex all the time going through your head'.

'Sorry, I am not sure we should be talking about this'.

'Sex in the morning,and at night time and anytime you can in the middle. I know how you all think, my two husbands were like it until I calmed them down a bit. Aren't you drinking your coffee? I imagine you are tired'.

'Sorry what, why'? David was confused and in shock.

'You know after all the sex'.

'We didn't have sex, okay happy now'? A flustered David broke out before he stamped his foot in an attempt to drink some of his coffee and not crinkle his face into a grimace.

'Why not? One of those are you? A gay boy'?

'My God Nanna, what are you saying to him'? Charlotte burst into the room. Hearing the conversation in the corridor she wanted to curl up and die but at the same time felt the need to rescue David. Sitting next to him across the table from Gladys she grabbed David's hand and looked at her. 'Nanna you can not ask somebody that. There is nothing wrong with being gay'?

'I know that, you seem to forget that I went marching in London for gay rights with your uncle Peter back in the 1960's. I had friends who had to hide their feelings back in the day before the legalisation and it was horrible'.

'So why are you being horrible about it then'?

'I'm not I am just trying to find out if he is gay or not. He wouldn't be much use to you if he was would he? If you are going to be a couple'.

'Nanna, he is not gay'.

'You spent last night together and you didn't have sex did you'?

'No he fell asleep, and I am not that easy'.

'He is a man, he should want to unless he doesn't want to'.

'Nanna he wanted to'. She paused and looked at David. 'You did want to, didn't you'?

'No'! Panicking he didn't know where to look. 'I mean yes, I mean I want to but we don't have to rush'.

'See Nanna he does want to'.

'I should think so a gorgeous girl like you. He should want to do it all the time. He better make it worth your while. You know, see how good he is before you commit'.

'My God Nanna. Stop! Come on David I want to show you out the back'. Pulling David with little resistance she stood and escorted him to the door and out the front of the cottage. 'Sorry about that, give me a minute whilst I go and kill her'.

Storming back into the kitchen Charlotte was furious but this anger was soon diffused when she saw her Nanna was in hysterical uncontrollable fits of laughter.

'Nanna what the hell was that all about'? She asked with anger but rapidly being overcome by the contagious laughter.

'Well you need to see if he can take a joke. I thought he did quite well'.

'Him, what about me? I almost died of embarrassment', she continued now starting to smile. 'He has probably run off now after that and will never come back'.

'I don't think so my love. He likes you a lot. I could see it in his eyes'.

A few minutes later David was joined outside by Charlotte who after a few moments of silent contemplation, she felt the need to apologise and try to explain again.

'I am so sorry about that, she was trying to be funny with you. I think she likes you'. Charlotte squeezed his hand.

'I haven't felt that uncomfortable since the first time I saw a sex scene in a film sat next to my parents when I was a kid. She is very straight faced and to the point isn't she'?

'Well if its any compensation, I wanted to the world to swallow me up'. The two started walking.

'Not really, no'.

'Well she promised to be on her best behaviour from now on and is doing us some lunch to make up for it'.

The two walked behind the bungalow where a ten foot mesh fence with a door in it spanned along the back of the property. Grabbing a bucket of apples, they walked in through the gate, David's heart beat was running at a thousand miles an hour as they followed a muddy track into the woodland.

'Would the fence stop them'?

'No but elephants are intelligent so they understand it is a boundary. Elsewhere there is just a stone wall about six feet tall but they don't try to get out. We will go down to the stream they are most likely washing in the morning sun light'.

The two left the path and into the heavy woodland area steeply down an incline.

'Is all this part of the property'?

'Yes, I think they are more interested in the isolated feel of it for their health spa'. Charlotte put her arm in front of David to slow him momentarily and grabbed his hand bringing him closer. As she slowly walked him into a clearing he saw the most magical sight he could imagine as three large elephants stood ten meters or so in front of them. Charlotte knelt down and he slowly followed suit to see one of the elephants spraying water over it's back from the stream. Looking brown in the spittle light getting through the leaves David was entranced by the beauty and magnificence he was watching.

'So the biggest one, the one closest to us is the male, he doesn't have tusks like many male Indian elephants so is called a makhnas. The ladies are slightly smaller and have a bigger rump'. Charlotte whispered with great enthusiasm in her voice. 'Now they know we are here so we can slowly stand but just for a few minutes I think if you stand still so they know you are not a threat. Normally we bring them up to see people so this is a bit different'.

'Are they calm normally'?

'Yes, we never have a problem with these three'.

'That is reassuring' David whispered back looking on in amazement, a view which Charlotte rejoiced to see the magic in his eyes.

Charlotte put down the bucket and walked towards the male elephant who lowered his head allowing her to pat and rub him between the eyes. His trust and comfort of her was spell bounding to David who couldn't help but giggle quietly with the pleasure he was feeling. Watching her with him continued the love David was developing for this almost complete stranger he could hardly have imagined existed a day earlier.

'Shall we go and see my friend'? Charlotte softly spoke to the elephant and led him by his trunk almost in a similar fashion to how she led David by the hand earlier. Coming closer she stopped him and fed him a few apples before turning to David. 'Go ahead, just pat him like you would a dog, he will like it'.

'What is his name'? David asked as he slowly placed his hand on his tough skin of his forehead reaching upwards.

'Oliver'.

'Hello Oliver, its a pleasure to meet you'. David continued to pet him and copied Charlotte's feeding method giving him an apple. 'Why Oliver'?

'We don't know, he was called that by the zoo who we inherited him from. They are intelligent so you can't change their names after they have understood it it theirs'.

Suddenly the Oliver took two steps backwards and made a few gruffly strong low pitch sounds in his throat before raising his trunk and trumpeting loudly knocking David backwards as he jumped out of his skin and causing Charlotte to laugh.

'He is being playful. He must like you and be happy'. She threw some apples down towards the female elephants and moved to David holding his hand. 'The two girls are just as friendly. The younger smaller one is called Sienna and the older one is Clarissa. What do you think now you have seen them'?

'They are amazing'. David stared forward before looking at Charlotte. 'You are amazing'.

Charlotte put her hand softly onto David's face and pulled him towards her opening her mouth and kissing him slowly. Her heart was glowing with newly found passion for him and she was becoming excited by him as she felt his tongue caress hers. With her heart beat rising and sensing his excitement growing she pushed her hand up under his shirt feeling his stomach spasm intensely as she pushed up to his chest.

Suddenly the spray splashed into them like a bucket of icy water breaking the moment as David gasped with shock getting the main bulk of it drenching his shirt fully. Wiping his eyes he looked to see Oliver standing looking pleased with himself as Charlotte almost fell to the ground with laughter.

'I think Oliver wanted some more attention from you'. Charlotte laughed looking at the stunned David.

'I guess so, I have never had a shower courtesy of a massive elephant before'.

'How did you find it'? Charlotte grabbed his hand leading him back to the house.

'Lovely, very sensual'. David laughed admitting the humour bchind it.

CHAPTER FIFTEEN

The two now drawn even closer together headed back to the cottage where David could smell the delicious scent of cooking before they even reached the kitchen door which they entered directly into the back of the bungalow.

'I have cooked you some chicken broth up my lovelies'. Gladys spoke with her back to them stirring a pot on the stove.

'Thanks Nanna, I think David might need to have a quick shower though'. Charlotte pointed the obvious to Gladys as she turned to see them.

'Oliver, let me guess? You will have to realise Mr David that Charlotte is Oliver's first love, he gets jealous you know'. She smiled at David making him feel more at home immediately. 'I will get one of my husband's old shirts for you to wear once I have sorted dinner'.

'Thank you' David smiled as Charlotte led him from the room.

The two headed to the bathroom where Charlotte started the shower holding her hand underneath it for a few moments testing the temperature.

'We better give it a minute or two to let the water get hot enough'. Turning she looked at David smiling as he undid his soaking shirt.

'Am I going first or do you want me to wait'? He questioned as she approached him.

'I thought as we have already just had one, we could maybe have this shower together'? She replied as David immediately felt full of energy. Charlotte pressed her hands onto his chest and pushed him backwards using his body to close the door behind him. Kissing him with intention she felt him pulling on her clothing as she heard Gladys call from the the kitchen. Gripping her fingers down around the waist line of his trousers she sighed and placed her head on his chest before stepping back and pulling away. Readjusting her ruffled clothes she smiled and kissed him again. 'Why don't you get in and I will try to be back in a minute'.

Kissing her again David felt excitation running through his body as he finished undressing and tested the water in the shower which was now steaming the room. Adjusting the temperature slightly her stood in the bath and pulled the curtain across before stepping under the water. Running the water through his hair he was looked down at his body a clenched his muscles trying to make himself look more masculine. Washing his more sensitive areas he heard the door slowly creek open to the bathroom. Listening he could hear the sound of a belt being adjusted and movement making him even more ready for Charlotte. Pulling back the curtain he smiled to greet her and stood frozen as Gladys collected his wet clothes stood looking at his full alpha male display on hand before telling him she had placed a towel on the radiator for him and some spare clothes in Charlotte's room. Within moments he pulled the curtain back and stood frozen crumpled over as he heard the door close. Now standing with his head in his hands mortified by his own actions.

A few minutes later Charlotte was sat at the table talking to Gladys as David sulked into the room trying not to draw any attention to himself. Sitting next to Charlotte she mouthed the word *sorry* at him as Gladys who was serving the food into bowls made a commentary of what she was doing.

'Just got some bread out in case you want to dip some in. Right I will go and get my tablets, start without me. Good to see the shirt fits relatively well'. She continued talking as she left the room.

'Oh my God, I am so sorry'. Charlotte whispered. 'I was going to come back but she asked me to look after the food whilst she sorted you some clothes out to leave on my bed. I didn't think she would go into the bathroom and get them. I am so sorry'. She stopped as David nodded. 'Did she see'?

'Everything? Yes'.

'Wow! The first time I get a serious boyfriend and my nanna sees him naked before I do'.

'Boyfriend'? David's head snapped up looking at her.

'I was hoping so'.

'It sounds really good to me'. The two kissed again to be separated again by the door opening and Gladys coming in. Waiting for her to sit down Charlotte squeezed Davids hand under the table.

As they started eating David felt slightly relieved by Gladys not mentioning the bathroom incident and so he felt he should try to lead a conversation with her.

'So Mrs Roderick, you have lived here for a whole one hundred years'?

'Yes my lovely, Charlotte has told you about the day on the beach and the King I presume'. She stopped as David nodded. 'We were here just a few months later on a permanent basis. It was a wonderful time as the village bloomed back then. Lots of business people coming through until the Great War anyway. That stopped things'.

'You have really seen the world change from here then'? David felt humbled by her longevity.

'Yes in the best ways I have seen advancement but also plagues David'. Grabbing Charlotte's hand she squeezed her lovingly. 'I have seen beauty and pure evil across the world since I have been here'.

'Were you not isolated from things living in such a small village'?

'No, the bad things tended to make their impact here a lot

quicker than the good but they could have positive long term impacts to. Like the Belgium's coming'.

'What is that? Tourists you mean'?

'No, you see when the Great War broke out it was largely over in Europe, so Wales and the Ceredigion area became a refuge you see for citizens who lost their homes and were seeking safety due to the fighting. It didn't take long either. My dad left for the war in 1915 but before then we had refugees stopping here. Well, when the German's invaded Belgium in August 1914 it made Britain declare war and offer a safe haven for thousands of Belgium refugees. A quarter of a million of them came across and thousands to Wales. Many came to Aberystwyth on the very track you arrived on recently. There were two ladies working for the university who arranged for nearly one hundred Belgium artists to seek safety in the town but we had a number of children and their mothers stop here with us. I remember my father building beds from the trees for the children and they stayed sharing Charlotte's room and the living room for a number of years, we had six people in all'.

'How long did they stay for'? David was fascinated by her life experience.

'Until the war ended and then in early 1919 they went away. I made some good friends back then as a child. I tried to teach them Welsh but they coped better with English. I kept in touch with my friend Emera who stayed in touch with us for the rest of her life until she died back when Charlotte was young'.

'How did you cope for four years with them living in your house'?

'I loved it, I had friends and my mother had other ladies when my father left for the war. So it was just good to support others and it was a big family. My mother had more help and chores were shared equally amongst the children and their mothers'.

'Did any stay'? David continued to question.

'No they were very keen to go back home and when the war finished it was just about getting the travel arrangements sorted. They spent Christmas with us though as we had been cut off due to the Spanish'.

'What do you mean'?

'The Spanish Flu outbreak at the end of the war. Aberystwyth being on a key train route at that time meant they were particularly worried about it reaching us. We heard of it in the summer when there was a small outbreak. Somebody my mother knew died in the August from it before her husband even got back from the war but it was the winter when weather got wet that they really worried about it. I didn't have to go to school for a month or more because they shut them all down and our Christmas celebrations were canceled. The mayor even tried to close the picture house but they wouldn't agree to it. We were off school until the new year but I remember then the teachers and many students being very poorly'.

'That's terrible'. Charlotte commented.

'Death is a natural part of life my love. We just don't like to accept that. The Belgium's stayed for one last Christmas with us and then back in the Spring then traveled home again. We had refugees from the English cities in the second war thirty years later but I was an adult then and got more involved in the war effort'.

'Your husband went to war'? David enjoyed the history lesson as much as his delicious lunch.

'Yes I lost him during the war. I coped by keeping myself busy not that I had much choice. My mother was still alive so she looked after the elephants with my children as I went into Aberystwyth everyday to support the war effort'.

'What did you do'? David asked with interest.

'Well, Aberystwyth was a strategic post for the British forces because it was remote but coastal. I worked two jobs, firstly I worked in the RAF head quarters which were in *Swyddfa Sir*, the building used as courts now but used to be the Queen's Hotel. I also worked as a accommodation assessor for the council as they had the training soldiers staying in hotels around the town so I checked the upkeep of this. Towards the end of the war injured soldiers especially from Dunkirk ended up here. I fell into that role I think because of my assets'.

'Sorry'?

'Nanna means she looked good and this was a morale boost for the soldiers'. Charlotte explained.

'Yes even I looked good back then when I was still in the throws of youth and my body was firm and attractive before time took its toll'.

'You are beautiful Nanna'. Charlotte held her hand.

'Not anymore my love. I am old and hanging on. The only good bit for me is seeing you now but as you know my eyes are going'. Nanna slowly stood up and walked to a cupboard pulling a packet of cigarettes out before looking back at them. 'This is what I have been saying to her David. She is young now but needs to get out and live a little. She needs to fall in love and have some children'. Walking to the kitchen door she turned and looked back at them. 'And even with my poor eyesight, you chose a good one for that Charlotte. He certainly is well endowed and ready to go'. Leaving the room, once again as silence filled the kitchen.

'She is something else' David muttered.

'She is my Nanna'. Charlotte smiled. 'I am just looking at the time, hadn't we better get moving if you are going to get to that meeting with Herman Splythe'?

'Yes, you are right. A shame really, there are other activities we could be doing'.

'No if we stop here much longer Nanna will have you doing cross-stitch with her'.

CHAPTER SIXTEEN

David walked into the historic Old College and spoke to the receptionist who directed him down the corridor towards the main chamber. Thinking about Charlotte he had to admit to himself that he had conflicting opinions about everything currently. On one hand he felt that she would be better off getting away from it and that this use of their land along with potentially him getting a new start in a big development opportunity in Aberystwyth would be a really good thing for her. At the same time however, he saw how alive she was with the elephants and how even he was overcome with joy and emotion seeing them out in the open country with her. As he walked into the large room there was over thirty smartly dressed people making him, dressed only in his shirt and tie feel a little lower class. As he looked around soon he spotted Herman Splythe who made his way over to him with another much younger well built man who was most noticeable by the scent of his very expensive and overpowering cologne.

'David, good to see you again. This is Mark Noland, he is the Head of Welsh Operations for Merriman Initiatives'. Splythe patted Mark on the shoulder.

'Good to meet you'. David confirmed with a handshake feeling that Mark Noland was demonstrating his clear power and responsibility with an overly strong and confident grip on David's hand.

'You, too. So I understand you are interested in joining our success story'?

'Yes I hope so'.

'Well why don't we go into the smaller office space next door before we start here and just have a chat. See if we can come up with something'? Mark gestured towards the door and David followed with Splythe accompanying him. Walking in through a small doorway they entered a tired but busy looking office space and Mark sat on the desk with his arms folded and looking at David. 'So David, I have to say I was concerned about getting the signature in place for the land that you and your brothers own but Herman tells me you have assured him of that and not only that but you are interested in joining our team. I am impressed that you spotted a potential opening before we took it further and have gone for the opportunity'.

'Yes well I think this town is perfect to develop and move forward, there is so much opportunity for untapped commercial development here', David found himself selling the future of Aberystwyth away.

'That is true David but as you will see tonight we are thinking a little bit more the sky is the limit long term here. But it is a slow burner, the process starts with the hotel and other plots around the town'.

'Yes I looked at those earlier'.

'Yes Herman, may have been a little naughty showing you them'. Mark gave Splythe who was stood aside David a short but deliberate look of displeasure before standing and pacing slightly before continuing. 'The thing is this David. We have a lot of potential openings here and from your background and with the references we got from your current employers there would be a very important role for you here'.

'References? I haven't asked them for references'.

'No but I know people that know people David so we have spoken to them'. Splythe confidently announced.

'We are suggesting a role a Land and Property Acquisition and Development Manager, I have an initial contract for you'. Mark passed David a contract which he under the pressure of the moment skimmed only seeing the salary clearly.

'That is a very generous salary', David couldn't hide how shocked he was.

'You will earn it if you take it. But the thing is we need to have 100% confidentiality here David. If you sign with us you need to understand the job is twenty four hours a day as and when we need you. Obviously, it will have set hours but out of hours at certain times linking to contracts acquisition may require it'. Mark looked at Splythe before continuing. 'Also this is not just hotels here. We are looking at industrial development. That may be a bit less popular in the town but essential for its growth. Should you agree to this then we expect 100% non disclosure to those who may be looking for information. Friends, family or people of interest'.

'Do you understand David'? Splythe questioned him.

'Yes, I do, I know construction is complex'.

'That also means in terms of what you are going to here tonight. If you sign that contract it will be legally prevention against informing others about our business at times'. Splythe explained.

'Look I am honored to be really offered this but I need to have a good think about this. My job in London would need to be considered and setting up back here'.

'London understands your potential decision and we would support you'. Mark confirmed.

'Okay thank you'.

'So David, as with the contract for the land we will need that back by Saturday. We need a clear staffing vision to move to phase two of our project and once the land acquisition is sorted we want to move forward with some pace. But for now I think we have a common understanding here so Mark has agreed for you to stand in on our conference. Please remember the bigger picture at the moment. We are going to be looking at changes for the long haul here'. Splythe opened the door as he spoke to David and shook his hand as if David had accepted the job right at that moment.

Slightly concerned by this but not wanting to cause a scene and with a genuine interest of the long term plans of Merriman Initiatives he followed out into the conference room where

Splythe and Mark told him to get a drink and some canapes whilst they prepared for the presentation. Walking around the large central wooden table and two smaller circular side tables with white tablecloths covering them he headed to the drinks and collected a glass of champagne. Tasting some bitesize and unrecognisable but pleasant food he was offered, David meandered around the tables looking at the name badges which displayed who each guest was and what branch or company they were from. He looked in surprise as he saw that people in the room were from different major cities in the United Kingdom and then others from other international cities including New York, Chicago, and Baltimore for the United States and at least two from various African countries. Within a few minutes the guests were asked to take their seats and David was shocked to find himself sitting close to the head of the main central table with his place badge reading *David Jones - Aberystwyth*. Sitting down he made a few pleasant exchanges about his nearest guest's journeys and then had his drink refilled before the lights dimmed making the projection at the front of the room a focal point. Before anybody spoke a video played amplified through speakers around the room as if it was in a large auditorium about Merriman Initiatives and the work they were doing worldwide. This included everything David was familiar with including commercial developments, hotels and health spas ranging from competitively priced accommodation to luxury. He then saw developments around the world which he was unaware of as the company identified their involvement in renewable fuels and environmentally sustainable development including claims they were investigating how to reverse global warming. A fact that David felt was more spin than truth in the vagueness of the video but was followed by a promise to ensure they supported other business becoming more environmentally friendly.

As the video package finished the lights raised slightly with the projector now showing a aerial shot of the Aberystwyth coastline as Mark Noland stood at the presentation lectern.

'Ladies and Gentlemen, that video which as you will be aware is updated bi-annually shows in a few minutes just some of the life changing, no world changing work we are doing with large companies and our investors around the globe. Indeed it is due to our success and out of the box thinking that we have developed some of the most successful recent trade developments in the business world and this is the start of another. The United Kingdom is leaving the European Union and whether you agreed or didn't is irrelevant. The people who are not successful will be the ones arguing that for the next thirty years. No, those who are forward thinking have accepted it and look at how they can make the leaving of the E.U benefit their business. The changes are already being seen in the stocks and shares world. The UK geographically can always be a trade capital and there is considerable increased interest with trade from China, India, Australia and the United States of America. If the UK is ready, this could be the greatest decision that we ever made. In actual fact it is unlikely that the E.U will stop trading with us. Why? Because they need our trade just as much as we need their trade. But more likely is we need to be ready. Our estimates are that in five years time the amount of inputs will have increased by 35% and thus exports will also significantly move upwards. But how is this going to happen? Where is the infrastructure? Bristol, Newport, Liverpool shipping ports are all running to full capacity. Sending business up to Scotland seems risky as they want to leave the U.K. So a new site is needed'. Mark stopped taking a sip of water and moved the slide onto a satellite view of Aberystwyth and the surrounding area. 'Aberystwyth, the jewel of Victorian Wales but left behind in a modern world. Relatively cheap land but at a premium. However, the coastal cove of Ceredigion Bay with its already deep waters to the south of the town give us a potential site. We are not going to drastically alter this beautiful seaside town. Why would we want to? The town itself will need investment into hotels, housing infrastructure and modern facilities which is currently being undertaken in phase one. That is not an issue at all. Where the investment will be needed is in phase two. Now I will hand over to our local Development Consultant Herman Splythe'.

'Thank you Mark, yes why Aberystwyth? Well just the location alone on a map of the British Isles should show that'. Splythe displayed a map on the projector. 'When taking the country as a whole we are actually in the centre of the UK geographically. Now there are arguments against that but we have calculated cost comparisons based on land fees to other already built up areas and using the proposed development of the rail lines which will be built along original tracks used previously in the towns history and the development of our road network which the government have already promised, this will be cheaper. How? Well simply put there is less political issues with building this port in a currently forgotten section of the coastline. Now the suggested stretch of land we are planning on developing is this area of farmland to the south of the town. Tanyblwch Beach which you can see here is about two km in length and the farmland behind is significantly flat and low lying for the area. This flat land continues a few miles inland to the village of Rhydyfelin. This would be where the entrance to the port on the land side is based. The river Ysytwyth as you can see runs parallel with the beach about 50m in land and we could dredge the land bridge and take the sea line 50 meters further in land. This would however aid our coastal defense during construction where we would use the river to build the initial port foundations using the beach and land to block nature until we are ready to remove it. The beauty of this development for the town is that whilst it would be large it is mostly hidden by Pen Dinas Hill. This means it will not have a visible impact on tourism of the town and employed laborers will not be put off living in the town. Now the farmland we would build the port on is owned privately but an offer for the farmer would be more valuable to him than us. There is no current large scale building on the land so it would be easy to develop from'.

'Okay do we have any questions from the floor before we continue'? Mark Noland announced looking out into the crowd.

'Yes, how do the people of the town feel about this development'? A female voice from the back of the room inquired.

'Well the initial feeling is that they could only gain from the potential investment so it is strong. The money invested will be coming direct from Westminster so it will see a surge in local town funding to ensure that this is successful'. Splythe answered confidently.

'Will this have any impacts on the actual town of Aberystwyth'? A second voice questioned.

'Minimal. Our initial directive is to update the town to have a more modern infrastructure which will start in the next two months. The shipping port dredging will begin the following year once Merriman Initiatives has negotiated the necessary contracts'. Mark Noland nodded as Splythe explained the plans.

'I am a little confused on the comment you made about costings. Why would it be relatively cheap in comparison to other areas? Are you not limited by the available landscape'? David questioned.

'Thank you Mr Jones. A very important question for our investors'. Mark stood up to respond putting the aerial view back up on the screen. 'You see the cost of building the land structures is much less than the sea port part. So ideal sites are looked for based on the suitability of the sea topography. The bay off the beach here increases in depth rapidly with a very steep descending underwater gradient and is an appropriate rock formation to securely hold structures in place. Obviously the closer this is done to the shoreline the cheaper it will be. The aim will be to build four separate docking bays for vessels but the potential to increase this and move around the coast further south could be a possibility in the future if our capacity is met'.

'What about storms? It this not a hard coastline for Atlantic surges'? The gentleman next to David spoke with interest.

'Obviously, the sun isn't always shining here. Occasionally there is a very strong storm but whilst this would close the port. There is no suggestion this would be any more frequent than the ports in Southampton or up in Scotland. The weather in this part of the country is often quick short storms and the brunt of the Atlantic weather is shielded by the southern tip of Ireland. Also the shape of the coast line supports lower turbulence and wave development in that part of the bay. We are currently purchasing another strip of land on the river Dovey which could be used to house ships during the storms if needed'.

◆ ◆ ◆

The investor meeting continued for another hour and the whole time David could see that the questions all had researched and logical answers. Following the meeting he took a slow walk along the back of the harbour and to the beach where this development would be constructed. Sitting on one of the storm defense rocks he looked along the quiet desolate beach with dilemma between his head and his heart. Looking at the site he couldn't believe it was suitable but then he realised his understanding of just what was possible was limited. He understood the idea of the port being directly accessible for shipping from the American North East Coastline and that the town wouldn't be largely affected by the port itself. He felt financially this could be a positive investment of unimaginable proportions for the town and indeed for himself as a potential employee. However, then he looked and with his heart he was sitting in one of the most tranquil and quiet places he had witnessed for years. He watched as a young couple walked a black labrador down the otherwise empty beach. If this development went through not only would the beach be gone but also the farmland behind it would be destroyed and become and industrial hub for the town. He felt uneasy about how the town would react to the development but felt it would be pushed through regardless if Westminster had approved it. Phase one was clearly to prepare the town and surrounding areas. The hotel for short stay visitors and the hotel and spa at Aberdyfith to give a luxurious near place to relax and possibly link it to a boat hold in poor weather on the Dyfi Estuary. The land they were going to sell alone felt a loss but the financial gain would set his brothers up much better. But what about Charlotte and Gladys? They had very little to gain and more to lose. He felt he could have found happiness but this was a secure future for him and if she trusted him he would ensure it was also a secure new life for Charlotte.

CHAPTER SEVENTEEN

Heading back to Ziggy's Coffee Shop he was hesitant but this feeling was forgotten when he saw that Charlotte was wearing one of the black aprons and helping serve orders to the tables. Watching her from the street he could see that she was really enjoying herself and had a natural service charm that customers were responding to. Heading in he was greeted by Ziggy who had Paul sitting by the bar as was customary in the early evening.

'Hello there good Sir. An interesting meeting? See you have your homework'. Ziggy quipped referring to the portfolio that David had been provided with.

'Yes we need to have a look together when it quietens down'. David stopped looking across the tables towards Charlotte. 'How is she doing? Are you short of staff or something'?

'I had to send Lynne out to go and get some more coffee from the storage garage and she offered to help out. She is a little gem. A natural too. If I could I would swap Lynne for her'.

'How long will Lynne be? I think I could do with talking to you both'. David questioned.

'Oh she is having a cigarette out back. She saw Charlotte working and felt that was just cause to go and do bugger all for half an hour. Can't say I mind though this is the nicest friendliest service our customers have had for a while', joked Ziggy.

Charlotte saw that David had arrived back and headed over with her empty tray. 'Hello, how are you'? She kissed him affectionately before continuing passed him. 'Do you want a hot chocolate? Your brother has taught me how to make one'.

'Yes that would be good. When you are both ready can you come and have a sit down, I need to you show this stuff'? David walked away and sat at a larger table clearing the cups left from previous customers.

'He seems quite stressed out' Paul offered looking up from his note book.

'I hope he is alright'. Charlotte stopped and looked across at him.

'You two don't know my brother well enough yet. He is always highly strung. He would get stressed out having a massage. I am sure he is fine but he will have all the information buzzing around his head from that meeting. He will just want to get it out before he forgets it all, that is all'.

'I hope so, I have a funny feeling about that folder', Paul looked across at David who was now sorting the glossy prints out.

'The last time you had a funny feeling, it was a bladder infection'. Laughed Ziggy.

'What do you think'? Charlotte showed them her hot chocolate deluxe and plated it up.

'Very good, don't tell Lynne'. Smiled Ziggy.

As if by magic at that point Lynne appeared questioning the comment made by her employer. 'Don't tell Lynne what'?

'That she is better at making hot chocolate than you are already' Ziggy responded.

'Well its not right making that rubbish anyway. This is a coffee shop not a sweet shop', a bitter Lynne fired back. 'I see lover boy is back'.

'Yes actually, can you hold the fort Lynne? We need to go and speak to him'. Ziggy asked moving around the bar.

'Well I will need a smoke break when you are done'.

'Another one, give you lungs a break, breath some oxygen'. Paul commented from the other side of the bar following Ziggy towards the table where David sat as Charlotte slowly carried across their drinks.

At the table David had ordered the items he wanted to show everyone and as Charlotte sat next to him across the table from Ziggy and Paul, he smiled as she placed the hot chocolates down for them and the two coffees across the table.

'This is all I can do, I wanted to be able to make you one when you got back' she smiled at David.

'I am impressed, thank you'.

'So what have you got for us David'? Ziggy asked looking at the documents in his hands.

For the next thirty minutes David described the presentation to the three of them who were getting progressively on edge as he detailed the development of the shipping port with their complete disbelief of the plans.

'This is the most ridiculous idea I have ever heard of. I mean firstly how the hell are they planning on getting the goods around to the rest of the U.K once it has arrived here'? Paul questioned the others.

'Well you see they are going to heavily invest in redeveloping the rail links to the town and improve the road networks. Also they said smaller boats could dispense contents to other ports around the country'. David answered almost like he was the one who had prepped for the presentation.

'But why would they choose here? Honestly I feel like this is some sick joke. I mean the weather here can be destructive at times. Surely the whole place would be financially costly the moment bad weather rolls in'? Ziggy debated.

'Well the main Atlantic storm surges are actually broken by the southern tip of Ireland and the shape of the bay means that more of the stronger waves hit the town than the southern beaches. Our weather is overly wet as opposed to stronger winds'.

'Okay, but what about the tourism of the town? Surely that will be about to take a hit'? Charlotte questioned David directly now feeling his answers starting to annoy her.

'Not really as the site will be largely hidden by Pen Dinas Hill and most tourists do not go south of the harbour side jetty so only if they venture that far will they really notice it'.

'Well environmentally it will be devastating I don't care what you say'. She batted back at him angrily.

'I am happy you went to the meeting David. I can tell you now there is no way I am signing that contract anymore and if I have anything to do with it neither will Joe. This has corruption written all over it. I have a good mind to go to the papers about this. Honestly, how can they take this area of outstanding natural beauty and destroy it with a shipping port'? Ziggy angrily confirmed.

'Look I get what you are saying but do you not think this would benefit us all in a small way? I mean look at how much extra people would be living here to use your business everyday'. David found himself defending the company.

'What about me? I have got nothing to gain from this have I'? Charlotte questioned him directly whilst starting to flick through the folder.

'You know what David'? Ziggy questioned him. 'If I didn't know better I would say you support this development. You were supposed to be going their to help us find reasons to argue against this. Why don't you tell us how you really feel'?

'I just can see that this could be an opportunity for the town overall. It could bring in significant investment'.

'Yes and destroy the place we call our home'. Paul snapped back. 'Now to me no price will do that but I guess I am not involved in the decision am I? I am going to sort out my equipment for tomorrow'. Paul stood and walked away not saying another word but clearly unhappy.

'I am just going to go and sit anywhere but here' Ziggy followed Paul.

'I am not sure why they are being so defensive, it's not like I have made my mind up about this development. I just think it is important they consider all the options'.

For a few moments Charlotte sat in silence looking down at the folder before looking at him with venomous eyes. 'I would say you have made your mind up totally. I don't know what is worse? The fact that I have just listened to you say that when I have just found this letter with a job offer. On which they claim they already have references collected for you in my hands? Or the fact that I am sat here only two days knowing you and I feel like my world has been shattered into a thousand pieces'?

'Charlotte please', David pleaded with her.

'No, you just shut up! Here I was just half an hour ago kidding myself that I wasn't falling in love with you and now I found out that business and money are more important to you than I am'.

'In love with me'?

'Yes stupid I know. Why would any crazy woman fall in love with you? I wish I would have ignored you on that platform. You obviously haven't thought about me at all'.

'Don't say that'.

'Say what? Say that you have chosen this evil development over me. Why shouldn't I? It's true you have not only agreed to sell your land to that evil empire but you have done nothing to help me'! Charlotte's voice was now making the rest of the coffee shop a silent auditorium. 'But worse than that you are going to take a job as one of those evil bastards as well! Well good luck with your job I hope it gives you all the happiness apparently that you couldn't see with me'. Now with tears streaming from her eyes and with her cheeks red with anger Charlotte stood up and headed towards the door. As she passed Paul she stopped and squeezed his hand looking into his eyes saying nothing before continuing. David watched her leave down the street hoping she would stop and turn to give him a chance to explain but the opportunity did not arrive as she left his field of view.

'Are you not going to go after her mate'? Paul questioned him publicly and loudly from a far as he continued to silently look out of the window. 'Well then you deserve to lose her then'!

'Paul please'. Ziggy said under his breath.

'Look, I love you and he is your brother so I am not going to kick him out of here but the only person he seems to care about is himself'. Paul now lowered his voice but continued so David would be able to hear him if he wanted to. 'She was like a gift from above when he needed it the most from what I understand. And what has he done for her? Nothing that's what. He was going to that meeting to try and think how we could stop them building on her home but instead he got himself a new job. No wonder that other girl cheated on him'.

Ziggy raised his arm to tell Paul to stop and headed to his brother who was now collecting up the contents of the folder he was given by Herman Splythe and Mark Noland.

'Are you going to let him talk about me like that'? David asked his brother without looking up at him.

'I would stop him if I didn't think there was an element of truth to it. In fact I think there is quite a lot of truth in what he said'. Ziggy stopped sitting down across the table from him. 'Did you go to that meeting knowing they may offer you a job at the end of it'?

'Yes but not in the way you are making it sound'.

'David don't lie to yourself. You weren't thinking of her, you were thinking of yourself. As you always do. Now let me guess you need me and Joe to sign that form to get you a job right'?

'Yes but'.

'Well I think you are lucky this is me and not Joe talking to you. I have gone to hell and back in my life in the past ten years and yet you didn't even think about coming and seeing me until there was a potential financial gain for you, did you? So I think it is time I played a game out of your handbook. You see Paul over there? The tall handsome guy with greying hair by the bar. I have lost contact with my son but I survive because of him. I survive because Joe and him are all the family I need. So what you need to do right now is get out of my coffee shop and find somewhere else to drink your hot chocolates from now on because you are not welcome here anymore'. Ziggy stood and walked back to the counter with the empty cups from the table. Turning he watched as David slowly left the shop not looking at either Paul or him. Standing his ground for long enough so that David would go out of view he walked to the store room where he sobbed without control. Within moments Paul stood with him and supported the man he loved.

CHAPTER EIGHTEEN

For hours David walked around the town on the warm summer night. For a while he was simply angry about the comments made publicly by Paul and then his own brother not supporting him but as time passed his mind questioned his own actions and he felt lower than he had a few days before. He wanted to support his family and be a better brother but he was just not wired that way. He was always the outsider following his two closer and older brothers around. Ziggy was the sensible one, Joe was courageous and then there was him, *David the other one*. He had started this day thinking purely of his brothers and of Charlotte and how to help but by the end of the day he was genuinely interested in the potential of this business venture but he had wanted to take Charlotte with him on this journey, not just leave her homeless.

After the sun had completely set he found himself comfortably drinking alone in a bar as he received an unexpected text message from Joe which read *Just been speaking with Ziggy. Can we come and talk you?* After several moments of non decisive contemplation from the bottom of his rum and coke David responded confirming his location in the bar on the pier overlooking the beach where Nanna first saw the elephants back in 1911. Within half an hour the two brothers arrived and sat without drinks opposite from David.

'Right then, come on'. David slurred slightly under the influence of the amount of alcohol he had consumed and was now acting as his protective clothing from anything they were about to pour on him. 'What now? Are you going to blame me for something else Ziggy? You want me to leave on the next train? You going to ask me to come listen to your fella spouting more about me'?

'No David'. Joe interrupted quite angrily before lowering his voice and taking a moment to relax his posture before continuing. 'An hour ago I would have dragged you to the beach and rubbed sand in your eyes but Ziggy and me have had a long conversation and would like to give you this'. He handed over an envelope.

'What is that then? Divorcing me from the family now are you'?

'No brother. That is the contract to give Splythe about the land. It is signed by both of us now so you can do with it what you like', Joe stopped and shuffled off the bench as a silent Ziggy followed.

'Why have you done that'? David looked up confused at him.

'You see David. We don't have perfect lives. Hell I am the only man who can seem to attract any woman in the town apart from the one I actually love and Ziggy is missing his own son grow up. But neither of us are prepared to stand on our morals and see you not get this job if you want it. We can't cope with you not getting this on our C.V's'.

The unexpected and brief meeting with his brothers did not help David develop an inner peace and so he kept drinking for a long time to come until he staggered back to his hotel room where he lay down and slept fully clothed and alone.

CHAPTER NINETEEN

Sometimes when drinking David would wake up fully awake and evidently unharmed by his indulgence whilst others he would wake up a broken carcass unable to move, think or open his eyes. Regardless what his body chose to do, it would always be an early rise. He woke up the following morning feeling broken but with the desire to fix his situation and that of his family and Charlotte. He loved his brothers and they needed to know that whilst he was not the most reliable long distance sibling he did care and would support their decision no matter what. Scraping himself out of bed after several attempts where the room slid from side to side like pirate ship fairground ride he steadied himself on the wall. After pouring his heart out to the toilet he forced himself to drink glass after glass of water and took a shower. Now with his stomach emptied of any contents and his damaged body washed clean he forced more water down himself and then took some drugs to calm the banging of the drums in his head. Walking slowly along the sea front he headed to the flat which Paul and Ziggy shared. Banging on the door in a similar rhythm to the pain in his throbbing head he lent against the wall pressing his forehead into the polished cool bricks by the grand entrance. Buzzing him up without checking who it was Paul was shocked and unsure of what to do when he saw David enter through the unlocked door.

'Hi, I haven't come to make trouble. I want to make amends with you and try to undo some of the damage I have done'. David said leaning against the dining room table. 'You were right the other day. I just don't know how to be normal'.

'Normal, normal is boring David. You just need to learn to

think about other peoples feelings'. Paul confirmed turning the kettle on.

'I am truly sorry mate. You have made my brother really happy for the first time in his life and I would like to be able to think of you as a friend if you will let me'.

'No probably not, I think you are quite annoying so just distant brother in law will do for me'. Paul smiled.

'Brother in law'?

'Well if you hadn't had shown up I may have asked him by now but you had to appear and steal the limelight with your attention seeking selfishness didn't you'?

'Congratulations brother'. David moved forward and the two hugged.

'Well I guess that means you are not homophobic', laughed Paul. 'So how can I help you sort this mess out so I can get you back on the first train back to London'.

'Well I figure there is one thing wrong in both of their lives. Ziggy needs to see Noah to make him happy and Joe needs to sort out his relationship with Heather'.

'That is two risky areas David. They could end up hating you if you make things worst'.

'But if it works. My brothers could be happy again'.

'Well I guess Ziggy is more likely to say yes to me if he has his son's blessing. Alright what is it you need from me'?

'I just need to know where I can talk to Noah and Liz'.

'No I can't do that yet'.

'Why'?

'Not until you have eaten properly and I have made you look less like a homeless drunk. If you go to see Elizabeth like that she is going to treat you pretty badly and if you go and see Heather like that then nothing you say will make her speak to Joseph'. Paul walked into the open plan kitchen and pulled a frying pan out of the cupboard. 'Right so I will make you a fry up and you can have some paracetamol and orange juice whilst telling me exactly what we are going to do for both of them and then how you are going to get that amazing girl you have let slip through your fingers back today'.

'I don't know Paul. I think she hates me, she really was upset'.

'Yes and that is the reason you have got to go and see her first'.

'I don't think I can'.

'Bollocks! You have to if you want her back. She will have just had a terrible nights sleep thanks to you and her whole world is being threatened to make things worst. So you need to grow some and quickly'.

'But she said she hated me'. David squinted as he swallowed the tablets.

'Yes and you can only hate somebody you really love. She was devastated because she thought she found somebody she could trust and love and you let her down'.

'I know'.

'Well the good thing for you is that everybody fucks up. But you just did it before the relationship even started. She was sky high and you crashed her down right at the start. This will depend on how much she really liked you now which I think I am pretty sure she felt like she had never felt before with you'.

'Really'?

'Yes, when she left I saw it in her eyes. I don't know why she would be interested in an older man being so young and beautiful but you can't judge taste. Sometimes the right bit of pixie dust is sprinkled at the right time. Once we have eaten, we will get onto it then'.

'We'? David looked up in surprise.

'Well no offense but I am not sure you are under the limit so I will be driving. Also if I do this for you I am guessing you will owe me one'.

'What do you need'?

'Well to start with something magical and unforgettable to happen so Ziggy will remember the moment I ask him to marry me'.

The two continued to talk and get to know each other for the next hour or so as they ate the breakfast that Paul had prepared. Feeling a lot more like a human David sat in the passenger seat of Paul's small van nervously thinking of what he could say to Charlotte as they drove towards the village. Driving to the end of the track leading to her bungalow Paul pulled up and looked down towards the house.

'They have elephants out back? My God, you never do know what the neighbours get up to do you'? Looking back down the street he eyed up the tea-shop. 'Okay look don't forget we are on a schedule but I figure you may need some time so I will read my book for a while in that old tea shop over there. *Esther's* the sign said. They look like they are open'.

David slowly headed down the track leading to the cottage where all was quiet. He knocked on the door and to his relief it was Charlotte not Gladys that answered the door. Still in her pink pajamas with her hair not fixed for the day and without make up she still caused David's heart to lose coordination. Looking tired from the most likely predicted bad nights sleep she avoided eye contact with him.

'What do you want David'? She said very quietly.

'Just a chance to talk to you. At the very least to say I am sorry. Please Charlotte'.

Leaving the door open she walked away and down the corridor into her bedroom. Sitting under her duvet she sat against the headboard with her knees up to her chest. David walked in slowly closing the bedroom door behind him and sitting on the edge of the bed.

'You had better make it quick'. She spoke defiantly trying to put strength in her voice. 'I have a meeting this afternoon with Trevor Thomas and Herman Splythe'.

'Why'? Worry filled David's voice.

'Well now I know what you are doing I think it is time I gave up this fight'.

'Don't do that, please', he begged her.

'Why? What is it to you anyway'?

'Well I hope it could be something. Look I know I really messed up but that is what I do. I like you. I really do and I was going to tell you about the contract they offered me but couldn't think how to do it. The evening with you and coming here yesterday made me forget who I am for a while and I went to find more out for you but like everything in my head it turned into a plan. A way to make my future more secure, with a really good job and potential, a new change that would help me move on but most of all it would give me something so I wouldn't have to leave Aberystwyth again'.

'But you have a good job in London, you have friends there and you can easily get a new place to live. Is this job which would really cost the town so much worth it just so you don't have to go back'?

'If it means I get to stay with you then yes'. David now had visible tears coming from his eyes.

'But I don't care about money. I just met someone who I really liked and wanted to get to know them. Your job doesn't matter to me. I would get a job as well, I wouldn't just expect you to give me everything'.

'I am so sorry, I don't want it to end now. I don't want to lose you'. David's tears flowed as his voice broke.

Charlotte leaned forward and pulled him towards her by his shirt kissing him. Within a moment after the uncertainty faded the two were kissing desperately as David slipped under the covers. Feeling her hands move down his back and pushed passed his belt onto his hips, he was ready to take this further as they heard the bedroom door swing open.

'Some man outside, says he is waiting for you Charlotte. Looks like there is one inside as well'. They heard Gladys say before walking away. Holding their breath in total stillness for a few more seconds like two children hiding, Charlotte ended it bursting into a fit of giggles.

'Who is she on about'? She asked.

'Paul was going to the teashop in the village. He said he would wait there'.

'Well he probably realised the doilies are brown and everything tastes of smoke and came back early'.

'A shame that is'. David buried his head into her neck.

'Yes, we had better get up'.

'I need you to get dressed as well. I need your help to make things right'.

'Who says I have forgiven you yet'?

'Well I was guessing that was being forgiven wasn't it'?

'Well maybe but I will need a much bigger gesture to completely forgive you'.

'Okay, I will have a think about it and add it to my list of things to do'.

David went out as she got herself ready for the day ahead. Meeting Paul outside stood by the van he smiled openly as the two met sending a message exactly what had just happened.

'So you two have made up then'? Paul questioned.

'Yes we would have made up a lot more if you hadn't come back so soon'. David quipped back. 'I thought you were going to get a cup of tea'?

'I did but everything was stained and brown including my cup and the tea tasted of burnt wood. The old lady serving me was almost as old as Nanna'. Paul explained. 'Talking of Nanna, she is very forthcoming isn't she? She said you were probably having sex. Sex mad she told me'.

'Yes she sure likes talking about it'. Charlotte smiled.

'Now here is a sight for sore eyes'. Paul gave Charlotte a quick kiss on the cheek and a hug as she got to the van. 'So you have forgiven him then'? She nodded back. 'Yes I must admit he got me too. But I told him he owes me one'.

'Me too'. Smiled Charlotte whilst looking at David.

'Good. Well I am sure he will impress us with his actions today'.

CHAPTER TWENTY

Sitting snuggly in the front of the van, the three headed to a small countryside outpost of Aberystwyth where David's former sister in-law Elizabeth Jones lived. Unsure of how he would tackle her, the three agreed it would be better if Paul as Ziggy's 'new' boyfriend should stay in the van whilst Charlotte and David should go in.

Upon arriving it was clear that Elizabeth had done well for herself as she let them into the house with much less debating than David had feared. The house was a modern build detached home which David guessed would be about four bedrooms due to its size and had ample land around it to make it a very nice family home. Looking at photos whilst they waited in the living room it was also clear that in the past few years whilst Noah had grown up, she had also moved on and found another man. Coming back into the living room Elizabeth who was about forty years old with blond dyed hair only possible to identify by a few darker roots. Sitting on the opposite sofa from them with a slim figure and dressed in a tight black tracksuit and exercise top she offered them both drinks and biscuits.

'So David it has been a long time since we caught up, how long has it been? Three years'? Liz spoke fondly to him without any of the disdain which he expected. 'How is Ziggy doing'?

'He has moved on like you seem to have, I am happy to see'. David looked towards the photos.

'Yes that is my fiance Marco, he studied here but came from Croatia. He works here and we are engaged to be married next year'.

'That is terrific news'. David genuinely was happy for her and she could see this in his reaction making her relax some more.

'How is he doing'? Liz asked with a smile referring to Ziggy.

'He is in a relationship with a nice man called Paul. The business is going well, I am sure you saw it in the papers'.

'Yes, I did. I have seen him but we don't talk. It's just a bit awkward still'.

'Yes well I think that is an improvement isn't it'?

'Maybe. Anyway what is it you want me to do for you David'?

'I want to give Ziggy the opportunity to see Noah again'.

'I don't know', she tensed visible as he suggested the idea to her.

'Come on. I get it when he was only six but he is four years older now and understands things more than we probably appreciate'.

'But he will be embarrassed. What will the other kids say to him at school'?

'Well he may need watching a bit and have it properly explained but how is he going to feel in ten years time when he realises his dad was sent away because he realised he was gay'? David paused waiting for Liz to look back toward him as she turned away ashamed of her own actions. 'It was a really hard situation I understand that and in the heat of it all you have probably said nothing that other people in your situation would have but Ziggy is a mess without his son. He loves him so dearly Liz. He wouldn't try and step in the way of you and Marco but just having the opportunity to see him would be like a new beginning for him'.

'I know you are right but I was so upset when it all happened. He just stood in our living room and said *I think I am gay and I am not sure I love you anymore.* We were having problems but it just broke me'.

'I am not judging you Liz, your world was turned upside down and your son was in the middle of it. But he has got used to Marco as I presume a step dad? Surely he must wonder where his actual dad is'?

'Yes but how will I tell him without him hating me. We have

walked past that coffee shop for the past few months and not once have I said his father is inside'.

'Look I don't think that should be a worry just let him know his father wants to see him'.

'I know I don't really know you but I lost my real parents very young'. Charlotte intervened. 'I was seven when I was adopted and I know by the time I was his age I would have done anything to see my parents again. Forget the reasoning behind why I was left behind, I just wanted to have that family bond. Don't get me wrong I loved my new parents but I just had a longing for them and to reconnect'.

'I don't think I can talk to him about this. I will get too emotional'. Liz stood and walked to the photos of Noah. 'I don't mind him seeing Ziggy as long as Noah is comfortable with it. If he doesn't want to I am not going to force it. But listen, if this happens you are going to have to talk to him for me'.

'Me'? David seemed shocked.

'Yes David, he used to love his Uncle David'.

'But I haven't seen him in four years'.

'Well he still remembers going out with you and Joe fishing last time you came. Listen, he is at school today but on Friday he is off for a training day. I could let him spend the day with Ziggy and see how it goes from there? But you will need to come and see if he wants to first. What do you think'?

'I think its amazing how much you are agreeing to considering you told Ziggy he was disgusting a few years back'. David questioned her suspiciously.

'Well, to be honest it is only recent but Marco and me are expecting. Only early days but it made us talk about parenting and I remembered how good Ziggy was. Noah deserves to get to know his dad alongside Marco'.

'Congratulations'. David and Charlotte both responded.

'We haven't told people yet. Not even Noah as its only a few weeks'.

'Don't worry I wont say anything to Noah or Ziggy', David committed.

'David. Thank you for doing this. Look he will be back home by four tonight. If you want to pop over I will make myself scarce. Just let me check with Marco'.

'Is that okay with you'? David looked at Charlotte who seemed shocked but elated that he had considered her and she nodded enthusiastically at him. 'Well I think that's a yes then'.

Sitting outside the house in the van, Paul sat nervously as Charlotte and David came out of the house with Liz after almost an hour. To his complete shock Liz who he had never really met before and was more beautiful and fit than Ziggy described waved at him from the door as the others walked towards him and got in the van.

'She waived at me'? Paul questioned.

'Yes, provided Noah is okay with it she will be a regular visitor I imagine'.

'You did it? She said he could see him'?

'Not quite'. Charlotte answered. 'But if David can explain and if Noah wants to see him then she is okay with it'.

'Oh my God, he is going to be so pleased', Paul almost getting emotional smiled with joy.

'You can't tell him until I have met with Noah. I need to make sure he is comfortable with it. Could make things tricky for you, are you sure you would be alright with that'?

'Don't worry if Ziggy gets a chance to see his son again then I will help however I need to. I can be as low camp as needed. David you have really done something here'.

David stood alone at the door of the house which looked a lot drabber than the previous time he had been there. Ringing the bell he was nervous but knew this one was better off doing alone. The door opened and Heather looked shocked to see him.

'David? What are you doing here'? She looked healthier but still tired all this time later to David. 'I thought you were living in London'?

'I am just here to try and sort somethings out and catch up with some people. Can I come in and have a chat with you'?

'I would rather you didn't. Its not exactly tidy in here. Sorry'. Heather closed the door and rested her head on the wood before opening it again as David was thinking about walking away. 'How about we go and get a coffee somewhere? Not at Ziggy's though'.

'Sounds good'.

'I will just grab my bag'. The door again closed and David stood waiting for a few moments before Heather headed out to greet him. They walked saying very little until they reached a coffee shop. Heather insisted on buying so David sat and was too polite to admit he couldn't stand coffee as the two cups were placed in front of them.

'So how have you been'? David asked taking a sip of the coffee whilst refraining from gagging as he tried to swallow it without tasting its bitter strength.

'I am okay, it has been hard you know. But life goes on doesn't it'. She nodded at him.

'Is that a statement or a question'? He smiled back at her.

'I am not sure. I am surviving. Like most people I guess. You'?

'I thought I was doing well but the lens has been altered so to speak in the last few days'.

'You up here with Kelly'?

'No'. David paused. 'We sort of broke up'.

'That's a shame'. She paused drinking from the mug before looking at him. 'How is he'?

'Surviving. He regrets it you know, walking away'.

Heather stopped in an attempt to say something as she welled up. She took a few moments as David placed his hand over hers to comfort her. 'Then why did he never come back'? She barely legibly questioned him whilst wiping her tears away.

'It broke his heart seeing you like that. He didn't know how to handle it. He still doesn't'.

'Neither do I David. But I have to handle it everyday when I see that room that our baby should now be growing up in'.

'He still loves you'.

'Then why isn't he sat here instead of you'?

'You know what he is like Heather. He doesn't even know where to begin. He let you down. He knows he doesn't deserve you back'.

'So why are you here then'? She questioned him.

'Because whilst I agree he doesn't deserve you. I can see that neither of you are coping without each other'. David looked directly at her. 'He is moving aimlessly through his life whilst you are hiding out in your house trying to avoid anything that means you have to move on'.

'That is unfair'. Heather snapped back. 'Do you think I want this? Do you think I want my heart to break every morning when the memory hits me lying in bed and I think about what we have lost? I lost my baby and because we weren't strong enough I lost my husband'.

'You can find him again. You know he still wears the wedding ring. He has never took that off'.

'I heard he was sleeping around'.

'He is trying to find something that is missing in his life. He needs you'.

'I don't need him'.

'I think you do. Or at least you need to clear the air with him so you can both move on'.

'I don't want to move on. I want the man I fell in love with back'.

'Then you need to find him because he wont come to you'.

'Because he is too damn selfish'.

'No'. David leaned in toward her. 'Because he is too damn scared to face you and what happened'.

'Well that makes two of us'. Heather pushed her chair back and stood up.

'Look my mobile number is on that card. If you change your mind or need anything. Just ring me. I am here until Monday'. David stood and hugged Heather who left quickly clearly needing to get away from the emotions stirred by their conversation. Sitting back down in the chair he didn't know if he had done a positive thing or not with her. He felt bad reopening old wounds but knew the only way she would move on was from meeting with Joe and he hoped he may have initiated that for her sake if not for his brother's.

The afternoon was quickly becoming evening as David met back with Charlotte and the two headed back to see Noah. David had not seen him since Ziggy and Liz split up and was shocked by how much he had grown. The two played together on his computer console for a while whilst Liz questioned Charlotte fully about their relationship and what she knew about Ziggy and Paul. Taking drinks in for them Charlotte sat by David and raised her eyebrows to suggest he was avoiding the necessary conversation with Noah.

'So Noah, do you know why we are here today'? David asked putting the joypad down.

'Mom said it was about dad', he said quietly clearly not wanting to face the conversation either.

'Yes'. David paused. 'The thing is Noah your dad really misses you and would love to see you again. Would you like to see him'?

'Yes'. Noah nodded.

'That's good Noah but you know he has had to move on from being married to your mom and his life is different now'.

'Mom said he owns the coffee shop in town'.

'Yes he does and above the shop his partner works who he loves very much'.

'Okay'.

'Well the thing is Noah is that'. David paused unsure what to say.

'Oh for God's sake David'. Charlotte pushed over him revealing her Welsh accent fully. 'The thing is Noah your dad is very happy in that relationship and that truly is what is important wouldn't you agree'?

'Yes, I guess so'. Noah looked bemused by the two of them meandering around the subject matter.

'Good. Because you want your dad to be happy like your mom is don't you'? She stopped as Noah nodded and smiled. 'Well the thing is your dad's partner is not a lady but another man. Do you understand'?

'I think so'.

'And you are okay with this aren't you? It doesn't really matter does it'? Charlotte said giving a face suggesting the whole conversation was a bit silly.

'They wont kiss in front of me will they'? Noah looked at David.

'I don't think so champ, not if you don't want them to'. David smiled.

'Are you two a couple'? Noah asked.

'Erm, yes I guess we are'. David said coyly.

'You love her'! Noah stood up and pointed at David. 'Yes you do'! He turned and hugged Charlotte before running to tell his mom about them leaving David and Charlotte sat alone in the living room.

'See. He is more bothered about us than his own dad. Kids don't care, it is only old out of date people like you who are nervous about it'!

CHAPTER TWENTY ONE

Heading back toward the Coffee Shop where Paul had arranged that both Ziggy and Joe would be present. David felt extremely anxious even though he had potentially accomplished two massive changes for the betterment of his brother's lives. Neither were aware of that at this point. He was still the brother who had sold out for a job and now he had some serious thinking to do. The land they owned had never benefited them and never would unless they sold it to Merriman Initiatives but that would allow them to start a chain reaction of business moves which would not only make Charlotte homeless but also change the town forever. At this point of the day his hang over had subsided with the emotional journey he had been on. Not wanting to drag Charlotte into another fight he agreed she could come to the Coffee Shop but she could continue practicing her hot drink skills with Paul whilst he sat with his brothers.

Entering the shop Ziggy who was arguing with Lynne at the counter told David to sit down and Charlotte walked David to the table before returning back to the counter. Joe entered the shop looking like he had just had a tough day at work covered in plaster dust. Tension was clearly in the air as Joe waited for Ziggy before the two sat across the table from David.

'I made a mistake and I am sorry' David started to break the cold stare from Joe.

'You damn right you made a mistake sunshine. I was ready to give you two black eyes yesterday for being so God damn selfish'. Joe was intense with anger towards David.

'Calm down Joe, he is here to apologise. Let's give him a fair trial'. Ziggy insisted.

'That is your problem Ziggy, you are too forgiving. Go on then tell us what you think it is that we need to hear'.

'I went into those meetings with the right intention of finding stuff out for Charlotte and how we could stop the council just pushing her out and selling the reserve to Splythe'. David stopped looking at Joe. 'You can doubt it all you want but look at it from my point of view. I didn't know initially what was going to be the full intent of their development. It seems unbelievable what they are planning'.

'But as soon as they told you, you got on board didn't you? Joe fired back.

'Well yes they did start to convince me it was a good idea. I am not going to lie to you'.

'Strange that, because you were lying to us yesterday', this time Ziggy gave him a hard time.

'Look at it from my side. I got here after finding my long term partner in a shower with some gym goer and then bumped into the most precious thing I have spoken to in a long time. A large company offer me not only a really good deal to sell a piece of land that for three generations our family has not done anything with. They also offer me a permanent job which would pay very decently indeed. With that job I could stay here and make a fresh start completely'.

'And you started looking at it like that all because of Charlotte'? Joe questioned at a more quiet and calm level. 'I am not being funny, she is lovely and you have hit above base with her. But you are going to risk your whole career back in London for someone you hardly know'?

'She is the best thing that has happened to me in years'. David looked over to her as she was even starting to crack through Lynne's defenses at the counter.

'But what happens when she realises how much of a self centered asshole you can be'? Joe questioned somewhat sarcastically.

'To be fair to him I think she saw him at his lowest last night and for some reason took him back', Ziggy suggested.

'I realise it was short sighted and by doing that job it would take me back to how I felt living in London but I don't know what else I can do? Property and sales is all I am any good at. What other skills do I have'?

'I don't know David but join the rest of us who don't know how they are going to make ends meet. Look at the two of us'. Ziggy's tone moved from opponent to adviser. 'Joe had to start his business whilst working for somebody else slowly gaining customers and not knowing where his next job was coming from. I took on this place not knowing whether I would get a single customer. You just need to stop, press the reset button and forget the past ten years or so and then see what opportunities there are. Wherever you end up, whether it is here or somewhere else'.

'That is what I thought I was doing looking at working for them. I wouldn't know what else to do'.

'If you stay in that career you might as well go back to London and slowly develop the high blood pressure which will kill you whilst you make some corporate leader like Herman Splythe rich. You just need to think about something that will excite you and make you feel fulfilled'.

'You might have to take risks, we both did, we still are in our businesses and there is a lot of pressure but we are both happy with our work life'. Joe added.

'I need to think about Charlotte as well in this. I want to help her if the land she lives on is sold'.

'Yeah and ideally you could think about doing something that gives us an alternative use of that land that means it makes more sense to not sell it', Ziggy reminded him.

'So you haven't actually handed the contract in then'? Joe questioned.

'Of course he hasn't. He would have told us he had, and besides he wouldn't dare talk with us if he had'.

'That's it'! David snapped happily banging his hands simultaneously on the tables.

'What, you did give the contracts in to Splythe'? Ziggy looked in shock.

'No, of course not'. David looked confused that they weren't following him. 'Look you said it yourself. I need to take a risk and do something new, something I would enjoy, something including Charlotte and something that would use the land'.

'Go on then tell us' Joe asked.

'Not yet. I need to go and get somethings. Meet me back here in thirty minutes'! David quickly shot up walking out the door after he practically leapt over the counter to kiss Charlotte before quickly running down the road.

'If his new idea still ends up being about selling the land to Splythe, I will kill him'. Joe commented.

'You wont have to, I will do it myself'. Ziggy smiled.

Thirty minutes later David burst into the shop full of hope and aspirations of his idea. He looked behind the counter and Lynne was stood on her phone. Looking across the coffee shop he was confused by who Charlotte, Paul, Ziggy and Joe were sitting with. The man had his back towards the door but from the look on Charlotte's face it was not a good conversation.

'Is that Trevor Thomas over there Lynne'?

'I don't know who he is but whoever he is, I think he is kind of sexy in that suit'.

Feeling confused by both Lynne's reaction to the balding, overweight man he met previously at the Tusk Trail and unsure of what was going on he quietly joined the table who were the only people left in the coffee shop.

'What is going on'? David asked quietly to Paul.

'Basically, they have either got to buy the land outright, get a mortgage or they have thirty days to vacate the premises'. Paul whispered.

David sat for a few moments and then slowly sneaked away

from the table, a move which confused and slightly annoyed Ziggy who was busy comforting and reassuring Charlotte. Trevor spoke contractual legal information at them but nothing was making sense to her.

'Lynne, I need your help. I am not sure how legal this is but I need Trevor Thomas out of this coffee shop for long enough to talk to everyone else before she signs something saying she agrees to being evicted'.

'What do you want me to do'? David saw a slight twinkle of mischief appear in Lynne's eyes.

'Well you did say you liked the look of him didn't you'? David looked over to an unsuspecting Trevor. 'Well I happen to know he is single and successful, owns a house, no mortgage or anything'.

'Leave it to me boy, I know what to do'. She pulled her rubber gloves off with her teeth in a provocative manner.

David walked back over to the table and interrupted the conversation as Trevor was in mid-flow.

'Right then, Trevor you are needed by the pretty lady at the counter I believe and I need to speak to Charlotte and everyone first'.

'I am sorry I don't understand', Trevor looked up revealing the blotchy marks from his stress delivering this news to Charlotte.

'You will do'. David gestured towards Lynne.

'But we haven't reached an agreement over this yet and I really need to push you Charlotte to agree on an early release'.

'What is a few minutes going to matter Trevor? Nothing will be resolved before business closes today'. Ziggy interrupted confirming to Trevor to head over. The table sat silent as he did and then Ziggy looked directly at David. 'You had better have something good up your sleeve brother because I don't know what else we can do based on what he just said'.

'What has he said'? David whispered leaning forward.

'Well basically if Charlotte and Gladys agree to move out early they will be financially supported but if not an eviction notice will be issued for thirty days time. Unless of course the money can be drawn up to get a deposit'.

David hugged Charlotte who was weeping with little strength left in her voice as the others talked.

'Look I think we all feel like the writing is on the wall here a bit'. David continued in a hushed voice. 'Even if we don't sell our land the council could force acquisition it from us and sell it to them. So I suggest we do something a little bit extreme but it might just create enough public awareness to stop this whole venture'.

'I don't like the sound of this', Paul commented. 'We have got businesses which doesn't need bad press'.

'What is it you have in mind David'? Joe asked.

'Well look, just bare with me on this one. Why is it that you all love this town? It has that certain something which most places lose. A link to its past which you cannot help but fall in love with. It is steep with important history and grandeur that most places don't have'.

'And how will this help us'? Joe asked.

'We have a large slice of land next to the castle ruins. The first part of the original town. Lets reenact the most iconic moment in the town's history. Let's bring the elephants back to Aberystwyth'. David climaxed his sentence with hopeful applause but got non.

'I am sorry but I don't see how that will help anything'. Ziggy pondered.

'If this weekend we brought those three elephants to the town when the tourists are all here on Saturday it would cause a big enough stir that the crowds could be massive. We then use it to spread the plans of Merriman Initiatives and spread the word of the land we own as well as the reserve'.

'And then what'? Ziggy questioned.

'I don't know'. David answered.

'So you want us to somehow bring the elephants from Charlotte's home twenty or so miles to Aberystwyth in the hope it gets some public attention. So we can bring down the whole development through bad publicity'? Ziggy seemed unimpressed.

'And what are we doing with our land'? Joe seemed unable to follow David's thought process.

'Well you see that is the second part. Last time the elephants got into an accident on Constitution Hill and it was covered up making many forget about them but this time we take them up past the Old College and to our land. We can then explain the problem of being forced to sell it regardless and see what impact it has. From there we can explain the amazing story of these elephants, hopefully get Gladys involved and see what else we can do to secure them'.

'You know what? Ziggy sat up straight. 'That is the most stupid sounding plan ever but I am kind of up for it'. He smiled and nodded at David.

'How the hell do you get three huge elephants down here anyway'? Joe asked.

'I don't know, wouldn't they fit in a removal lorry or something'? David answered with his own question to the biggest hole in the plan.

'Until they fell over and into the side of the lorry and then fell straight out onto the road'. Paul answered for him. 'No you would need to walk them here surely'.

'Twenty miles along the roads here, you can't do that with them. It will either scare them to death or cause a horrific accident'. Ziggy suggested.

'What about walking them along the rail track, there is only one train every three hours. It would be the quickest route'. David suggested.

'But you might damage the only public transport from the big cities into our town. We want good publicity not being told we are irresponsible and stupid'. Paul suggested back.

'We could walk them along the coast line if we get the tide right'. Charlotte finally spoke out after listening to the conversation and regaining her posture as the stroked David's arm in appreciation.

'How long would it take to walk them that distance'?

'If it was flat terrain probably about eight hours but it would include wetlands, the sandy beach and waiting for tides so I would put it more to double that'.

'Well if you wanted to be on that beach for mid-day Saturday we would have to leave at a very early time with no guarantees'.

'If we found a secluded spot we could probably camp'? Suggested Charlotte.

'Camping with three massive elephants, is that possible'?

'They are pretty well behaved. If we tie them with rope to a tree and feed them they will sleep like a dog would'.

'That is three bloody big dogs'. Paul laughed.

'So we get them to the beach by the Saturday lunch and parade them in front of the crowds. We will need to think how we spread the message about Merriman Initiatives'.

'We can spread the word on social media. I can get onto that' Paul jumped in. 'That will stop Merriman getting their way with the local papers and stopping the story being blocked'.

'If it catches on enough the BBC will probably jump at it. They will always try and find a unique Welsh event to report on' David added. 'So please link them in the stuff you put online'.

'So how many people do we need to transport the elephants Charlotte'? Joe asked.

'If would be sensible if we could have at least five people. One for each individually and two more to lead the way'.

'How would we do it'? Joe continued.

'Just like you were walking a dog', Charlotte explained.

'Three bloody big dogs', Paul laughed again.

'Okay so we get them onto the beach and then walk them along the promenade to our land and then what'? Ziggy questioned.

'Then we need to have some sort of enclosure to keep them in so the public can come and meet them'. David answered.

'Would it need to be much'? Joe asked. 'We don't have much time'.

'They could do with somewhere to be taken out of the crowd if they need a rest. Any shelter will do'.

'I can get wood from the timber yard and quickly put up some sort of make shift shelter for them and put a fence along to stop the children getting to close. How strong does it need to be'?

'They are very well behaved so just strong enough to keep the children out'. Charlotte answered.

'How will we pay for it'? Ziggy questioned.

'It wont cost that much. If I explain to them that I can get them advertised on national television with what we are building they may give us a good deal' Joe said confidently. 'If I can get support from a couple of people I should be able to get it up and sorted in the morning. I take it I could use hay to create some clear barriers for them'.

'Yes we use hay with them for over the winter', Charlotte nodded at him.

'Excellent, then it looks like we are actually going to do this'? Ziggy questioned.

'What can possibly go wrong'? Joe laughed.

'Well I am guessing we will probably be breaking about ten laws so probably quite a lot but I think if we don't try then we will regret it'. Ziggy said before turning to Paul. 'What are you thinking honey'?

'Just who will clean up the elephant shit when they take a dump on the promenade. You can't use a poop-a-scoop for that can you'? Paul laughed.

'I am thinking who will clean up behind Herman Splythe when he sees this'? Ziggy laughed before getting serious again. 'So first thing in the morning we need to get over to your house Charlotte and get ready to set off. So if we have you, David, Paul and myself with the elephants. We are going to need somebody else really? What about Lynne'?

'Oh my God! Lynne'! David shot up and rushed towards the counter where everybody else watched following him as he disappeared towards the stock cupboard. Stopping as he pulled the handle down he heard cries and yelps which made the idea of abduction and kidnap run through his head before he dared to peek through the door where he greeted to a naked Trevor on his hands and knees with a half naked Lynne spanking him.

After a moment of silent observation in which he saw that Trevor was fully self engaged with this activity he closed the door trying to erase the vision from his mind. Walking back to the table he sat down quietly with the others watching. 'I think you are going to need to give that store cupboard a deep clean. But on the plus side I think we can get Trevor on our side if Lynne is. Because by the looks of it he will do anything she wants him to'.

'Anything'? Ziggy asked with a grimace on his face.

'Yes', David nodded uncomfortably.

CHAPTER TWENTY TWO

Following a few more discussions and organisation of how they were planning on doing this unlikely and potentially law breaking feat people made their way excited home, unsure but all agreed. That night Ziggy would discuss the idea with Lynne and if she thought it had legs then she would need to convince Trevor to give them the cover and not report it in to Herman Splythe and the council. Joe was sorting out the building work and labour to prepare them for the arrival on the Saturday. Paul would help on the Friday daytime covering the elephants progress on video and then upload this on a makeshift website advertised by social media on the Friday evening into Saturday. Ziggy would sort out tents and camping equipment and leave it in a car near the agreed camping site. David and Charlotte would need to plan the route and get the elephants ready but first they had to talk to Nanna.

They agreed that this had to be done straight away and caught the next train back to the village where they waited for Nanna to get back from the pub and watching her soaps. They used that time to plan the route using Charlotte's knowledge of the local area she gained from years of exploring as a young lonely child. When Nanna got back she sat and listened to Charlotte going through the plans and said very little in return until she was finally asked what she thought with both David and Charlotte waiting with baited breath.

'Do you know how big this was in 1911'? Gladys asked them.

'Yes Nanna, that is why we are going to do it again. To remind the public about them and hopefully save this place'.

'I don't care about this place anymore', Gladys shook her head.

'But Nanna, we want to try and save it'.

'I don't want you to worry about me or this place anymore. It is time for you to move on'.

'I am sorry Nanna, I thought you would want us to do this'.

'I do. Just not because of this place'.

'I am sorry I don't understand'.

'We do it to show the world how amazing this whole town is and to save it. Forget our little sanctuary. It is time these animals were brought and looked after by professionals. And if we can give the town this one more reminder of its roots then I think you are right David. I think the town will remember and stop this development'.

'Nanna, you are okay with it then'? Charlotte smiled feeling the necessary permission had been granted.

'More than okay my love. What time do we leave in the morning'?

'Nanna, you want to come'? Charlotte looked at David with concern.

'Darling, I have looked after elephants here for over one hundred years. If they are doing one final journey then I am doing as much of it as I can with them'.

'I am not sure that is a good idea Gladys'. David stepped in.

'Listen you two. They are legally my elephants and they only leave this place with me'.

'But Nanna what if you get hurt'?

'Hurt? I am one hundred and twelve years old and smoke. What else as exciting as this is going to happen in my life time? You know the doctors said my sight will be gone completely in a few months. I don't mind that though because I have seen everything that I need to. I still remember seeing those elephants back in 1911 and it would be the happiest day of my life to see them there again whilst I still can. I don't have long left Charlotte we know that, but this could be my last memory of doing something most people will never be involved in, let alone at my age'.

'I just don't know if we can Nanna' Charlotte held her hand.

'Look I am sure between us we can make this happen' David stepped in. 'You may not be able to do some parts of the journey but I am sure you can join us on significant parts of it, would that be okay'? David asked Gladys.

'That would be lovely', she responded with a huge grin of happiness on her face.

'Do you think that will be possible'? Charlotte asked him.

'If we get somebody with a car to drop her at certain parts of the journey where it is flat we can push her in her wheelchair I am sure. Thinking about the campaign on social media it will make it a little more amazing'.

David and Charlotte helped prepare the elephants with plenty of hay to eat the night before their unexpected long journey. Following this they checked their map and agreed on the route they would take which included the criss crossing of several rivers and wetland areas as they approached the sea allowing plentiful water for the elephants to be able to drink. As Charlotte helped Nanna, David showered and lay on his make shift bed on the tired old sofa looking through the photographic history of the elephants that Charlotte had collected to give Paul to use online. Resting his head on the pillow placed on the arm of the sofa, he lay thinking about the next two days as the door opened. Standing at the door, Charlotte smiled in her white dressing gown with her wet dark brown hair combed backwards over her head. Joining David as he sat up she sat opposite him on the sofa.

'Thank you for today'. She said shyly.

'What for'?

'For coming up with this, the most ridiculous but wonderful idea. For showing me that you care about me'.

'You don't need to thank me, I figure I owe you one after the other day'.

'But this is going much further than I could have expected'.

She leaned across and kissed him slowly melting David as her mouth parted allowing his tongue to touch her soft blood filled warm lips. The freshly showered sent of her wet hair raising his senses further.

'I think with a thank you like that I hope the next day goes well, besides I should be thanking you for forgiving me'. David smiled at her before kissing her again as the two lingered over each other both wanting more but not daring to prompt the other. For a moment Charlotte rested her forehead on David's chest which was covered with a t-shirt dampening it with her hair.

Looking up into his brown eyes, Charlotte became more serious making the decision to take the lead forward. 'I think we should thank each other properly'. Pulling his hand she felt her heart racing as she stood up pulling him with her towards the door. Not looking back at him, she let go and quickly wondered down the corridor and listened in on Gladys' room before turning and taking both of his hands. Walking backwards and leading him into her bedroom. Feeling electrified by nervousness and excitation she kissed him as he closed the door behind them slowly longing for more but enjoying the moment ever more as a result.

CHAPTER TWENTY THREE

David awoke in the small single bed he had felt so complete only hours before but now alone, the room seemed empty. Still naked he leaned out of bed and pulled on his underwear before realising all his clothes were left on his make shift bed in the living room. He normally spent a long time waking in the morning and would set three separate alarms to coax himself out of bed. But today with the prospect of the journey they were taking and the highly rewarding memories of his previous night he floated onto his feet. Wondering about Charlotte and hoping she would reenter the room to carry on their discovery of each other physically from the night before, but it was not to be. He knew looking at the time he had slept in and she was probably panicking in the bathroom. Picking his crinkled t-shirt up off the bedroom floor he pulled it over his head and opened the door hearing the low level chat of several people in a different room. Quickly diving across the corridor into the sanctuary of the living room his heart sunk as he entered the room to see Ziggy and Paul sharing a cup of tea with Gladys.

'Well here he is, sleepy head'. Ziggy announced. 'Of course with the day ahead I am sure you got yourself straight to bed'?

'He looks like he has hardly slept, strange that' Paul chuckled.

'Well definitely, because his sheets on the sofa here were hardly ruffled. A lot less than his hair'.Ziggy confirmed.

'That is because he was busy having sex'. Gladys laughed.

'Oh my God'. Paul winced.

'Woke me up, all I could hear for hours was sex, sex, sex', she continued with a wink at David.

Feeling the presence of somebody behind him. David's relief

was massive as he felt Charlotte's arm around his chest as he turned to receive a loving kiss. Shocked that she was fully dressed he soon made his weak excuses and made his way to the bathroom from which he emerged ten minutes later a new man. Quickly drinking the tea she made for him and eating freshly made toast from Gladys he made his way out onto the backyard where the elephants were tied by a rope to the fences. They stood well behaved, not testing or pulling on them at all as if they understood the importance of their upcoming journey. Ziggy, Paul and Lynne stood staring at the huge wonderful animals in awe as David joined them.

'Lynne, good to see you here' David greeted her. 'Have you managed to talk with Trevor about what we are doing'?

'Yes I have', Lynne responded taking the cigarette out of her mouth and smiling in a first for David. 'Don't you worry about my little lover boy. He will do as I say, he will follow your instructions fully'.

'Thank you. Nanna how are you feeling'?

'Ready to go young man', she responded sat in the wheelchair she used for long distances.

'Right then, recording Paul'? David looked for confirmation to Paul who was recording the journey both on film and photography using cameras from his business. 'Well then if you are ready Charlotte, open the gates and we will head off up the village'.

'Okay, I will lead Oliver as he is the most likely to be stubborn. David you take Clarissa, Paul and Ziggy take Sienna, and Nanna you can lead the way being pushed by Lynne. The appropriate people took the relevant ropes nervously across the fences as Charlotte walked over to the large gate which had not been opened in a significant amount of time. Pulling the gate slowly to not cause a stampede if the elephants decided to, she guided the others to give slack on the ropes and give the elephants time to acclimatize to the new situation as they put their backpacks on. Carrying mainly food and water for themselves and the elephants the group were relieved to see little excitement from their three lead travelers. Once fully packed up Charlotte took the lead at first pulling on her rope and thus directing Oliver who barely fit through the gate. Pulling the rope tightly as she changed the direction she then held it with some slack as they walked forward. Explaining her actions to the others as a measure to prevent the rope injury anybody should their elephant suddenly pull on the rope unexpectedly. Next up David took the lead and after a few tugs on the rope he convinced Clarissa to follow him. Feeling slightly overwhelmed David kept the rope tight but once he stopped walking Clarissa responded and he felt more at ease feeling she understood he was moving her for a reason. Finally Ziggy and Paul started to move Sienna and she responded well even with their panic bickering as if they were arguing how to start up a new car.

Once all three were out they started heading up the track away from the bungalow being led by Gladys who was sat proud in her wheelchair being pushed by Lynne. Entering the main street of Aberdyfith they walked at the pace of Lynne and the three travelers slowed momentarily as they felt flat cold concrete on their feet for the first time. Heading up the high street they were an incredible sight which caused a distraction even in their tiny hamlet. As they continued Esther and her daughter rushed from her tea shop in the quickest fashion possible for a lady in her eighties. Offering Gladys a box of freshly prepared sandwiches as they went on their way she cheered with happiness at the sight. Reaching the public house at the end of the road they were greeted by a crowd of people which joined Gladys at the front of the convoy and started walking with them relieving Lynne of her duty as they headed uphill out of the village. Stopping as they entered the woodland Paul moved ahead leaving Ziggy in charge of Sienna to photograph the now growing troop coming out of the village. Gladys stopped to look at the elephants leaving the village on the same road they entered it over one hundred years prior. Giving her a moment they stood silently as a tear ran down her cheek knowing she was beginning the last great journey she would take. After a few moments the group continued onward and up into the woodland along the same road which David discovered the village in his desperate attempt not to lose Charlotte only a few days previous. Looking forward at her as she turned to check on the other two elephants he caught her eye and the two smiled before she turned away again. He was happy. How his life had changed due to meeting this girl was beyond measurement. Regardless of how this would work out he felt this journey marked his new start in his life, a life where he would be more daring in his personal life and look forward with less fear. Suddenly from the front of the convoy a voice called out identifying an approaching car as they all came to a halt and moved the elephants into the vegetation at the side of the road. The car slowed slightly at first and then considerably as the man driving passed in his white family saloon almost veered off the side of the road in shock at what he saw. The elephants pulled sharply on the ropes away from the road not sure what to make of the vehicle. They had only ever seen trucks moving slowly on hay deliveries back at the reserve. David felt his feet dragging across the floor as Clarissa pulled him but soon stopped as he heard Charlotte's voice shout at them to be calm. Within a few moments they continued and now started heading over the peak of the hill and down the small single tracked road towards the main road which they would encounter a much higher rate of passing traffic of a much greater size and speed.

Standing twenty meters from the main road they saw a regular car doing the national speed limit and contemplated what their best option was before attempting the under two mile length of road which would lead them down to the Dovey Junction train station path which they needed to take to get into the further wetlands and Dyfi river. It was the first of two stretches of main and busy road they would take. It was the largest bit of danger from traffic on the journey putting the safety of the elephants and their unqualified handlers at risk.

'I don't know how we are going to keep them calm if a lorry comes past or a fast sports car'? Charlotte fretted to David.

'Can we not just walk them through the woodland either side of the road'? He responded pointing towards the bank.

'No the one side is cut through by the rail line whilst this side of the road is also a steep incline, they could lose their footing and get injured'.

'How about one at a time with a few of us directing them'? Paul commented from the back.'We could use the people from your village to surround the elephant from the road side to make it calmer? I don't know if that would work'?

'Okay yes that makes sense. We can tie the two girls to the trees and then lead them individually to the end of the road'. Charlotte nodded.

Whilst the others took a quick break her and David worked together to move the females and tie them to two different secure trees with enough movement room for each elephant. Turning they took the rope and led Oliver to the the main road where they grouped the villagers in a line a few meters ahead of the elephant and a few meters behind. Two people went ahead and two more stayed back by about twenty meters so they would flag down any vehicles to slow before it caused any stress. This was the first time that David really considered the dangers of what they were doing and he prayed silently that the passage down the stretch of road that was less than two miles would be a safe one. Within a few hundred meters the first voice shouted car and the two pulled the rope towards the side of the road towing Oliver. Directing his head into the leaves of the trees and distracting him from the car which slowed considerably as it saw the adult male elephant with a line of people either side, he remained calm. Sensing a method that worked they did this three more times with Oliver before reaching the pathway which tailed off the road. Walking him onto this path they took him a suitable distance from the road before securing him to a sturdy looking tree. Returning for the second time they collected Sienna as Lynne went ahead to start the journey with Gladys along the roadside. A move which nobody even questioned, forgetting their safety as to being so preoccupied with the elephants.

Walking Sienna was a smooth journey and they completed it quickly getting to the safety of the footpath at the same time Lynne and Gladys did. Heading back to collect Clarissa, David and Charlotte passed Ziggy and Paul on the road. Soon they were greeted by an expectant Clarissa who sniffed at David as they untied her and walked her onto the road. Again as with the first two when a car came they pulled Clarissa's focus into the bushes. This even worked as a lorry passed by to the relief of all involved. Coming around the final corner one of the lookouts turned back and shouted car to the main group. David and Charlotte pulled Clarissa into the undergrowth as they had done several times now. This time however, as the car passed the driver deemed it suitable to sound the horn several times immediately spooking her. Before he realised what was happening David felt the rope rip through his hands as he cried out from the burning pain. Clarissa jumped wildly backwards jolting her head upwards and knocking Charlotte backwards a meter or so into the trees where she hit the ground and lay still. Clarissa spun into the road and ran quicker than David thought possible for an animal so large along the road and down the path towards the others. Watching in shock, David could only hope nobody blocked her route. Turning he saw Charlotte had not got back to her feet and quickly he ran over to her where he found her lying on her side in the leaf litter.

'Are you okay'? He pleaded as she turned to look upwards at him.

'Bloody idiot hitting his horn'. She smiled and sat up as David placed his hand on her face to direct a kiss which she stopped seeing the burn marks on palm of his hand. 'Oh my God! Is your hand alright'?

'It was my fault I should have put some gloves on, it will be alright'. David continued as he pulled her to her feet.

'Where did she go'?

'Down the path thankfully'.

'We better go and find her, if she falls on the train tracks she could get seriously hurt'. Charlotte ran ahead as David shook his head in disbelief at her determined courage and slowly followed on her trail.

Getting to the path where they had secured the elephants. Charlotte saw Sienna and Oliver still and everyone making their way out of the quickly gained cover found urgently as Clarissa gamboled down the path. Running along the path Charlotte stopped at Lynne who was stood with an empty wheel chair.

'Where is Nanna'?

'She just got up I couldn't stop her'. Lynne answered pointing in the way of the Clarissa's route.

'She is 112 years old, anyone could stop her'! Charlotte shouted in disbelief as she got towards the train track.

She quickly got to the track crossing leading to the island platform at Dovey Junction where a train was at the platform and passengers had disembarked the train with a buzz of great interest in the air. Walking onto the platform Charlotte knew that Clarissa must be at the centre of this but she could not see her at that point and was more concerned about Nanna. In all her years she had never seen Dovey Junction full from end to end with people and tried to maneuver around them as quickly as possible. Getting toward the front of the train she looked over the edge of the track following the target of the passenger's cameras to see Gladys stood with Clarissa stroking the front of her trunk.

'What happened'? Charlotte asked the driver who was stood by his door at the front of the train.

'I was just slowing down to pass through, I have to rarely stop going this way through the station away from Aberystwyth but just slow right down as we pass through. Well lucky really because I saw this massive elephant and the old woman just stood on the track at the end of the platform'. The driver pointed to the position on the track where he saw them. 'The old woman seemed to be pulling the elephant out of our path onto the Pwllheli track so we could get through but I thought I better stop and check she is alright'.

'She if fine, just getting involved that's all'. Charlotte smiled down at Gladys who waved up to her.

'Do you know her'? The driver asked.

'Yes, she is the most important person I know'.

'Why is that'?

'She saved me in this very spot twenty years ago that's why'. Charlotte smiled not looking at the driver who shook his head in confusion and disbelief.

'Well I better get these people back on board they may have connection trains in Wolverhampton or Birmingham New Street'. The driver said before turning and blowing his whistle whilst signaling to get back on the train.

'Wolverhampton'? Charlotte turned excitedly grabbing the man's hand to his surprise.

'Yes it's one of the main stations on the line'. He answered confused. 'It takes about two and a quarter hours on train from here'.

'So you have been there'? She looked at him with wide eyes.

'Yes I live there actually'. He answered.

'You live there'! Charlotte almost jumped up excitedly. 'You are the first person I have met from Wolverhampton. This is amazing. Tell me about it. It is as wonderful as it sounds'?

'Well erm, I think it's okay'. The driver took a few steps away feeling very uncomfortable with the bizarre conversation he was now trapped in.

'What is it like? It is as grand as I imagine it to be'? She continued to question him enthusiastically.

'Charlotte, I have been looking for you'! A overly welcoming David appeared behind her and pulled her by the arm as she turned towards him.

'David, he is actually from Wolverhampton. He can tell me about it a bit more'. She smiled with almost an unhinged excitement in her eyes.

'It's alright, she has always dreamed of visiting, don't worry'. David tried to cover the slightly uncomfortable conversation the driver found himself in.

'This place is bloody weird, no wonder hardly anyone stops here, inbred the lot of you'. The driver continued to curse as he shut his door. Out of the window he shouted down at them, 'Get them off the track, I am going to have to report this in, not that anyone will believe me'. Within moments the train pulled away slowly as it passengers continued to photograph the elephant and Gladys on the linking track.

'What is it with you and Wolverhampton'? David quizzed Charlotte as she hugged him.

'I just want to go there that's all'. She looked up. 'Take me there one day, promise me'.

'If I must'. He shook his head looking at the departing train.

'You are the best boyfriend ever'! Charlotte smiled kissing him before letting him go and turning to Gladys. As she climbed down to the track David watched unable to hide the smile resulting from her terminology of their relationship had sparked inside of him. 'Nanna come on we need to get you both off this track'.

David climbed down and grabbed the rope still attached around Clarissa's neck as Gladys was helped across the tracks by Charlotte back towards the foot path where the others waited with Oliver and Sienna. Sitting for a few minutes to rest Charlotte now organised Gladys to be taken home to rest for a few hours before being picked up later. She would then brought to the rendezvous site where Paul and Ziggy had parked with the camping equipment. After a few minutes Charlotte and Gladys hugged. David watched seeing how much love Charlotte had for this elderly lady and understood how these gentle giants could bring people so close together. They had shared a lifetime of love with animals some people would never got to see.

◆ ◆ ◆

After a few minutes the villagers wished the party well and watched with Gladys as they headed onward with Oliver and Charlotte leading the way, followed by Paul, Ziggy and Sienna. David and Lynne now walked with Clarissa at the back of the line. This was the first time that David felt the warmth of the sun on this rare stereotypical summer's morning coming out from within the shadows of the tree line. The convoy headed along the side of the rail line along a public footpath which started as a path but then turned into a muddy animal track clearly used by cattle more than humans which entered a field where they had to take a detour to find the farmer's gate. Heading through the field the human travelers found it more difficult than the elephants coping with the saturated field seemingly shaded from the sun's drying effect. Using the rail line as their guidance they soon passed through a small woodland section and then a more friendly dried out field before the main road drew alongside with the rail track. At this point the journey had hit the most difficult point, the River was potentially too dangerous for the human's at this point and it would lead to further crossing due to its meandering should they attempt to cross now. The road was hugging the edge of a steep hill and squeezed them between it and the rail line so there was no escape from the regular fast traveling oncoming vehicles. At this point they had no option but to use the rail line. Checking the time they estimated they had an hour before the next train would come down the track on its journey towards Aberystwyth so ventured onward. Increasing their pace with the ease provided by the solid dry track to follow within ten minutes they had covered the distance needed pulling onto the field to the side.

As they walked through the field David watched Charlotte leading them using her knowledge of the local area better than he could with the aid of a map.

'You really like her then'? Lynne abruptly broke his happy mindset.

'Yes Lynne, I think she is wonderful'.

'She certainly looks supple'. Lynne started admiring her ample curves.

'Lynne'! David responded in shock.

'Well it is good you like her. I gotta hand it to you this is pretty impressive what we are doing'. Lynne seemed to soften. 'You know this is only the start of a painful few months for her'.

'Maybe, but hopefully we will be able raise some awareness and get people behind this cause. You never know what we are going to be able to achieve'.

'I didn't mean that David. Can't you see it? It is pretty obvious'?

'What'?

'Gladys is not a well lady, she hasn't got long left'.

'No, I know she is old but she is fighting fit apart from her eyes'.

'David. Trevor told me about her health last night. He is worried she will not make this trip. She has cancer'.

'What'? David looked in horror at Lynne.

'When I told Trevor about the companies plans last night he explained to me everything about Gladys and the property. She is getting worse by the day. She is hiding it but the only place she will be able to cope before long is a hospice. As far as the council are concerned they extended the lease a few years but now she is poorly she will soon need constant help'.

'But she has Charlotte'. David rubbed his chin as he considered the news he had just received. 'She is going to be devastated. Why hasn't she told her yet? She can look after her'.

'She can't David. She is not related so they are not recognising her as a potential carer and she has no legal argument to stay in the property'.

'She is her adopted daughter. That is legally related, Trevor knows that'.

'No she is not legally anything. Gladys never adopted her. She kept her without permission'.

'What'? David snapped looking more concerned.

'I don't know the details David. I think you need to speak to Trevor when he delivers our lunch'.

David didn't speak another word to Lynne as they continued their journey. Playing the conversation they had over again in his head. *How could she not be legally adopted? How could Gladys have gone this long without telling her how poorly she was? What should he do?*

◆ ◆ ◆

Within the thirty minutes they reached the last road they would see for a couple of hours before they met the estuary and wetlands heading toward Ynyslas sand dunes. It was here they sat and waited for Trevor to deliver their food as arranged by Lynne who was enjoying a much needed cigarette when he arrived. David watched as the two shared a passionate embrace without the cigarette being extinguished. Within minutes everybody had sandwiches brought from Ziggy's Coffee Shop as everyone apart from Lynne tucked into their food. She was more content eating the sandwiches from Esther's as she preferred the slightly drier sandwiches she had packed for them.

'You are very quiet, are you okay'? Charlotte asked David as the two sat on the grass looking down towards the estuary away from the others.

'Yes, I am just a bit overwhelmed I think'. David lied to her.

'We have done the hardest bits now. Just down to the estuary and then along the beach all the way to Borth' she smiled at him reassuringly.

'Yes. I just want to go and check with Trevor about a few things'.

'Okay'. She nodded as he squeezed her hand and stood up.

David walked over to Trevor who was now putting some

empty plastic tubs into his car as David approached.

'David, how are you'? He said in a frosty fashion clearly still resenting him for moving in on his original object of affection.

'I need to talk to you'. David said directly.

'Well I don't know, Lynne told me to take some crisps to her'. Trevor responded clearly realising what they were about to discuss and wanting to avoid the conversation in any possible way.

'She told me to speak to you Trevor. I can get her if you want'?

'No, no that wont be necessary'. He quickly responded.

'Look Trevor. I have no issues with you. As far as I am concerned you have been trying to protect Charlotte and when you met me you were doing nothing different. But I want to protect her now and you know something I need to know more information about in order to do that. Now from what I can tell you and Lynne are an item so we have both done well from this situation'.

'Okay but lets go for a walk, yes'? Trevor hushed his voice.

The two walked away from the others down the quiet single track road which Trevor had parked along as they started the conversation.

'So Gladys is poorly'? David questioned.

'Yes I am afraid so. She has lung cancer which has spread to several parts of her body. She ignored it for a long time but now is too weak to have treatment'. Trevor's voice shook as he held back his emotions.

'I don't get it. Why wouldn't she tell Charlotte'?

'She hasn't told anyone really, she needed me to take her to the doctors in town you see. If she didn't get a lift off me then Charlotte would have realised she was going there and to the hospital regularly'.

'So you have been holding this inside, having to hide it from her'?

'Gladys said she didn't want Charlotte to worry and make herself ill. Charlotte is a really intelligent girl but she will never accept someone she loves is going to die. Even if they are 112 years old'.

'But doesn't Gladys think she will be hurt by not being told'?

'I don't know David. I just wanted to follow Gladys' wishes'. Trevor's eyes started to fill with tears which caused David to pat him on the back.

'I don't blame you Trevor. I understand what you have done but she needs to know. How long do they think she has'?

'Not long. A few months at best. She is struggling walking long distances now. The drugs are hiding the symptoms although she did a lot of that herself making sure she was away from Charlotte when she was not good. She is on pain killers now also but she can feel it getting worst. I am guessing she is sort of seeing this as a final responsibility which is why she is so keen to take part even though she clearly shouldn't be'.

'This could be her last fond memory is what she said last night'. David remembered.

'It literally could, she really should not be doing this'. Trevor said.

'My God, I need to talk to Charlotte. She needs to know Trevor'. David looked and received an agreeing nod. 'This is going to turn her world upside down'.

'It's not just that David'. Trevor almost choked on his own words with clear regret.

'What is it'?

'Charlotte doesn't know the truth about a lot of things'. Trevor looked away ashamed of himself.

'You need to tell me'.

'I only found out when she had the terminal diagnosis and confided in me on the way home. I wasn't sure what to do. I just don't understand how it all happened'.

'How what happened'? David felt he was getting more impatient.

'You see in this situation normally Charlotte would have a good argument that the council should allow the continuation of the tenancy because she has lived their her whole life and she has supported her elderly relative'.

'Yes that makes sense, so why can't she do that'?

'Because they are not related'. Trevor sighed.

'No but adoption is legal, surely that counts as the same weight in court doesn't it'?

'David it's not that straight forward'. He paused as he wiped a lone tear running down his face. 'My God, what is she going to do'?

'Trevor you are scaring me'.

'Gladys never legally adopted Charlotte. In the eyes of the law there is no historical account of her becoming her guardian'.

'But I don't understand? Charlotte said she did, she has lived with her for twenty years surely she would have realised it by now if not'.

'She never legally adopted her and according to the council Charlotte does not exist anymore'.

'But how? How did she keep her if she never adopted her'?

'They lived in a remote village in the middle of Wales. Charlotte never went to school but was home educated, she has never had a job other than in the village where it has been cash in hand. She hasn't appeared on a register for nearly twenty years, legally she does not exist'.

'But doctors, dentists surely they have to have records'?

'Gladys always used private or the nearest local doctor for Charlotte. No questions asked'.

'But surely she would notice her life wasn't the same as others'?

'Why would she? You can only know how different you are if you can see a template of normal life. She has lived in that elephant sanctuary for her whole life almost. That is anything but normal but how would she know any different'?

'But surely she would grow up to not be able to socialise and do normal stuff. She is amazing, she is bright and caring and just amazing'.

'Don't get me wrong David. There may be something very wrong here in terms of how they did it but Gladys and Simon brought her up really well. When she was young there were lots of us in the village but gradually people moved to the town or away and she just stayed'.

'That is why you are so protective of her isn't it'?

'I am not going to lie, I like her a lot but I want her to be happy, you seem to do that. But yes, when you first walked into that pub, an outsider could be dangerous here and I needed to try and get you away from her'.

'And Herman Splythe'?

'I figured out his game shortly before you arrived. He wouldn't care if they were both kicked out on the street but I have managed to convince him that it would be bad press if Gladys wasn't supported and in turn I am trying to ensure he gets something for her too'.

'So does Herman Splythe know about all this with Charlotte'?

'Yes, to some degree'. Trevor confirmed.

'I am going to have to tell her'.

'It is going to break her'. Trevor shook his head.

'Finding out from Herman Splythe would be a lot worse'. David felt stick to his stomach.

CHAPTER TWENTY FOUR

Joe's team were busy at work as he stood looking at the pile of wood which needed to be a secure stable in the next twenty four hours. His team were hard workers and this was most likely an unpaid job so he couldn't present his stress to them as they dug a moat and placed the secure fencing around the edge of the field. The land which nobody had taken any notice of before and had always just been an unremarkable place was now sparking interest in the local community with some people questioning what was happening and others outraged that this land was being fenced off. Either way he thought, they would be more shocked when they would see what was about to arrive. Turning he looked back at the pile of timber and considered his options. He was struggling. He was so high on the idea of building the housing for the elephants he hadn't considered the size of the job fully and with his team only working for another hour he would struggle to be ready in time. He could build it but would need another person. Getting to work he set up the main support posts ready using one of his men to help him but as the time pushed on he soon was facing a very long and probably unsuccessful day ahead. He hadn't felt this stress and responsibility in a long time. Sitting on the pile of wood he put his head in his hands and cursed himself.

'Fucking idiot', he sighed cursing his own ideas.

'I think we can both agree on that'. Heather stood looking down at him with her dark brown hair tied in a pony tail and dressed looking ready to do some DIY.

'Heather, what are you doing here'? Joe stood hardly able to speak.

'David has been hassling me to come and see you for days. I wasn't going to but the last time he spoke to me I heard the oddest sound in the background on the phone. An elephant'. Heather laughed and smiled moving towards Joe. 'He told me the most craziest story going and I said I bet you were there with him but he told me you were back here putting all the hard work in whilst they were getting the glory'.

'How can you even bare to talk to me'? Joe interrupted with tears in his eyes.

'I haven't been able to for so long now that it seems like I put my life on hold because of it. I knew I would want to scream at you'. She stopped wiping tears from her eyes.

'Why don't you? I don't blame you for anything you say to me. I have no right to anything from you other than hatred'. Joe found it difficult to look at her.

'Because I just want you to do what I needed when you walked away' she sobbed as she reached for his hand. 'I just want my husband to hold me'.The two embraced as tears flowed from them both unable to talk as for the first time they shared their hurt.

'I am sorry, I didn't know what to do', Joe whispered through her hair.

'This, that's all I needed' she responded gripping him in.

'I am sorry to interrupt this touching scene but Joseph I was wondering what on God's green Earth you are building on the land I am going to be buying off you'? Herman Splythe stood smugly in another immaculate pin stripe suit. 'I hope you are going to undo this damage pretty quickly unless you want less money'?

'We are not going to be selling to you Herman'. Joe moved clearly against him as Heather kept hold of his hand sensing the tension.

'That is an unfortunate shame'. Lines of concern spread across Splythe's face as he looked at Heather and then back at Joe. 'I think I probably understand. This is your brothers doing isn't it? That girl has opened her legs and he opened his heart and now money doesn't matter'.

'How do you know about that'? Joe aggressively responded.

'I have seen the news reports about those bloody elephants. I wish I would have had them put down when I had the chance'. Splythe turned and looked around. 'So let me guess. You are bringing them here for some strange reason'?

'Yeah and you can do whatever you want but we are not selling', Joe boasted defiantly.

'Well lets keep an open mind here then Joseph. You say you are not selling but I am sure Mrs Jones here would love some financial security. You know, in case you want to try again'?

'You what? You son of a bitch'! Joe erupted as Heather pulled him back whilst Splythe didn't even flinch in his game of upsetting a volatile Joe.

'Calm down Joseph. All I am saying is I am getting this land whether you want to play ball or not'.

'We choose not to'. Heather calmly suggested.

'Okay well, I had better make some calls'. Splythe paused. 'It's a shame really as not only are you now forfeiting your share of the land cost but if you make this difficult I am going to pull everyone of the council contracts your company has won. You have worked so hard for since you got yourself back on your feet'.

'You are a nasty piece of work aren't you'? Heather scowled at him.

'It is just business little lady. Nothing for you to worry about. But your estranged husband here has to simply make a decision. Drop this stupid fantasy of bringing them animals here, which by the way are my property. Or he will lose every council contract he has in the next few hours and find himself responsible for some work that doesn't meet legal health and safety requirements back at our offices a few months back'.

'You bastard. That was all done as an insurance policy then'? Joe shook his head in disgust.

'It is just business Joseph. Well look I don't want to ruin this little reunion. I tell you what Joseph, I will let you leave the mess you have made and I will sort the clear up once you are gone. You just get that contract to me by two this afternoon or you start losing the money that keeps you afloat during the winter. Good day to you young lady'.

The two watched in disbelief as he turned and walked away without a care in the world. Sitting back down they contemplated their next move.

'What now'? Heather asked.

'I can't not give him it. I will be bankrupt if I don't'.

'Okay look, I think what we do is this. I will get as many people to help us here as possible'. Heather moved over to the basic frame Joe had created. We will build the frame whilst you go and give him that contract'.

'Give him it'?

'Yes. If he wants to play it underhand then let him think he is winning for a few hours. When those elephants rock up tomorrow, public pressure will stop them in their tracks'.

CHAPTER TWENTY FIVE

Soon after Trevor left, the party moved on as David mulled over his need to tell Charlotte the truth about her life. He wanted to protect her from all of this but realised that by not telling her it would only make the inevitable news more devastating at a time when she would be facing a massive change and heartbreak simultaneously. She would have questions and if she found out today she would be able to ask Gladys for the answers. As he was walking David decided he would tell her when they had set up camp for the evening but until then he would hold this information privately.

Entering a Site of Special Scientific Interest had two benefits to the group. Firstly they had a lot of different walkways and were better maintained increasing the pace of the group but secondly the landscape and natural beauty they were experiencing around the site of Ynys-hir was stunning. The convoy could see the five miles ahead of them all the way to the coast that they would need to walk as the land gently sloped downward to the sand dunes and sea of Ynyslas in the distance. As they trundled through the area along a loose gravel and dried mud track the convoy came to a sudden halt. David handed his reigns over to Lynne leaving her with Clarissa and headed up to Charlotte who was stood still with Oliver at the front. Looking at the floor she looked unsure of what to do which was soon understood by David.

'How do we get them across that'? Charlotte asked him without looking upward.

'It is just wide enough for them to get stuck in isn't it? David turned looking back at Oliver's legs.

'What's wrong'? Shouted Paul from behind with Sienna and Ziggy.

'Cattle grid'. David responded before looking at Charlotte. 'I didn't even consider this as a potential problem'.

'What can we do'? She looked at David for answers.

'There must be something around that can act as a bridge or something across it. You know some planks of wood or something'. David said as Ziggy approached to help out.

'We could use the rope'. Ziggy suggested.

'How would that work'? Charlotte looked unsure.

'We have an awful lot of it wrapped around the elephants. If we tightly wrap that around the grid it will form a bridge for them. It might not hold but it is likely they will always have some of their weight on the metal. The problem is the gaps if they miss place their step. But hopefully the rope will take the weight for a few seconds'.

'Sounds good to me' David looked at Charlotte who nodded agreeing with the idea.

For the next half an hour David and Ziggy used the rope gained from the elephants and wrapped it under the two end iron girders which lay horizontally across the gap making the cattle grid. Pulling them tightly they made two tracks across the grid, setting each approximately the width of the elephants legs apart. In the meantime the others stuck as close to the elephants as possible who were too busy enjoying eating the local wild flowers which were in bloom to cause any problems from their lack of restrain now being applied. After testing the rope tracks across the cattle grid using their combined weights and jumping up and down the group accepted it was time to lead the elephants across. Charlotte led each over guiding them via their trunks as the others stood either side trying to give some support stopping each elephant moving sideways under the strict understanding if one did slip they must move out of the way and quickly. After a few moments of worry each elephant successfully made it across and then rested as the ropes were retrieved before being put back on as reigns for each one.

Striding down towards the sea level they soon reached the outer fringes of the Dyfi estuary and hugged the side of the farming fields as best they could to avoid getting swamped down in the muddy salt marshes. The tide was out however which made it much easier to make pace. Paul left Ziggy in charge of Sienna as he was overcome with the natural beauty of the environment they were in and had to use the chance to take some shots of the nature around them. The natural beauty of the landscape was staggering to David too who had forgot how compelling the area was. They were walking a clear succession of landscapes on their journey which at this point were all within his vision. Moving down from the hills with dark majesty of the Cambrian Mountains behind them and through the diverse summer wildflower woodlands and meadows they now overlooked the dynamic estuary which would separate the Ynyslas sand dunes and the postcard village of Aberdovey which was not yet in view. Paul took photographs through passion more than duty now being able to chronicle this journey through the most incredible backdrop where the elephants did not look out of place.

As they reached the Ynyslas sand dunes it was early evening and at that time there were still tourists and locals using the beach. Stopping for considerable time at a busy freshwater stream the group let the elephants have a long drink as the long beach walk in the morning would have few opportunities for freshwater drinking. Sitting in their caravans on the approach to the sand dunes many tourists could not believe the passing site and rushed out to take photos and videos of the event which was exactly what David hoped for. The more coverage the journey had the more people would spread the word. Whenever people asked they told them they were taking them back to Aberystwyth seafront to remember the historic day in 1911. At this point everybody in the group agreed to remain tight lipped about the demonstration against the plans of Merriman Initiatives. Moving from the caravan park along the estuary the group arrived at the edge of the sand dunes where people returning to their cars from the beach busily took photos and started the essential spreading of the news that the three elephants were heading towards Aberystwyth. As they headed around the northern edge of the dunes across the narrow low tidal flow of the river separating them from Aberdovey they could see people on the beach across the water taking photos and trying to organise themselves for long distant selfies with the elephants in the background. Walking around the sand dune system the group headed onto the main beach where they looked for a suitable camping site. The beach was stunning and David who had forgotten why he loved Ceredigion Bay in the past ten years was now finding himself constantly reminded. A Site of Special Scientific Interest due to its beauty he walked taking in the visions around him. An endless golden sand undisturbed by development made the most picturesque beach which was shallow and flat until it met the sand dunes. Walking down the few people who were present all came to inquire about their journey. Soon they spotted a sand dune cove which would protect them from any wind during the night and thus was perfect for them to set up camp. Convincing the elephants to walk over the line of pebbles and boulders that the tide had worked consistently to bring to the top of the beach, the group staked the elephants rope into the ground to secure them from wondering. Ziggy and Paul headed back to their car which they had left at the start of the day in Ynyslas Dune Car Park to collect the camping equipment. For the next hour the group put up the four tents which could hold two or three people that they had managed to collect off friends. As they completed the tent construction Lynne received a phone call and announced that Trevor had arrived with Gladys in the car park before heading over the dunes to help bring her to the group.

With the sun becoming lower in the sky the group rested whilst Paul documented their campsite fully and David found time to sit with Charlotte. He knew the time was not right yet, he had to wait until Gladys had arrived but was aching inside as he approached her. Sitting on the edge of the dune with a dark blue sweatshirt on to keep herself warm now the sun had started to dip, he stopped to look at her before sitting. The sun made her skin glow a golden colour and showed her stunning natural beauty. Sitting next to her she hugged into his arms and turned for a long kiss before looking out to sea holding his arm around her neck by his hands.

'How are you doing'? David asked.

'Pretty good actually', she smiled and kissed him. 'I love this place, it is my favorite place in the whole world'.

'Yes I had forgotten how nice it is. I have been to many places on holidays in the last few years but I forgot that I had this on my doorstep when I lived here'. David looked across at the elephants before turning back to Charlotte. 'I never imagined being sat here with someone as pretty as you and three adopted elephants though'.

'I never imagined I would be sat here with the elephants either. Certainly not due to completely random acts of kindness from a man I met on the train from London'.

'No you imagined he would be from Wolverhampton', David laughed. 'Look I wanted to help and don't forget we are trying to help the town as a whole to not be destroyed by those evil bastards'.

'Well I am grateful anyway and I think you are pretty nice'.

'Thank you, I suppose I am'. He smiled again.

'I am scared about tomorrow'. Charlotte sighed.

'Why'?

'Well we go to that beach and this goes well or bad. It doesn't matter does it'?

'Why?

'Because on Monday you are going to head back to London aren't you'?

'Lets get through tomorrow first and decide how we go forward afterward. If this goes well tomorrow who knows and if it doesn't maybe you should come back to London with me'?

'I can't do that'! Charlotte laughed in a shocked response to his suggestion as if it was the most unimaginable idea possible.

'Why not'? David turned to face her. 'If Nanna ends up in a home which they pay for you may need to start again. You could come and do it with me'.

'But not in London'. She quickly rebutted the idea.

'Okay yes I get it might be a big change but we can visit each other regularly'. David offered.

'Well not really. I can't go much further than the village'.

'Have you never been any further than Dovey Junction to Aberystwyth'? David asked in a struggle to believe the answer which he already knew and Charlotte shook her head confirming his beliefs.

'Nanna didn't want me going any further in case I got into trouble and didn't know what to do'. Charlotte explained.

'I bet she didn't'. David shook his head in disbelief.

'What do you mean by that'?

'Its just a bit unusual that is all to never travel any further than your home village and local town these days'.

'You have to understand Nanna is very old and has lived in that village her whole life so I guess she got used to its safety'.

'How do you mean'?

'Well think about it'. Charlotte turned to David and smiled. 'Since my Nanna has lived there, the world has witnessed at least two wars involving the whole of the world. More recently there has been terrorism and other horrific things happening. But whilst the last century of horrific acts of crimes against humans rights has happened my Nanna has lived there protected from the evils of the world by the isolation of that village and has carved a life of happiness without needing to know about all the horrible things going on around her in the wider world'.

'But don't you think you have missed out in life only knowing the village and it's people'?

'I feel I should have visited Wolverhampton but it is a bit far'.

'No I mean look, she is right in some ways. The world can be a horrible place but when I think about the life I have led since I left this place. I have met so many people who all have had an impact on my life. Sure some of them haven't always been positive but they have shaped me into me. I mean look at Kelly. I never want to see her again but actually if it wasn't for her I would have missed out on concerts and eating at Michelin Star restaurants'.

'Well we have got one of those Michelin Start restaurants in Ynys-hir now'.

'No but think how different your life could be if you would have risked getting on that train and visiting Wolverhampton by yourself by now. Just what could have happened and how your view of the world could change'.

'But why would I want to do that? Take a look at what we are doing now. We are walking three magical animals across the most beautiful landscape you have ever seen. People don't get to do that. But we do and I am getting to do it with you. The strange man who I met screaming at himself on Dovey Junction platform'.

'Alright, I think I am losing but we will need to talk again after tomorrow', David stopped and smiled at her before stroking her hair from her face. 'I am really happy you came to speak to me on that platform'.

'Good. Hey do you know how Nanna is getting across these sand dunes? I have just thought, they can't get the wheelchair over the sand it will get stuck'. Charlotte stopped as David smiled and grabbed her hand pulling her to her feet and towards the top of the dune they were sat on. 'You know don't you'?

The two walked up the dune with out David explaining. As they got to the top Charlotte could hear laughter and soon saw the reason for it. Sliding down the ridge of the adjoining dune towards them was Gladys being pulled by Trevor and Lynne on a bright red plastic snow sledge. Smiling from ear to ear Gladys was laughing loudly which could be heard from the top of the sand dune and Charlotte watched as they approached.

'Nanna!' Charlotte shouted joyfully as she passed them. 'What on Earth are you doing'?

'Living my life lovely, living my life'! Gladys beamed through her smile as she started sliding down the dune towards the camp.

Running down the dune Charlotte caught up with her at the bottom in fits of uncontrollable laughter alongside Trevor and Lynne who were now lying exhausted in the sand next to her. As Charlotte approached, Gladys asked for her arm in support to stand and then she let go taking a few unaided steps forward.

'Are you okay Nanna'?

'I couldn't be happier my lovely'. She turned with tears in her eyes. 'Look at that. Have you ever seen something so beautiful? My lovely children on the beach with the sun setting behind them. That is the greatest thing I have ever seen'.

'Oh Nanna, I am happy they got you here'. Charlotte hugged her as Ziggy came over with a camping chair for Gladys to sit in. Helping her down she sat looking towards her elephants unable to stop her alternating bouts of smiles and tears as she absorbed the experience. Placing a blanket over her Charlotte sat with her as David looked on from a distance.

Meanwhile Paul packed up his camera in order to head back to the shop for the evening where he would upload all the information, photography and footage to publish the website before using social media to raise its profile.

'You happy with what you are doing'? Ziggy asked stood over him.

'Yes I have it covered, don't you worry', he smiled and stood kissing Ziggy.

'Do you want me to walk to the car with you'? Ziggy asked him.

'No, its alright I will ask David to come to check out how he wants me to help in the morning'. Paul confirmed.

'No worries'. The two hugged and Paul headed towards David leaving Ziggy who watched him head over the top of the dune.

Walking towards Gladys and Charlotte with his own folded camping chair Ziggy placed it next to them and enjoyed the sight of the elephants resting in front of them.

'I will wait until David is back and then we will go and fill the buckets with drinking water for them before we sort our barbecue out', Ziggy confirmed with Charlotte. 'This feels pretty special doesn't it Gladys? You must be pretty proud of your granddaughter for doing this'?

'I would be proud of her regardless of what she did. She is a good girl my Charlotte'.

'Yes she is'. Ziggy smiled across at her. 'She certainly has David smitten'.

'Do you have children of your own Mr Jones'? Gladys asked causing Ziggy's heart to quiver with emptiness.

'Yes I have a son. Noah. He is eleven years old'. Ziggy said quietly.

'I bet he is a handful like you and your brother'? Gladys questioned.

'I hope so'. Ziggy smiled before walking towards Lynne and Trevor who were busy showing signs of affection to each other. 'How are you two doing? Are you hungry yet'?

'I think we might just go and lay down for a bit first', Lynne said with a naughty shake of the head as she grabbed Trevor's hand.

'Jesus! Well you just keep the noise down. Try not to ruin the moment for Gladys, Charlotte and the elephants with sounds of seals humping in a tent'. He laughed turning and shaking his head in humorous disgust before getting a shocking vision. Looking twice in disbelief he stared momentarily paralysed by confusion as standing at the top of the dune was David with

Ziggy's son Noah. He was taller than the last time he saw him from a distance and his brown hair with its central parting was longer than before but it was definitely him. For a moment the two seemed unsure but before he could react Noah started running towards him and within moments he was in Ziggy's arms. Ziggy held him so tightly as tears streamed from his eyes and he laughed whilst sobbing and asking him what he was doing there.

'Uncle David has sorted it dad, mom says I can see you'. Noah explained excitedly trying to pull himself back off his blubbering father as David approached from behind.

'You did this for me'? Ziggy stood looking at David with a red blotchy face whilst the rest of his body shook with emotion.

'I had to make it up to you, I had to make it right'. David responded as he welled up slightly.

'But how did you with Liz'?

'She has softened about it, and we had a good chat the other day didn't we Noah. He is fine about it all aren't you'?

'As long as you don't kiss in front of me', Noah said pulling a face much to the amusement of Ziggy.

'You don't mind that I have a man as a partner now'? Ziggy questioned for final confirmation.

'Uncle David said you were happy. I have missed you'. Noah said with a sweet smile.

'I wish Paul could meet you', he said pulling Noah in for another hug.

'That is why he has gone to be honest'. David said causing Ziggy to look up confused.

'He knew about this'?

'Yes, he hasn't met Noah yet but he helped me get to Liz and then he thought you should spend your first night with Noah on your own so you could catch up properly and he would meet him tomorrow'.

'The night? You are here for the whole night? Your mom is okay with that'?

'Yes. It means her and Marco can go out so I think she is quite pleased'. Noah explained.

'Marco hey, who is he then?' Ziggy looked across at David.

'Liz is getting married Ziggy'.

'That's good. Good she is moving on'.

'Hello Noah'. Charlotte said walking over. 'Are you okay'?

'Yes thanks'.

'You knew as well'! Ziggy laughed looking in disbelief.

'She helped me a lot on this as well' David confirmed.

'Thank you. Both of you'. Ziggy was elated and had not felt so happy in years.

CHAPTER TWENTY SIX

For the next hour or so Ziggy and Noah worked together on the fire which they made from drift wood and used it to cook their sausages and burgers which the group sat together and ate with Noah being the centre of attention from all the adults. Following dinner Ziggy promised he would take Noah to meet the elephants and the two headed off. Charlotte had felt that David had gone into himself since Noah had arrived and after dinner as she helped Gladys into her tent so she could rest. Looking for David she climbed high on the sand dune before spotting him sitting further down the beach alone. Not sure what the issue was she headed over to him taking a blanket as the sun was now nearly gone and she could feel the chill developing in the air. Sitting down next to him she could feel worry radiating from his body and felt she now needed to support him.

'Are you alright? You seemed quiet earlier and then at lunch you weren't saying a lot. Now you have wondered off. Its not about Noah and Ziggy is it? You should be really proud of yourself, they are really happy together'.

'No it's not that' David sighed.

'Well tell me what it is then'. Charlotte grabbed his hand and pulled on it. 'You said no more secrets, come on. I can't help if you don't talk to me about it'.

'I want to but I don't know how to tell you'.

'What? It can't be that bad'.

'I found something out earlier and I don't know how to tell you because I don't know how you will cope with it nor what I can do to help'. David got emotional and wiped his eyes as he looked at her.

'David'? Charlotte looked at him with wide concerned eyes. 'I am getting a bit worried now. Tell me, please'.

'Okay but just promise me you will not just react without thinking it through first'.

'David'! Charlotte getting more desperate now insisted on some more information.

'I spoke to Trevor earlier and he told me something you don't know. He doesn't know how to tell you but I know I have to. I found out that you don't know everything you think you do'.

'What do you mean David? Stop using riddles and just tell me what he said'.

'He told me that you were never legally adopted by Gladys and that as a result you don't legally exist as you are not registered anywhere and there is no record of you with the council'.

'That is ridiculous'! She looked at him in disgust and anger. 'Why would he say that'?

'The only reason he would is because it's true'?

'No don't be stupid'.

'Charlotte, he is telling the truth. Gladys never legally adopted you and just kept you at the house'.

'That is not true'! Charlotte snapped at David before she started sobbing. 'She wouldn't do that to me. She is a good person'.

'I am sure she had a good reason'. He tried to hug her but she pulled away in response.

'But she could have told me. Why didn't they adopt me'?

'I don't know'. David sighed looking out to sea before continuing with the revelations. 'That's not all'.

'What else can possibly be worse than that'?

'Nanna isn't well Charlotte, I mean she really isn't well'.

'Now I know you are lying, look at her tonight she is glowing with happiness. What is wrong with you'? Charlotte now stood up abruptly and raised her voice in anger. 'I thought you were different but you are not a nice person. This is because you want me to go to London isn't it? How selfish are you'?

Charlotte stormed away back towards the campsite leaving

David upset and not sure of how to respond to her understandable explosion of emotions from his unexpected news.

With her head throbbing by the confusion and anger merged with worry and a feeling of being scared, Charlotte headed into camp wanting to go to her tent and avoid any conversation. Gladys however was directly in front of her before she could get to her perceived point of safety.

'What's wrong lovely'? Gladys questioned seeing how upset Charlotte was.

'He said you lied to me, you didn't adopt me and you are not well. Why? Why would he say that? It is ridiculous, why would he say that'? Charlotte got more erratic as she went through it again in her head.

'I think we need to sit down for a talk Charlotte'.

'Why? It can't be true, why are you all doing this to me'?

'Come and find me when you have calmed down'. Gladys simply walked away towards her camping chair leaving Charlotte numb with worry and stood feeling more alone that she could imagine.

After a few minutes Charlotte joined Gladys and sat next to her in the chair Ziggy was using earlier. Saying nothing she stared passed the elephants out to sea waiting, not able to say anything which would start the conversation that she knew they must have.

'I have always loved you my Charlotte. I have always seen you as daughter let alone my granddaughter'. Gladys paused. 'You parents didn't want to keep you. I overheard their conversation on the train one day and offered to take you for myself'. Gladys stopped as Charlotte broke down silently in front of her, shaking with emotion. 'I saw you and fell in love. I couldn't imagine why they would want to give you up for adoption and I couldn't face seeing you go into a home until someone found you. We looked into adoption but they said we were to old and couldn't do it. So I approached your parents and we came up with a decision that we would look after you and take you in as our own regardless of what the authorities said we couldn't do. That day I arranged they would leave you and then we would arrive on the next train and take you home. That way nobody could see us and report it'. Charlotte sat with her head in her hands non responsive as Gladys looked at her. 'I love you like my own. You are my daughter I wouldn't keep anything from you unless it was to protect you'.

'You have been lying to me for twenty years. At which point did you decide to never tell me that my parents just didn't want me or that I no longer exist? You were just going to leave it were you until you died and I would have to find out for myself'?

'No I had put things in place'. Gladys grabbed Charlotte's hand which was quickly pulled away.

'Things in place for what? When you die? You are dying aren't you? You don't even think I am worth being honest to about that do you? What am I going to do? There is no record of me! I don't exist! I have no history'.

'I put things in place to look after you'. Gladys calmly reiterated.

'Like what? There is nothing you can do. I am going to be homeless, jobless and can't do anything about it. Literally I can do nothing because of these lies. What am I going to do'?

'Trevor will look after you'.

'How? What am I supposed to do? Just live in his house doing nothing'? Charlotte stopped dead as her own thoughts caught up with what was just said. 'You have been manipulating him haven't you? You knew if he kept coming to see me and was supporting me when you died that I would need someone and then we might end up together. All that talk of meeting a stranger on the train was just your low level reverse psychology wasn't it'?

'He would look after you and you would be safe'. Gladys stood firm with her belief.

'But I wouldn't be happy. And what happens if something happened to him? You just can't program everything like this, it is wrong'.

'He wont stick around for you'! Gladys bit back slightly in a tone of knowledge and authority.

'David'?

'He was just after one thing, which you already gave him. What is left now for him here? He is going to be on the next train out of here and you will be left. Trevor wouldn't do that he is a genuinely kind boy'.

'Yes, who has his own life to lead, not one that you decide for him. I don't love him! I don't want to be with him, I want to be with the stranger I met on the train, exactly as you said I would'.

'You are too young and naive to know what you are talking about'.

'Well I can blame that on you can't I as I never went to school and have only ever met people in the village so I wouldn't know. I haven't even been to Wolverhampton'!

'I was protecting you from the cruel world'.

'You were protecting yourself more like! You didn't want me to go away and discover the world because you knew I would find out'.

'Don't be a silly girl'. Gladys shook her head.

'No you don't get to talk to me like that anymore. Look around Gladys'. For the first time in her memory she didn't want to call her Nanna. 'All of this. All of this was done for you and me. By him.By David. He may well get on a train tomorrow when we are done. I don't know that but what I do know was he has been more honest to me in the past twenty four hours than you have for my entire life'. Charlotte stood to walk away but turned back and looked at her. 'You know what the worst part of this is? You have been the center of my world for the past twenty years and now I know that the center of my world is just as deluded and as evil as the people you told me you'd protect me against. I have not lived a real life because of you'.

'Your life has been wonderful because of me', Gladys shook her head.

'But that is it isn't it Gladys? I have lived the life you decided for me. Not my own life full of mistakes I made for myself but just living a life based on one big mistake you made. I have never dared go anywhere because I didn't have the confidence to do so, and that is what you wanted'.

Turning Charlotte headed out of the camp into the now dark surroundings. Unable to cope she sped up ensuring she was out of range as the uncontrollable sobbing she held inside burst outward. Hurt she couldn't carry her own weight and sunk down onto her hands and knees before collapsing forward into the cold damp sand. Lying on the side of the sand dune she rested her head down as her breathing slowed. Hearing the sea lapping in the distance she accepted her life was now a lie. She could not be loved because someone who loved you would not lie to somebody they loved for so long and leave them never knowing their own story. She was as alone in the dune as she felt in life. Her life would end with Gladys' and then she would have nothing. She was worthless and forgotten in a world that was bigger than she could cope with. She could not live in the world because nothing was true. The decision she made at that moment was as dark as the night around her but was made with no conscious thought as she was cold from her heart outward. Thinking nothing she slowly stood up hollow and with no more emotions. Empty of love, she lost no more tears and walked towards the water. Reaching the edge, she moved beyond it and slowly continued into the low lapping waves. Looking ahead she didn't feel the cold around her legs as it accumulated the numbness she was experiencing. She looked into the blackness of her future with no more light ahead as the waves caressed her body pulling at her very soul.

Coming back towards the camp David was feeling hopeless

and uncertain. He was muttering to himself as his head could not cope with containing the argument he was having with himself any longer. He wondered slowly dragging his feet along the sand whilst his feelings swayed backwards and forwards with the sound of the water ebbing in and out contemplating whether he should have told her everything. Charlotte was now hurting because of him trying to be the man she needed him to be. He felt sick with upset not at the way she reacted but at that he had made her feel that way again. He wanted to protect her but also couldn't face her yet as he looked up the beach to where the camp fire had started to reduce now people had presumably settled for the night. Stopping, he sat on the cold sand and looked up at the moon over the sea which was just breaking through the clouds and starting to reflect on the water. At first he didn't notice the shape in the water as he looked beyond it deep in thought. But his eyes spotted it moments later. Sitting forward he strained to see the outline of somebody's shoulders and head in the water, only shown up by the gentle disruption to the calm surf around them. Standing, David walked towards the water stopping as he reached the edge looking outward trying to see if his eyes were playing tricks on him completing shapes from shadows being made thirty meters out. As another larger waves passed the object it rotated like a cork bobbing in the water and David's stomach knotted as Charlotte's pale face stood out clearly against her dark hair in the water before sinking mellowly into the darkness. Shouting her name he made his way as quickly as he could into the surf struggling against the resisting water which held him back with more strength the closer he got.

Approaching the area he saw her last, now with water pushing him around from his elbows down, he tried to steady himself on the bottom shouting her name and spinning around looking in all directions. Another wave crescent gave an apparition ten meters away momentarily. Jumping into the water he swam against the mixing of the tide and desperately grabbed under the water before spotting her in the water being carried away by the current. As the next wave approached he jump with it and the two of them were drawn together as he manage to clasp his hand on to her wet hair. Grasping and clamping tightly to the final strands of his connection to her he was thrown under the water and spun but refuse to let go. Disorientated he hit the surface seeing her lifeless body slip over the next wave giving him an opportunity to grasp her blue sweatshirt and tug her back so he could grip under her arms and aim for shore. Really pushing against the tide he shouted her name and was relieved to see her eyes open. After a moment of clarity between the two her survival instincts were awoken as her mind came back from the darkness. Crying out she panicked and then kicked under David's aggressive insistence moving them finally towards the shoreline. After a minute of exhaustive kicking David felt the shallowness beneath his feet and took the weight of her body dragging her towards safety. With the shallow incline he was still over ten meters from dry land as the water went below his knees and at this point he picked her over his shoulder desperate to get her out of the water. Her body convulsed with cold as feeling entered her once again bringing the pain back in. As he reached the sand he continued a few meters before he fell forward from exhaustion cradling Charlotte as they hit the sand. Lying on the sand he supported her head as he gasped for air and he tensed his body resisting the desire to shiver from the coldness of the water. He said nothing as he captured his breath just looking down at her for a few moments until she looked up as she coughed and sobbed.

'What the hell were you doing'? He shouted angrily. 'You nearly died out there'.

'I'm sorry, I am so sorry'. She cried.

'I nearly lost you'. David rose to his knees pulling her upward raising her head and looking at her in the moonlight. 'What were you doing'?

'It's all a lie isn't it. I have nothing, I have no one'. Tears flooded down her sand covered face.

'Look at me'! David shouted pulling her eyes up directly to his by holding her head at an uncomfortable angle. 'You have me. Do you hear me? You have me'.

'I can't cope on my own, you have your own life. You are a success. I can't be a burden on you'.

'Listen I didn't have a life until I met you, I thought I did but I didn't. You are part of my life now and I am here for you. I want to be here for you but you have got to let me be, you have got to let me love you'.

'But we hardly know each other', she sighed.

'I know how this feels. I know when you hurt I hurt. I know I want to hold you in my arms and not let you go until you feel better'.

'I want that'. Charlotte looked with some hope at David as he held her.

Feeling her body shivering more violently as the cold set in, David pulled her up to her feet and walked her to the camp adjusting his arms so he could hold her as they walked. Silently they unzipped the tent and David helped Charlotte pull off her wet clothes before putting a dry top of his on her. Wrapping her hair in a towel he lay her into the double sleeping bag and dried his short hair quickly as his pulled his wet clothes off. Laying down behind her he wrapped his arms around her, holding her and pressing his body against her trying to warm her up sooner. Feeling he had her safely back with him David drifted as the adrenaline wained and their bodies warmed each other. Awakening slightly as she rolled over he kissed her as she pressed her lips against his. Holding his body against her she needed to tell him and did it with almost inaudible confirmation which he felt through the lips that she gave him as he drifted asleep.

'I love you'.

CHAPTER TWENTY SEVEN

Charlotte awoke with a startle hearing Noah shouting to his dad in the distance down the beach. Lying in David's arms she felt warm and safe as he kept her close to him, protecting her even in his sleep. As David stirred he pulled her closer and silently they lay looking into each others eyes. David had so many questions for her and would need to make sure she was okay after the previous night but for now he just needed to be with her and not let her go. Kissing, their dry lips moistened as they opened against each other and he felt himself becoming more needing of her. Moving his arms under her t-shirt he pulled it up to where she wore it around her neck like a scarf not wanting to let her go for long enough to remove it. The two held each other's warm bodies against each other never losing eye contact. Slowly rocking, this was different to the first time. There were no nerves now, just the need of togetherness from their connection. This was not discovery but confirmation and they used each other for support whilst watching each other face to face. The two lay not willing to let each other free for some time following.

'Did you mean what you said last night'? Charlotte looked hopefully at David.

'Yes, every word of it'.

'You said you love me'? She pushed further wanting further confirmation.

'I do love you and I nearly lost you last night'. He said bringing her hand up to kiss.

'I am sorry, I felt like I had nothing left and I couldn't see forward. Everything I have done has been based around this lie'.

'You can have me moving forward if you want to'? David looked at her hoping she would agree.

'But you need to go back home and be you. I can't be an anchor on you'. She couldn't cope stopping him living his life.

'We will figure something out, I am not letting you go, do you understand'?

'Yes, I wont do that again'.

'How do you want to handle everything today'?

'I want to give Gladys her final memory and get to Aberystwyth. It is what we said we were going to do'.

'What about Gladys? She does love you. She did things the wrong way but she was trying to protect you'.

'But she lied to me for so long', Charlotte looked away unable to face the painful truth.

'I know but sometimes lies are told with good intentions'.

'For now let's just get on with today and I will think about how I can deal with her and this whole situation later'.

'What about Trevor'?

'She has manipulated him like she manipulated me. He is a victim of all this. He has been played by her and Herman Splythe'.

'He has really took a liking to Lynne', David smiled.

'Then he has a chance to be happy even after all of this'.

'So do you. But you have got to trust that I am here for you'.

'I do. I was just so scared'.

'Everybody is scared, and anyone who claims they aren't is just another liar'. David pulled her into him and she rested her head against his neck. Wanting him again she felt a responsibility to get up and start the day but she realised that life was about her now and she took his hand to show him her need.

The morning was a slower start than expected for many reasons with some emerging from their tents much slowly than others. Ziggy and Noah were busy playing in the surf as Charlotte and David headed to the Ynyslas Sand Dunes visitor centre to shower and freshen up. As Charlotte headed back over the sand dunes drying her hair she came across Lynne who was heading back toward camp also.

'You look like you had a busy night then'? She smiled at Charlotte who didn't answer. 'Me and Trevor have been pretty active ourselves'.

'That's good to hear'. Charlotte retorted in an uncomfortable uncertain response.

'Is it Charlotte'? Lynne seemed to get more intentional in her tone. 'It's just that I know you and my Trevor have a past'.

'Not really, just a long time ago. It isn't something I think about'.

'You can say that but I know Charlotte'. Lynne opened her eyes as if to make a point.

'Know what'? Charlotte was confused.

'How you look at my Trevor. How inside your body yearns for some of his love'.

'No it really doesn't. I am with David now'. Charlotte wanted to get away from the conversation as quickly as possible.

'Good. I just wanted to check that there isn't a problem here. So we are not awkward in anyway'.

'Well we wasn't but I am feeling a bit awkward now'.

'No need. I just needed you to know how things are and I am happy for you and David'.

'I understand you really helped him to try and catch me on the train the other day. Thank you for that'.

'True love can't be stopped. That is something you learn isn't it'.

'Yes, even if they hurt you'.

'He has hurt you'? Lynne suddenly looked angry as if she was about to find and tackle David.

'Not him'.

'Oh you mean the old lady? Well look I think you need to look back at all she has done right for you. Think about how different life would have been if you didn't have her. You can change your life going forward, you can't undo the past. No matter how wrong she may have been, it is clear she did it for you'.

The two were distracted as they saw Paul rushing to the camp and followed him in where he was very excited to speak to everyone about the coverage they were receiving. As Charlotte and Lynne arrived Paul was busy telling David and Ziggy about response on the internet.

'It had already gone viral since a train passenger put it on social media and by the time I put the website address out there, thousands of people had seen it'.

'That is incredible'. Charlotte chuckled.

'No there is more than that. It has been picked up by the BBC who asked me for the footage and want to do a telephone interview with one of us. They are going to be at the promenade to film us arriving and from the sound of it they are not going to be the only ones there'.

'What do you mean'?

'I mean thousands of messages on social media from people traveling to see us arrive. The response was huge before I even uploaded the full story and made the website active'. He continued with excitement in his voice. 'We have really been noticed on a big scale'.

'I wonder if Herman Splythe has noticed'? Ziggy questioned.

'From the number of missed calls on my phone I would say so'. Trevor interrupted.

'We had better get moving then' David announced.

The set off was prompt leaving behind Trevor and Paul who took the tents down whilst the others headed off. Gladys stayed with them in camp, she would meet them as they traveled through through Borth and then to the shop at Aberystwyth to ensure she could get to the seafront in time to see them arrive.

As they headed along the beach on the beautiful summer's morning more people started to join them walking a respectable distance but alongside them wanting to be part of this fascinating story. The public presence multiplied ten times as they arrived in the small sea side town of Borth at the end of the long stretch of sand. Greeted by the owners of the local zoo who donated food for the elephants, the team rested as they planned the next stages of their journey. The route would now take them up the steep hills via a quiet connection road between Borth and Aberystwyth where they would go as far as Clarach Bay. They then would use the low tide to walk the elephants from the bay around the temporarily exposed low tide sands and to the seafront in Aberystwyth, recreating history.

After a short break on Borth Beach the convoy headed up the boat ramp towards the road where several police cars waited. Approaching the officers who were stood at the entrance to the narrow road they were planning on taking, David felt his suspicions that they were not here in support of their journey start to come reality.

'Good morning officers'. David smiled as he and Charlotte led Oliver towards them.

'Sir, are you in charge of this party'? A lady spoke back to him.

'Well I guess we both are'. David pointed at Charlotte.

'In that case I am going to have to inform you that I cannot permit you to continue this journey as you are potentially putting lives of the public at risk and you could cause a public disturbance with this being a non planned or risk assessed event that does not have a council permission to go ahead'.

'This is ridiculous, we have traveled all this way without a single problem. Surely you can let us continue'? David tried reasoning with the officer. 'We are closer to Aberystwyth than we are to going back home'?

'I am sorry sir, this decision is not mine but I must enforce it. I cannot allow you to take the elephants any further'. The officer stopped as the public gathering was now being recorded by several members of the crowd. 'Please I insist, can you turn around please sir'?

'This is stupid. Just let us pass'. Charlotte got more annoyed as it became clear they were facing a problem. 'This is them trying to block us getting to the town isn't it'.?

'I am not sure what you mean'? The officer answered.

'Herman Splythe from Merriman Initiatives, one of the town's councilors. He doesn't want us to get to Aberystwyth because it will lead to everyone knowing about their plans to destroy the place'.

'May I remind you both that false allegations about councilors is against the law', the officer was now feeling pressured due to the awareness of camera's recording the incident.

'We are not making it up'. David pulled his back pack off before pulling out a small folder as he turned to the gathering audience. 'This is documentation from a meeting I went to earlier this week where Merriman Initiatives identified their plans to build a massive shipping dock to the south of the town. This is being kept quiet as the town is slowly taken over by the company until they have enough of a foothold to bring this plan in'.

'This is not the point here Sir. I am unable to let you keep going and moving these pets through'. The officer continued wishing she could turn a blind eye to this.

'Actually madam I don't think you understand completely'. Paul appeared with Gladys in her wheelchair as the crowd parted to let them through. 'Sorry to interrupt but I think there has been a misunderstanding here. This young lady is called Gladys Roderick and she is the legal guardian of these wonderful creatures. You see she was in Aberystwyth when the original photo of the elephants was taken back in 1911. Hard to believe I know but that makes her 112 years old'. Paul stopped looking around and realising the crowd had gone very quiet as they listened waiting for him to make his point. 'Her family were asked by the council to look after these elephant's grandparents and they would have the land they lived on to do this for as long as needed. Now unfortunately, the council led by Herman Splythe has decided the land should now be sold to Merriman Initiatives for a health spa and therefore Gladys and her adopted family will be homeless. This means that according to the paperwork which luckily Glady's was given by her parents, she is no longer responsible for these elephants and thus she is carrying out her final obligation of returning the elephants to their actual owners who are the council. Thus the continued travel along this route is in the interest of public safety otherwise my friends will be legally allowed to leave these magnificent animals with you to look after'.

'Let me have a look at that paper work please'. The officer looked at it with another lady before turning back and smiling at them. 'This looks genuine and it does explain that as long as you have the property you are the guardians. So you have been evicted'?

'I can confirm that as Gladys Roderick's accountant'. Trevor stepped forward.

'Well then I guess I have nothing else to do'. The police officer stepped aside.

'So we can keep going'? Charlotte asked excitedly breaking her smile when her eyes crossed with Gladys.

'No, that road is winding and narrow in places. You cannot go down that way as it is too dangerous'.

'So how will we do this'? Charlotte looked at David before the police officer interrupted.

'I will use our cars to close the road for an hour from here to Clarach Bay'. The officer smiled at the amazing news and support she was giving. 'Give us ten minutes and then I will radio down when you can start walking up it'.

The news sparked applause by the gathering crowd who soon followed the elephants up the steep incline and along the winding road as it squeezed between farmland. Today they were making impressive pace due to the clear pathway and surfaces they were walking along and as the sun rose into the sky the group felt positive. Reaching the police road block at the other end of the section, they turned and headed along the long straight road towards the beach in Clarach Bay. The road had now also become lined with people all recording and supporting the convoy as they passed through. Arriving at the shingle beach, the group stopped for a lunch break. The meager sandwiches they had planned to eat were quickly replaced by offers of picnic hampers by others who arrived at the beach wanting to share in the moment. Ziggy and Noah sat talking with locals and people who had traveled large distances as David and Charlotte finally got to sit down and rest. Almost forgetting the night before they chuckled as they looked at all the people trying to have photos with the elephants and how much of an event this had become. The public had demonstrated they cared and it which made Charlotte feel more positive about the world around her knowing that these people had come from far and wide to join them.

Charlotte's mood was short lived as several high end black cars appeared along the road behind the people gathering to see the spectacle. Walking to a higher vantage point she felt sick as out of the car Herman Splythe and several other men in suits headed along the road toward them. Running back down to David she warned him of the approaching threat and they got everybody to move back down to the elephants in an attempt to head off before the menacing party reached them.

'Going somewhere Mr Jones'? Splythe raised his voice without stretching it to a shout. 'I just wanted to come and finish this deal off that is all'.

'What is he on about'? Charlotte looked at David as the blood drained from her face.

'Little girl did you think all this was real? Did you think he actually loved you? That is very sad'. Splythe chuckled he grabbed a very quiet David's hand and shook it.

'What is going on David'? She looked at him with tears forming in her eyes.

'This man is a genius that is what is going on. You see he knew the biggest barrier to us getting hold of your land was these magnificent beasts and what to do with them. But by doing this little trip you have all officially vacated the land. Well now they are off the land and so we will be able to begin the bulldozing your little farm just as soon as the diggers arrive. You see I can thank young David for this. Now all that is left to do is wait for the trucks to collect these creatures and our business will be over'.

'How could you do this to me'? Charlotte cried at David. 'After everything we have been through? I thought you loved me'?

'I do'. David reached out to her but was repelled by her quickly moving away. 'This isn't what I planned. He is lying'.

'David if I was lying, how would I have the agreed contract to sell your land'? Herman turned to the man next to him who pulled out the contract David was given by his brothers. 'Now I know this is a difficult situation so I will let you two have a little chat but when the trucks arrive we will be securing the elephants. So I suggest you say goodbye to them properly'. Splythe turned calmly and walked away leaving the group in disbelief.

'He has set me up'. David turned pitifully looking at Ziggy as the others stared in confused anger. 'Ziggy I wouldn't have done this. He has set me up'.

'He has the contract David. How did he get the contract'? Ziggy demanded.

'I don't know, he must have stolen it from me some how'. David begged.

'How David, when exactly? You must have seen him for him to steal it'! Ziggy stormed away and David followed catching up with his brother who was looking out to sea at the water's edge.

'Ziggy I didn't do this. I need you to believe me'. David asked.

'I want to David but he has the contract and besides I think it is someone else you need to convince first. Don't you'? Ziggy looked over towards Charlotte who was sat on a large boulder further down the beach clearly shaken by the news of this betrayal.

David turned away from his brother whose son stood watching and headed across the beach with a heavy heart. Approaching Charlotte he stood behind her not sure how to speak to her. Before he could say something to reassure her, she sensed him and spoke not turning to look at him.

'You know, the last few days have been the very best and worst of my entire life', Charlotte told him whilst continuing to look out to sea. 'My whole life has been turned upside down and I don't even know who I am anymore. The person I loved most in this world for the last twenty years has been lying to me. I met you and stupidly like that evil man said I have fallen in love with you. Do you know how hard that is for me and how childish that makes me feel? I fell in love with you. Not last night, not when we first made love but that moment when you called me back to you at the train station in Aberystwyth. I turned and just fell for you at that moment. I am so scared David. So scared about Gladys dying, losing my home, about Oliver and the girls and what will happen to them. Last night I thought there was nothing left. Then this morning I realised I was wrong because I had you. That scared me more than anything because I knew it meant my life would have to change. I knew I would have to go to new places but I would have you to protect me. But I guess Splythe was right. I am just a stupid little girl who thinks I fell in love'.

'You're not stupid. I feel the same'. David pleaded resisting the urge to try and turn her around to face him.

'Do you'?

'Yes'.

'Then you need to do something for me David, and you need to be totally honest about this because if you lie to me now I need you to know I can't live with more lies'.

'Anything'.

'You said Splythe was lying. I want to believe you. I want this morning to be the first day of the rest of our lives. Our lives together. I need you more than anything but I don't need another liar in my life. I am not strong enough for that. I need to know what happened and that you love me enough to be honest. If you gave him that contract then there is no us David and I can't look at you again. If this is some evil scheme of Splythe to undo everything we are doing and you are telling me the truth, I love you more than anything', Charlotte stopped speaking and started trying not to burst into tears.

'What are you saying'?

'I am saying if you did as he said when I turn around you need to be gone and never make me have to look at you again. But if it is not true, still be here and I will believe you against him'.

Charlotte had made the first decision of her new life. As much as it hurt she was taking control and would not allow David to be a part of it if he was being untrue again. Wiping the tears from her eyes she started to turn hearing the sound of movement and making her worst fears build. Her heart jolted as a warm hand interlocked strongly with her fingers and spun her round. David grabbed her other hand and looked into her eyes.

'I did not give him that contract. Everything we have done is for you. I love you and I am never going to stop loving you'. He said with tears streaming from his face.

'I trust you'. Charlotte cried. 'I love you'. The two kissed with salty tears fueling their emotions, holding each other tightly.

'If you do then so do I', Ziggy interrupted patting his brother on the back before turning and heading towards Splythe. David and Charlotte tightly holding hands followed whilst wiping their tears away.

'You really are the snake they all say you are. That young lady, that amazing young lady has been through a hell of a lot this past few days and it is all due to you and this evil plan. You don't care who your company hurts do you? Why tell her that lie? Just to really hurt her emotionally as well as removing her from her home? Well you may be able to take our land and her home but you will not stop them or us being a family you cold son of a bitch'.

'Mr Jones, I have the contract right here. Why do I need to lie to you'?

'Because you have been embarrassed and your pride hurt by David choosing us over you, and it has taken the shine off this deal. Because you offered him a job in your soulless corporation and he has thrown it back in your face'. The crowd were now gathering around to see the encounter again with people recording it on their phones. 'Let me see that bloody contract again'. Ziggy demanded as Splythe was handed it again flashing it to Ziggy. 'Well it may be the genuine thing, I don't know how you got it but it is dated for tomorrow so at this moment in time that land is still ours and we are taking these elephants there. You can pick them up from there'.

'You can't do that', Splythe proclaimed. 'I am the legal owner of them now and demand you to hand them over to me'.

'The police informed us we needed to take them to a place they would not cause any public damage and in the most direct route possible. So we will do that for you by taking them into Aberystwyth and to your newly acquired land'.

'No wait they are perfectly fine to stay here'. Splythe demanded turning looking back to the police.

'Well I think you will find until they are safely moved they are still our responsibility. So you can have them upon delivery in Aberystwyth. Now be a good chap and clean up the elephant dung when we have gone'. Ziggy turned mouthing at the others to move quickly as they walked away leaving Splythe and his men watching. Quickly the group untied the ropes and started heading over the low tide exposed beach that would take them around the cliffs to Aberystwyth.

'Dad, is all of that true what you just said'? Noah asked Ziggy and they led Sienna with them from the main beach.

'I have no idea son but he can't make his company look bad. It was more about politics than legal truths'.

'Are we going to get arrested'? Noah continued.

'I hope not. You're mother will not be pleased if we do'.

Heading around the cliff face the group had renewed energy for the final part of their journey as they left the crowd behind them making it a more intimate end to their trip. Off the beach in the gentle sea they were joined by several canoes and a bit further off shore the coastguard who wanted to ensure they were not trapped by any change in the tide. Walking hand in hand Charlotte and David moved forward in their journey together with a now more acceptant Oliver in tow almost showing his understanding of the events with his change in behaviour. Behind them Lynne walked with Clarissa whilst Ziggy, Noah and Sienna followed behind. As each cliff edge was passed they drew closer to the unknown of how the town would react.

CHAPTER TWENTY EIGHT

Gladys was shocked to see that the promenade was full of people waiting to see the arrival of the elephants. The volume of people was making her gasp as she was brought down in her wheelchair from the coffee shop by Paul and Trevor who had been working on the social media awareness campaign. Using Trevor's understanding they announced the point of the trip to the public and explained carefully the plans of Merriman Initiatives. The promenade was not packed to the point of not being able to move but was full from the town pier to Constitution Hill which was at least half a mile in distance. People were picnicking on the beach and paddling in the water. Others were sitting eating fish and chips which could be smelt even by Gladys as they approached the beach. The town square was full with motorbikes from those who had traveled to see the spectacle and people leaned against their cars all wanting to be a part of this special event. Gladys felt like she was back in her youth with excitement. She felt that the day was just as important now as in 1911 and that this would be a nice way to say goodbye to her final three elephants. As they walked slowly down towards the bandstand where Joe had reserved some space for them earlier in the day, people recognised her from the stories and photo's posted on the website. Soon a clap of appreciation for her work begun making her weep with happiness. Turning to look down onto the beach and water she looked onward hoping that soon the travelers would make it home as she ignored the aching in her chest and eyes.

The journey had taken its toll on the whole team as they rested in the final cove before they would come around the cliff for the Aberystwyth seafront. David sat on the pebble beach with Charlotte and Lynne waiting for Noah and Ziggy who were scouting the best route around the final rocky outcrop before they would reach the beach. Lynne sat and looked at Charlotte resting her head on David's shoulder as he tried to reach Joe on his mobile phone but with little success.

'So what is next for you both then'? She questioned them when he moved the phone away from his ear. 'I mean I don't want to scare you young lady but in an hours time this little journey we have been on will be finished for better or worst and you are going to have to get on with normal life'.

'I don't know'. Charlotte said unsure of how to respond from the unexpected question.

'You are going to need to go to the police I bet'. Lynne continued as lighting a cigarette.

'What do you mean'? Charlotte asked.

'Well you not existing and all. You are going to have to tell them all the full story about how you ended up with Gladys and these three'.

'I suppose I do'. Charlotte looked at David. 'Do you think they will arrest Gladys'?

'I am not sure, she is very old now but possibly'. David responded.

'Do you want her to get arrested'? Lynne quizzed.

'No of course I don't'. Charlotte snapped quickly.

'Why not'? She puffed through the smoke.

'Because she thought she was doing the right thing. In her mind it was the only thing she could do'.

'Exactly me girl. That is why you have got to forgive her fully because you don't know how long she has and if you drag this out. You will be the one regretting it'.

'I know'. Charlotte nodded.

'You didn't answer me David'. Lynne looked towards him.

'What about'?

'Well what are you going to do? London? Aberystwyth? I think this girl needs to know'.

'I know, we are going to work it out once we are finished'.

'You see that you do'.

Noah and Ziggy came back up the beach from the water's edge to the others where Noah couldn't wait to speak to David.

'Uncle David, there are millions of people there'.

'What'?

'I don't know what Paul did but the sea front is the busiest I have ever seen it brother'. Ziggy smiled. 'It is incredible'.

'Well then we had better give them the visitors they have been waiting so patiently for then'. David stood pulling Charlotte up to her feet. 'Are you ready for this'?

'Yes'. Charlotte smiled and hugged David as Ziggy turned to them.

'We really need to go, we haven't go long until this tide turns this into a disaster not a celebration. It is coming in quickly and will trap us if we don't go round soon'.

The group quickly collected their bags and with the coast-guards watching from a far they pulled the elephants around the tricky final blockage of a large concrete wall containing a pipe which signaled their arrival back into the town. Taking their time to avoid a hazardous slip the team were knee deep in water as they first saw the crowds waiting for them. Television cameras were at the front, standing waiting for the first glimpse of them emerging into view. Hearing applause and cheering spurred the team onto the pebble of the beach as police cleared people back allowing then to start walking along the beach where the tide was still low enough to walk around the ground water pipes leading water back into the sea. Handing the rope to Charlotte, David walked hand in hand with her and enjoyed the beaming smile of pride and joy on her beautiful face as they waved to the crowd and regularly stopped for photography. Walking around the bandstand the elephants and their entourage came into Gladys' view. Charlotte walked Oliver up to the edge of the promenade wall and handed the his rope to David who watched as she walked up the steps and to Gladys. Smiling, David watched Charlotte conquer her fears hugging Gladys and then directing Oliver's trunk to her so she could stroke him before Paul was sniffed out. After a few minutes Charlotte moved back down and confirmed with David that she wanted to take them into the water so the exact memory could be recreated. Speaking to the others they all agreed they had come this far so David and Charlotte led them down to the waters edge and into the steep incline meaning after a few meters the water was up to their chests and the elephants were enjoying their mixed salt water bath.

Gladys shrieked with pleasure as her mind was taken back to 1911 where she first saw elephants enjoying mixed bathing with people in the sea. Looking out at the elephants she saw the same majesty and beauty with the same pier behind them contrasting against the blue sky of the summer time. For moments she forgot the pain and remembered only happiness as her life's work was finishing and she would soon be handing her adopted children to somebody who could continue to look after them once she had gone. She looked around at the crowds who were taking in the same memory she had locked in her mind for so many years. It would not mean as much to them but it would be remembered and talked about. It meant everything to her in her final days and she could see that for Charlotte it was the start of a new life with a lasting memory of happiness.

Ziggy sat on the sand resting and watching the unforgettable sight before them. Noah jumped up to his feet waving when he saw his mom in the crowd by the paddling pool on the promenade.

'Can I go and say hello dad'? He turned hoping not to upset

Ziggy.

'You go for it big man'. He smiled watching him run up the beach as he followed him to his mother. Looking up it was the first time in years he had made eye contact with Liz and he was quite relieved of the distance between the two currently. To his shock and unexpected relief she smiled at him and waved showing her forgiveness from time and moving on. Mouthing *hello*, Ziggy smiled back as he felt a warm hand cradle his causing him to turn away.

'Hey fella'. Paul stood looking at him and collected his second hand as he turned.

'Hey you. You did a good job advertising this then? How many people are here? Must be a few thousand'?

'Yes, but its you I wanted to talk to'. Paul gulped air down with a nervous swallow bringing Ziggy's attention to his clammy hands.

'Why what's wrong? Are you okay? You look a little pale'. Ziggy looked closer to his eyes as if to inspect his health.

'No, no I am fine just wanted to ask you something that's all'. Paul released Ziggy's hands turning momentarily before looking back at Ziggy. 'We have been together almost four years now and I know we practically do everything together. You know with work and then living in the flat together. I knew it felt right all that time ago but realised that you had Noah missing from your life. Now he is back with us and that void is filled so I think we should be more open. All the people we love accept us and any that don't quite frankly must have their own problems. So I was hoping that now your family is complete again and even David seems happy that we could complete our relationship'. Paul pulled a small box from his pocket and lowered himself down to his knee. Momentarily looking at the sand as there was a gasp from the crowd behind them, he looked into Ziggy's eyes. 'Ziggy Jones, will you do me the honor of making my life complete and marrying me'?

'Paul? Why now? In front of thousands of people'? Ziggy asked with a tear running down his face.

'I have been waiting for so long, but you were never truly happy. Not until you saw Noah yesterday. I needed a magical moment to ask you. I think this is it, I am not interested in anyone else, just you. Although I think they are waiting for an answer. Ziggy, will you marry me'? Paul looked on nervously along with the crowd who now were in an expectant hush.

'Yes, of course I will. I love you'. Ziggy fell down to his his knees where Paul placed the ring onto his finger before the two embraced each other as the crowd applauded and cheered in rejoice.

The crowd stayed a respectful distance from the group who now celebrated the news with them and hugged each other in celebration. Some of the press gained access to small inflatable boats in an attempt to recreate the *Mixed Bathing in Aberystwyth* photograph which the original event was captured from. Back in 1911 the elephants were then taken to Constitution Hill where mystery and a sequence of unknown events led to years of rumor and innuendo. Today however the plan was to take the elephants along the promenade and round the front of the Old College onto the land which the brothers had owned. So after they had frolicked in the sea with the crowds watching fondly the group headed back up the beach as the crowds parted taking photographs which they continued to upload spreading the word of the completed journey and linking it to the website Paul had built. Walking slowly up the ramp off the beach; David, Charlotte and Oliver waited for Paul and Trevor to bring Gladys to them and walk in front of them. For Gladys it was a a fitting end to her life's work leading her adopted children to the land where hopefully the news of their journey would have raised enough awareness to come up with a solution for them to be looked after now she could not longer continue to do so. The convoy took their last mile along the sea front and headed around the front of the Old College before making their way towards the land.

◆ ◆ ◆

David looked ahead and could see that Joe was waiting hand in hand with Heather next to a gate opened onto the newly fenced off land. Towards the far side of the field which had a stone wall running along it there was a quickly constructed barn full of hay for the elephants as well as an area for the elephants to play in the hay. The church next door agreed to a supply of water and Heather had brought a trough to fill with water from a local farm which the elephants would be able to drink from. Looking ahead in appreciation and impressed with the job Joe and his team had done, Charlotte smiled as they wheeled Gladys to the fence line in front of them. By the time they were ready the press were fully recording every moment as they took the elephants onto the land one by one and took off the rope which had guided them since they left their home. David stood with Joe and Ziggy. Charlotte walked ahead with Oliver to inspect the grounds before returning to them with a big smile on her face.

'I have got to hand it to you mate, this place is incredible'. David looked around. 'The fences are really sturdy and the barn looks great'.

'Thanks, I had a little help though'. Joe pulled Heather in for a hug. 'I understand you might have something to do with that'?

'Well I figured I owed you one, just don't mess it up this time'.

'No sir. What do you think of the barn Charlotte'?

'I think it's wonderful Joe. Thank you both'.

'Don't mention it. It looks as if this journey has been worthwhile already'? Joe pointed at Ziggy and Paul who were talking to Noah.

'Yes we have been busy, haven't we'? David looked at Charlotte for confirmation before looking at Gladys who was with Trevor and Lynne in the distance. 'Talking about things that need to be done'.

'I know'. Charlotte sighed and turned heading over towards Gladys who was watching the elephants in the field investigating their new surroundings. Seeing Charlotte approach she smiled as she sat next to her on the grass overlooking the whole scene.

'They look happy don't they'? Charlotte said looking out to the field and placing her hand onto Gladys'.

'Yes lovely they do'. Gladys smiled down at her. 'So do you with that young man'.

'I am happy, he did all this for us'.

'I know, he is a good man. You just make sure that you keep him being a good enough man for my little angel. You make sure he looks after you once I am gone because you deserve to be looked after'.

'You make it sound like you are going to die tomorrow Nanna'. Charlotte wiped a tear from her eye. 'We still have lots of time left for me to show you that I don't need looking after. I can fight my own fights'.

'I know you can love but it doesn't mean you don't need somebody to be with and to look after you. We all need someone to look after us. That Ziggy needed Paul, you need David, I have needed you for the past twenty years'.

'You haven't needed me Nanna, you have looked after me'.

'And I needed to do that. You were right what you said at the beach. I have been selfish'.

'I didn't mean it, I was just upset'.

'No, you did and you were right. At some point I lost sight of helping you grow up and become an independent person and I wanted to keep you safe. Safe but at home with me. You need to make sure he lets you spread you wings'.

'And do what? I don't have any qualifications or experience'.

'You just trekked three huge Asian elephants nearly thirty miles across every land possible from nothing. You can do anything you decide to if you only let yourself'.

'I don't even dare go further than Dovey Junction'.

'Well that is where he needs to help you'.

'Why did you never tell me about my parents'?

'I didn't think it would ever help you knowing they didn't want you'.

'I know they didn't want me or they wouldn't have left me, it just would have confirmed it for me'.

'I just thought it was best left alone'.

'Do you know where they are now'?

'They did keep in contact for a short while. The last I heard they were in Dublin but that was nearly twenty years ago'. Gladys paused as Charlotte tried to compose herself. 'They didn't deserve you my love. You were as beautiful then as you are now. They were only interested in themselves. You should have been their little girl but it didn't seem to make any dent on them'. Gladys stopped putting a tissue to her eyes. 'But to me you have always been my little girl. I am just sorry I just held onto you a little bit too tightly and for too long. But I need to let you go now for your own good as I do with the elephants'.

'How long do you have Nanna'? Charlotte weeped quietly gripping at her hand.

'Not long, weeks maybe, but I can feel it spreading. I wont be able to get around much longer'.

'I am so sorry for shouting at you yesterday'.

'Don't be. You just look ahead now my girl. You hear me, I hope that David is the man but regardless how it goes you just keep looking ahead and be the wonderful girl that I saw all those years ago'.

'I am so scared'.

'That is a good thing. Just face it and you will be amazed at what you can do. I wasn't ready to take on an elephant sanctuary sixty years ago but look at us now'.

The two hugged and talked more watching the elephants with the gathering crowds around them. Time heals all qualms but for Charlotte limited time allowed her to forgive and she was determined to make sure she spent as much time as possible with Gladys whilst she could.

Herman Splythe approached the field with his team and several police officers in tow. Dressed in his executive blue suit he had no crease out of place and looked as defined as ever with his perfectly presented grey hair and designer glasses shined to perfection. Walking directly towards the group David realised that the trouble was not over. Splythe approached, standing on the outside of the gate he waited for Joe who soon opened it to allow him and his team onto the field. Smiling like he had won a great victory he stood looking at them all before pushing his glasses up his nose and turning to Joe.

'I have got to say young Joseph I am quite impressed with this structure you have managed to build. I mean I do remember distinctly coming to see you yesterday and in our little meeting telling you that as a council officer I specific prohibited further construction on this land'.

'Why would he do that Splythe'? Questioned Ziggy. 'I think you will find that it is completely legal for us to build on this land as long as the structure is not permanent or is in the interest of the general public. I would say from the amount of people getting to see these beautiful animals and the recreation of them in the sea that this is in public interest, wouldn't you?

'Quite. Well anyway it will be of little consequence really. Indeed you have given us time to empty out the bungalow formerly occupied by Mrs Roderick and my men have delivered all their belongings to the only known location we had. Your coffee shop Mr Zigland. I trust that is okay by you'?

'I don't know what ridiculous law you have managed to manipulate to turf an old lady out on the street but you will get yours someday pal'. David mouthed at Splythe.

'David, I am very reasonable. That is why I offered you an excellent job the other day. Don't be silly, I am well aware of the legal ramifications of the old lady needing medical attention so I have arranged for her to be placed in a home under our expense. In Leeds'.

'In Leeds'! David blew with anger.

'Yes well the law says it must be to a certain quality and I think you will find that the home I have chosen is excellent. Its private. She will get the best care there if she chooses to take it'.

'Very good. You know she wont take it and leave Charlotte alone'.

'From what I understand she will be leaving her alone much sooner than she thought. That is a shame really because with you having to keep your job back in London now I am removing my offer, she could do with somebody to look after her interests'.

David lunged towards Splythe who stood his ground with a smile on his face as Ziggy and Joe pushed him backward. Quickly Charlotte headed over to calm David down pulling his face to look at her. With a few reassuring words he backed down stepping away from a smiling Splythe.

'She is a good influence on you David. If you would have touched me I would have pressed full charges'.

'You are disgusting do you know that'? Charlotte turned and rebutted at him.

'She is feisty David. She is going to find it hard to get a job with that attitude but then again maybe she will be able to go to the job centre with Trevor who I will also be letting go. Oh wait, no sorry you need a National Insurance number to work don't you my girl, silly me'.

'Are you actually here for something Splythe because otherwise we need to really talk to the town about your planned developments'? Ziggy asked.

'Now I am pleased you have mentioned that. You see you have already said quite a bit back in Borth. You just be careful what you say because should the wrong wording or claims come out of your mouth Mr Zigland, then I am afraid you could find a disparity lawsuit on your hands. It's a bit awkward you see as we have some history trying to make a deal. Now you are not happy you can't just go and spread unconfirmed rumors about us. It's bad business practice'.

'Yes very clever. Well I think the message is pretty much out there now anyway'. Ziggy looked around at the sea of people coming to see the elephants.

'True, I am sure in a weeks time that people will remember this for what it is. A rescue of three homeless orphaned elephants by the good people working in collaboration with Merrimen Initiatives'.

'What'? Charlotte scowled at Splythe.

'I really must thank you all for your help in this. I mean it wasn't essential, we had already signed the deal to take the land off your hands but you insisted on delivering the elephants to their temporary home before we can sell them to a good zoo'.

'I didn't give you that contract'. David shouted. 'How did you get it? Get someone to break into my hotel room did you'?

'No David. I never said I got it from you did I? Well if I did I must have gotten you three mixed up. You brothers all look the same. No it was Joseph that finally stepped up and delivered the contract to me yesterday. I just knew he would see sense in the end'.

'I'm sorry guys, I had no choice'. Joe hung his head in shame.

'Yes so there we have it. Everyone is a winner. Well apart from the fact that Joseph agreed to forfeit his share in the sale to pay for the cleanup of this monstrous construction he has built and pay for the security we will need. I am sure your brothers will share their percentage though Joseph'.

'People will see you for what you are Splythe one day' Ziggy snarled.

'A strategist'. Splythe smiled. 'I hope so that would be quite flattering. Anyway, if I could ask you to vacate this land now as it is property of Merrimen Initiatives'.

'Isn't there a cool off period in that contract or something'? Ziggy asked angrily.

'I made sure that it was exempt which is why you are getting so much for it Mr Zigland. Sorry you should have checked the details with your solicitor. Anyway if you can vacate the land now please, come along'.

'Don't worry, I just want to say goodbye to them first'. Charlotte headed towards the elephants.

'I am afraid not young lady. They are property of Merrimen Initiatives now. If you go any further you are putting your well being in danger and I will have to ask security her to escort you off the land'.

'Do what you have to do'. Charlotte turned defiantly and headed straight to the elephants where she pressed her hand on Oliver's forehead speaking to him. Within a minute Splythe called security who were slightly reluctant but soon escorted Charlotte off the property to meet the others.

Walking around to join Gladys the group felt deflated as Splythe gave his orders to his team to secure the site fully. Sitting on the grass they watched the elephants with the crowd as the weather changed and clouds rolled over them mirroring their feelings. For the the group it was failure. For Gladys it was goodbye and the emotions she felt were sadness but relief of finishing a long journey. Merrimen Initiatives had won the battle but for her it was the elephants who mattered and they were now being looked after and soon would have professional keepers. As the crowds started to thin the group walked towards the sea front.

CHAPTER TWENTY NINE

After a slow subdued walk, Joe and Heather split away to head home as the others made their way to the coffee shop which had been shut all afternoon. With bags of clothes and belongings piled up outside Ziggy chuckled at Splythe's childish effort to disrupt them as all the furniture was placed in front of and blocked the entrance to the shop door. Working together the group moved the furniture and took the important belongings into the shop placing them on the floor and in the storage room before sitting down together to try and digest the days events.

'I am so sorry, I thought it would have more impact than that'. David looked shamefully into his hot chocolate.

'Don't be silly, you made all of this happen'. Charlotte squeezed his hand across the table. 'If it wasn't for you then we wouldn't have done anything. You made people remember the elephants. You got us all here'.

'For what though'? David questioned. 'We haven't stopped them getting the bungalow, we have still for some reason sold the land to them. They have everything and now you and Gladys are homeless'.

'We wont let them end up on the street David. We have a spare room in the flat we can set up for you both, don't worry about that'. Paul interjected. 'It isn't luxury but we can sure make it comfortable'.

'That would be brilliant', Charlotte confirmed before looking towards Gladys sat next to her. 'You would be happy with that wouldn't you Nanna'?

'I couldn't be any happier than I am now my love', Gladys smiled looking tired at Charlotte.

'Hey listen. Why don't you take Gladys and have my hotel room tonight? She looks tired after today and I think it will be quicker than waiting for Ziggy and Paul to sort the room out. I can stop at their flat tonight'.

'Are you sure? I wanted to spend some time with you'. Charlotte questioned David.

'Yes, I don't go back to London until Monday, we can talk tomorrow'.

'Okay, I will get a few of our things and put them in a backpack. Can you help Nanna into the wheelchair for me'? Charlotte stood and headed to the back as Paul and David helped Gladys into the chair before wheeling her outside to wait for Charlotte.

'David, walk me to the sea front', Gladys asked.

'Charlotte will be out in a moment, we should probably wait'.

'No I want to talk to you for a minute'. Gladys insisted and David pushed her to the front where the two sat in the diminishing light of the cloudy sunset with David perched on a bench next to her.

'She wont be long Gladys, I presume you want to tell me something before she gets here'?

'I just wanted to make sure I didn't miss the sunset', Gladys stopped to capture breath revealing some of the pain she was in to David. 'I also just wanted to say thank you. You didn't have to do that today and all of this stuff. My Charlotte was in love with you the first time she met you I know that'.

'So why did you tell her I wasn't trustworthy'?

'Just because she fell in love with you doesn't mean you felt the same. I see differently now. I might be going blind but things still come into focus. You have given me my final happy memory between you two and I never thought I would see that again. You have given her a very special memory but you have got to give her more. I have made some serious mistakes with her David. She needs to see more places, meet more people but you need to keep her safe for me'.

'I will, I promise'.

'You know I am really happy she has found you now it is all out in the open but there is another thing that she needs to know about. Not yet but I really think when she is in a stronger place she deserves to know'.

'What's that'?

'Her mother was expecting a little boy at the time'.

'What'?

'He was born six months after they left her with us. I have a name and address from a long time ago. It is with my banking details'.

'Why don't you tell her? She should know'.

'She will know, when you think she is ready David. But she is to fragile now. She would blame him. He was not to blame for her parents selfish decision. He was as innocent as she was'.

'Why didn't you just leave this? I have got to keep this from her now'.

'When I am gone, she is going to feel alone. Having family is important'.

'She is going to be pissed. I can't believe there is another secret. Is there anything else Gladys? Because you seem to have more hidden layers than an onion. Is there anything else I need to know'?

'Just that I have a little bit saved up for her when I go'.

'She wont be able to get it, she doesn't legally exist yet. You can't have left her anything in your will'.

'Oh it's not in a bank David. It's in our special place'.

'What the bungalow? They wont let us back in there'.

'No, when the time comes just ask her and she will know where I mean'.

Charlotte appeared behind them crossing the road and sitting next to David on the bench wrapping her arm round his waist and looking out to the sunset.

'Are there sunsets like this in Wolverhampton'? Charlotte asked.

'No, I have been a lot of places and there is no better sunset than on this coastline'. David looked out to the horizon with her. 'I can honestly say that is true'.

'God has done a good job of painting the sky tonight Charlotte'. Gladys softly spoke looking out to sea taking the orange and blue collage in. 'He is giving us one that we can share together and remember'.

'I suppose I should get you back in though Nanna, it is getting cold', Charlotte looked passed David to Gladys.

'I am fine. I want to see the sunset tonight and share it with you my love. David can you let us have this time together? I want to end this special day with my Charlotte'.

'Not a problem. Are you okay to get her into the room'? David looked at Charlotte who nodded before kissing him and looking at him with a thanking smile. 'I am sorry we didn't quite pull it off today. I don't really understand why Joey gave him the contract. I guess Herman won in the end'.

'He hasn't won anything David'. Gladys turned away and smiled at him. 'You have both found each other, Ziggy has his son, Joey has Heather and even Trevor has Lynne. That land will not bring him what he wants. This place is too special for people like him. You mark my words this isn't over yet'.

David headed off back to the coffee shop leaving Charlotte and Gladys sitting holding hands looking at the sun sinking below the water as the sky darkened on their adventure. Feeling the cold Gladys looked weary as the clouds blew over leaving the moon in the sky, so Charlotte took her to the hotel where they would share a bed. Soon after showering Charlotte lay next to Gladys and watched her before quickly falling asleep feeling secure and safe with this lady who she admired and loved with all her heart. That night she had vivid dreams about the elephants both good and bad. From the best parts of the trip to finding David had done a deal with Herman Splythe.

Suddenly waking with a jolt in the early morning she felt the need for water. Getting out of bed she went into the bathroom. Heading back into the room Gladys was struggling to put an extra pillow under her head.

'Nanna, I will help you'. Charlotte lifted her weightless stiff body and placed her down onto the extra pillow.

'Love, do you mind opening the curtain slightly? I want to see the sea this morning. I can hear it through the window. I would like to see it for a bit'.

'No of course not Nanna, do you want your glasses'? Charlotte opened the curtain for Nanna revealing the dim early morning light showing the calm bay accompanying the sound of water lapping on the beach. Giving Gladys her glasses she lay down with her and held her hand as she closed her eyes.

'I love this view' Gladys said softly. 'You look beautiful when you sleep my Charlotte'.

'I love you Nanna', Charlotte whispered as she fell into sleep.

'I love you too'.

CHAPTER THIRTY

Apart from the pile of unwanted furniture which was now pushed to the side of the shop window on the street outside it was a normal morning in the coffee shop. Ziggy was busy cooking his mini breakfast meals in the kitchen listening to Lynne be as vile as she could muster to each customer in a way that was unique to her and made the abuse customers received when visiting Ziggy's in the early morning special. The coffee shop was not busy but steady which for half nine on a Sunday morning was as expected. Leaving the kitchen Ziggy headed around the shop to collect the empty cups and plates further suggesting he needed to either find a part time assistant or replace Lynne with somebody competent. Standing looking at the wall he decided he would replace some of his existing framed artwork with some of the more captivating photos that Paul had taken of the elephant's journey back to the town and select a modern version of their beach experience printed in black and white. He smiled to himself thinking about the trip and how proud he was to have been involved. He smiled more now his son was back in contact with him and accepted Paul and his relationship. His eyes then cast down to his hand where the black and silver ring was proudly worn and brought a feeling of happiness and completeness he had never been able to feel since he last spent time as a dad with Noah years previously.

'You happy people, you make me sick'. Joked David from behind as he hugged his brother.

'Well I think you must be quite happy. Have you just come from the hotel'? Ziggy questioned as the two sat in a booth. 'Lynne, hot chocolate for David please'.

'No I just came from yours via the elephants then straight here. I will let them have a lie in, Gladys was exhausted last night. To be fair so was I'.

'Is Paul up yet'? Ziggy questioned.

'Yes he was getting in the shower as I left so I imagine he is on his way'.

'So what is your plan today'? Ziggy asked. 'Spending a bit of quiet time with Charlotte? Have you decided what you are going to do yet'?

'What do you mean'? David acted naive to the decision he had to make.

'Well are you going to go down to London or are you going to stop here'?

'I don't know'. David clearly displayed the fret in his mind from his change in body language as he paused and waited for Lynne to put the mug of hot chocolate down without contemplation of its presentation. 'I want to stay but I have so many loose ends in London, and a job. A secure well paid job'.

'But you have Charlotte here'.

'I know but I can't just not go back'.

'Why not? Maybe a clean quick change will make it easier. What happens if you go back? Do you live with Kelly again? Do you do a full months resignation and not see Charlotte in a time when she is going to need you'?

'I don't know what to do', David shook his head as he drank the sweet hot chocolate exciting his brain in the early morning.

'Look can I just tell you what I think and then I wont hassle you again unless you want me to'? Ziggy looked at him fully intent on doing so regardless of his brother's reaction.

'Go on'.

'You have savings right'? Ziggy waited for David to confirm. 'So a deposit in London is going to be more than here. You also have a load of money coming presumably tomorrow morning from the land sale. No matter how tainted we cannot stop it now. You are in a safer financial state than most'.

'I suppose so'.

'So quit your job. You hate it anyway. Move back here and stay with us until you can find somewhere to rent for six months. Get a job and then look forward. But the main point is you will be here with Charlotte. She is the best thing that has happened to you in years. She has made you, you again'.

'But renting would eat away at my savings especially with no job'.

'Stop being such a business man and think with your heart not your head. Would you rather a small house in cold wet old Aberystwyth with the woman you love this winter or would you like a contemporary flat with an urban design. In other words small. Living on your own thinking about her every night and worried that she isn't going to bump into a man who will stay here for her'.

'Gentlemen, how are we this fine morning'? The two turned as Joe sat down with a coffee. 'I trust you both had spectacularly romantic evenings'? He waited with a smile on his face. 'No? Just me then. Well I must say I am happy it is Sunday today not Monday because I am shattered'.

'I am a bit surprised you have the nerve to come and sit with us after handing the contract over to Splythe'. David looked at him.

'Wait a second young David. I think you are not aware of the full chain of events here'.

'Go on then' Ziggy interrupted. 'Do fill us in on how it became you selling our land to that scumbag'.

'I didn't really get a choice in the matter. I was working on the fencing with Heather which by the way I think I owe you a thousand favors for. Herman approached me and held me at ransom for it'.

'How'? David looked unimpressed contradicting his own actions earlier in the week.

'He said I would lose all of my existing council contracts if I didn't get him the contract by the end of the day. I can't survive without them during the winter months. I had to do it'.

'Alright I get that but why didn't you let us know'? Ziggy

asked puzzled.

'Well I figured the wheels were already too far in motion at that point. Besides I am not so convinced he is going to get the last laugh'.

'Why is that'? David looked up from his drink.

'Well hopefully in the next few minutes I will be able to explain to you'.

'What do you mean'? David questioned.

'I have a visitor on her way to see us. Actually that looks like her now' Joe looked out onto the road where a lady carrying a office satchel headed over towards the coffee shop acknowledging Joe as she did so. Heading into the coffee shop Joe stood to greet and introduce her to the others.

'Gents this is Sara Fischer from the planning committee of the County Council. They oversee all the towns in Ceredigion not just Aberystwyth'. He stopped as they sat down. 'Basically, Herman gave me a few hours to get him the contract and so I headed back here in the of chance you would be back. You weren't but Paul was so I told him about it. He was pissed off that we were basically being blackmailed so I looked up online who managed developments and managed to get a contact for Sara. I emailed her and luckily she picked it up agreeing to speak to me quickly'.

'So what did you talk about'? Ziggly questioned Sara who was sitting patiently through Joe's explanation.

'Well basically Joe told me about the situation and I am obviously quite sympathetic to your cause. But I had to go away and do some research so I told him to do what he thought best and went through potential outcomes if my understanding was correct'.

'What do you mean outcomes'? David quizzed her keenly.

'I have spent a long time on this last night and had to call in some favors to get historical documentation about the site but I think you can stop the sale for definite'.

'How'? David leaned forward.

'Well simply put Mr Splythe has been cutting far to many

corners on planning applications and the sale of land has to have legal checks just like any property does which if not carried out can lead to serious issues'.

'What do you mean'?' David quizzed her further.

'Okay, your land for example was brought by your grandfather and has legally been passed down two generations to you but that land also has many gravestones bordering it which as part of the condition of selling to your father must be individually considered before any acquisition for development'.

'So you are saying that we can't sell it without permission of the church'? Ziggy asked.

'This is where it is difficult because it is so old and protection of burial site laws are different now to when your grandfather purchased the land but certainly while selling the land is probably okay for the right reasons, the suggested construction on it however is very difficult to agree with'.

'My God. So he was just going to ignore everything'? David looked around in shock.

'He was going to use his position to cut through red tape he said. So basically he was going to get it passed through under the table. Can he do that'? Ziggy looked at Sara.

'Could he have done it? Yes probably. Can he do it? Not legally. Will he be able to do it? Not following the massive public support of your awareness campaign no. I have been speaking to some colleagues confidentially about this and they think we have a good case to oppose development of this site'.

'I think I like what you are saying but I am not a lawyer. Can you put it in really simple words for me. Does this mean it is still our land'? Ziggy asked with excitement.

'That will depend on what you want to do. You will have the option to cancel the sale as there is a legal cooling off period or we will enforce the sale of the property for a basic evaluation back to the council where we will use it in an agreed way'.

'Which is'? Joe asked.

'It is agreed public land for recreation and for church usage. So in other words I don't think it will be able to be used to keep the elephants on but it will probably just be used for a picnic site'.

'Hang on a minute', Ziggy needed more confirmation with a growing smile on his face. 'You are telling me that stuck up idiot has brought land from us using all sorts of underhand methods meaning he can't pull out now and in a few weeks time you may be able to force him to sell it to the council for less than he paid for it and stop any use of the land'?

'Yes, if I can get to the right people today I will be contacting him tomorrow morning'.

'What about the elephants'? David questioned. 'What will happen to them'?

'They are and will until sold be council property and therefore council responsibility'.

'Will you keep the reserve open'? David asked.

'No, it was out of date and not a sufficient site so they will be sold to suitable homes but it will be done correctly. The sale to Merriman Initiatives of the reserve land is legal and above board. However, the council can't afford bad press on this. They made national news yesterday, people want to know what will happen to the elephants'. Sara stopped to look at her watch before standing. 'I am going to have to press on but Joe I will keep you informed of any progress'.

'Not a problem, thank you. Oh what about Charlotte'? David stood as she prepared to move.

'Ah yes the young lady. Well I spoke to a colleague who will give you a ring. Apparently, it is rare but not completely unheard of. They will have to get her in and interview her thoroughly as part of a series of checks to ensure she isn't lying about this to get citizenship but if she can answer the questions, she should be registered within a few weeks. I must warn you though, the elderly lady is going to be questioned about it. It could be pretty serious for her'.

The three brothers sat contemplating the conversation with a new feeling of success amongst them for the next few minutes as they talked back through what she had said to them.

'So do we want the land back? I mean Joe, he said you had

agreed to not get your share. That means we will only get two thirds of the original price', David explained.

'Hey look as far as I am concerned, I have got back with Heather. We are in a good place and with my history the more money I have the more likely I am to sway. No way should we buy it back from them. Imagine him having to answer to them suits higher up than him when they find out they are losing money on the land by being forced to sell it back at market value to the council after what he has offered us for it'.

'Yeah, he has played a very devious game here with us and almost won. If he was successful he would have changed this place for ever and not in a good way. I say we keep the money and just sit back and enjoy the ride, he is getting what he deserves. And Joe, we will split whatever we get with you fairly'.

'Definitely', David added. 'I wouldn't want to have to face Mark Nolands though'.

'Who'? Joe looked at him uncertain.

'He is the man in charge of their whole Welsh operation and Herman's superior I think. They were so confident this was a done deal. They thought I would snap the job up without a question'.

'Well they didn't bank on you falling for a complete stranger did they'? Ziggy smiled. 'And talking of beautiful strangers here she is'. Ziggy smiled at Charlotte who walked over to them looking out of character and pale. Her hair pulled back revealed the rings around her bloodshot eyes showing her pain and anguish. 'Are you alright Charlotte'?

Standing next to them she shook her head as tears streamed from her eyes and she looked away in avoidance as David stood reaching to hold her. Feeling her crumple into him at first for comfort but within moments as a necessity when her legs gave up below her. Lowering down onto the bench she pulled herself deeply into him as she sobbed unable to catch breath as David tried to calm her. Quickly, Ziggy went to get some tea for her nerves, returning to the table as David spoke softly to her.

'It's Gladys isn't it'? David held her whilst looking at Ziggy as she nodded unable to speak through her distressed state. 'Charlotte, I am so sorry. She is not in pain anymore though. She didn't have to suffer for long'.

'Charlotte, have some green tea, it will settle your nerves a bit'. Ziggy passed her a mug across the table. 'Have you let anyone know yet'?

'No, I just panicked and came here, I thought she was just asleep'. Charlotte tried to compose herself before taking a sip of green tea. 'That is disgusting'.

'We had better go and let the hospital know'. Ziggy said to David.

'She was still talking to me this morning' Charlotte explained interrupting their exchange. 'She asked me to open the curtain so she could see the bay as it got lighter. I put an extra pillow behind her head and fell asleep holding her hand'. Charlotte sobbed preventing her from continuing momentarily as she swallowed to remove the teary mucus in her throat. 'The last thing she said to me was that she loved me'. Again unable to continue she sobbed as David held her.

'That sounds like a lovely way to go to me Charlotte'. Joe lent forward insisting softly. 'Relatively sudden, watching the sea holding hands with the one person I held closest to my heart'.

'But I was so horrible to her the other day', she reared up sighing to get more air inside her.

'She didn't hold that against you', David said holding her. 'She loved you and she knew you loved her. She got to finish her life in the most extraordinary way. She told me last night on the sea front how special seeing those elephants back on that beach was to her. I think she knew she didn't have too long left and that is why she wanted to watch the sunset with you. Because she wanted some more time together with you'.

'But I should have known and rung a doctor'.

'Love, sometimes it is just the time. She was poorly. It was her time'. Ziggy reached across and squeezed her hand. 'Why don't we head over and call the doctor'?

Charlotte nodded and the others left David to comfort her for a while before heading to the hotel room and organising the collection of Gladys from the hotel.

CHAPTER THIRTY ONE

The rest of the day seemed to seep away into a blur of under-whelming pointlessness for Charlotte as they vacated the hotel room and took her belongings to the flat. Charlotte followed the others without a real interest in where she would stay. She replayed her arguments with Gladys over in her mind and blamed herself for putting her through emotional trauma in her final days. Once all of the belongings were moved she slipped out of the flat feeling suffocated from the attention David was providing in the kindest way and she walked. She walked along the beaches with her sandals in the surf trying to process her new life by closing the her old one. Eventually walking in the low tide under the pier she reached the section of the beach where the elephants had bathed only a day earlier and she felt close to Gladys' spirit for the first time that day. Sitting down on the promenade where she had gone to hug Gladys the day earlier when the elephants arrived she looked out to sea imagining them bathing in the waters again. Unaware of the passage of time she felt David approaching but didn't turn as he sat next to her asking if she was okay.

'I never truly understood what people meant when someone dies and they say you feel numb'. Charlotte responded with a slight sniffle. 'But I have felt numb all day. I know you were trying to support me earlier but I just needed to be alone for a while. Because I am alone now and I know you are here with me but she is the only person I have known my entire life or at least since I was a child. Everything I know, every fact, every opinion or idea I have stemmed from her. Now she is gone and I have no idea how to live a life without her. I really don't. I know I will find a way but I just don't know how'.

'Day by day, that's how. You survive to the funeral and then we stop looking backwards and look forward, together. You and me, here, together'. David held her as she sought reassurance of his promises in his arms. 'She will be watching over you, somewhere, she loved you more than anyone'.

'I know she is, I can feel her here. I know it sounds stupid but as soon as I got here I felt her with me. I don't feel numb sitting here. Knowing she saw the elephants here yesterday and that we sat on the benches last night together here watching the sunset. She is with us now I can feel it. That is why she asked me to open that window last night because she wanted her spirit to be able to come out here. I know it sounds silly but I can feel her'.

'It doesn't sound silly at all. It sounds exactly what she would do. Sit here with the final images of her memory projecting in front of her. She knew you would come here and she would want you to know she was here whenever you need her'. David stopped as Charlotte lifted her head off his shoulder and wiped the tears from her face looking out to the water where the elephants frolicked a day earlier. 'Listen, I will go and get a hot chocolate for us and some coats and give you some time alone with your thoughts and memories. We can stop out here as long as you need'.

David was gone for quite sometime and Charlotte did feel alone but believed somewhere near Gladys was with her as she watched the evening sky darken slowly on the quiet Sunday night. Happier memories filled her mind from childhood. The occasional tear leaked out in correspondence to them as she played through a collage of moments she had in her thoughts. Sitting beside her, she felt David was accepted by Gladys now and she trusted like today he would continue to protect her and keep coming back. He placed a coat over her shoulders and looked out to sea not saying anything but showing he was there for her. Turning to look at him as he passed her the large take-away hot chocolate she was taken aback slightly by the grin on his face which suggested he had done something mischievous. But with no confirmation as he simply turned looking towards the water. She took it no further and sipped the hot sugar rich comfort which would allow her more time sitting hoping that Gladys was with her. She didn't register the sounds at first with her mind being so far away but turned to see them beyond David's smile. Oliver seemed determined to run into the water and Ziggy released the rope in order to let him get their quickly as Clarissa and Sienna followed with a huge trumpet accompanied by Paul and Joe.

Gripping David's hand he turned to see a smile return to Charlotte as her heart filled with joy and fond memories. As she watched the elephants wade in the waters with the sun setting behind them, Charlotte turned to see the young child sit by her side and hold her other hand. Looking at her with a reciprocated loving smile they locked eyes and understood before turning back to look at the elephants. Charlotte was safe and happy protected by the two people she loved.

CHAPTER THIRTY TWO

'It is really good news Charlotte', David tried to convince her knowing it felt like she was losing another part of her past.

'I know', she turned smiling to him before looking across the field where they fed on the hay. 'You know, I don't think the security guards are coming back'.

'What makes you say that'?

'Well it is just that they have been gone for fifteen minutes now and they even took their chairs', Charlotte directed David's attention to where the two men had been seated when they stopped earlier en-route to the cafe.

'In that case you should say goodbye properly then'. David climbed over the fence before landing on the other side looking at her.

'Are you sure'?

'What can they do anyway? They are at fault for leaving them unattended. They left them for ages last night giving us time to take them to the beach for you. Besides that in a few weeks time they are going to be moved and yes we can go visit but you should make the most of the time that you have them here. They are your brothers and sisters'.

Smiling at him she quickly climbed over the gate and rushed to the elephants where she hugged Oliver as David watched from afar. He knew the more time she could spend with them would help her especially as they waited for Gladys' funeral to be sorted.

'Lovely image isn't it'? David was startled as he turned to see Herman Splythe in another pristine pin stripe suit of a grey tone matching his immaculate hair. Behind him were his security crew who had clear gone to collect him following Charlotte and David's arrival that morning. 'You spent some time with them last night as well I believe'?

'Herman for God's sake. You won. She is grieving so that will save you the money of finding a home. Just give her a chance'.

'I will do more than that David', Splythe stopped looking over to Charlotte as she approached and gripped David's hand.

'What do you mean'? David looked at him.

'I will give you what you want. You can have the elephants back and this land', Splythe looked at Charlotte. 'You can keep the creatures'.

'What is the catch? Why the change of heart'? David looked puzzled at him.

'After all this press there is no more plans for this town. You both put a stop to that. No you just sign a contract and you will get your land back and Merriman Initiatives will get its money back but will ensure all legal fees and expenses are covered. What do you think'?

'Sounds like are covering your tracks to me'? Joe interrupted accompanied by Ziggy as they approached their brother's side.

'Oh good, the whole inbred clan are here', Splythe chuckled.

'That is not a nice way to talk to people you are trying to do business with Herman', Ziggy suggested.

'Well lets not pretend this is what I planned, but you should be happy. You didn't want to sell the land to me. Sign a few forms and it is yours again'.

'So they must have found out about your dodgy dealings then and you think undoing the deal will cover it'? Ziggy pushed.

'I think it would just be for the best if we forget this whole deal', Splythe explained.

'It is a shame you put a non cool off period clause into the contract isn't it'? Joe smiled.

'I am sure we can come to some arrangement gents', Splythe seemed increasingly desperate.

'No thanks. We don't want it back'. David turned with Charlotte and headed towards the elephants before being spun by

Splythe's hand on his elbow. 'Now, now Herman. Don't push it'.

'You listen to me David. Don't make a silly mistake here sunshine. I know people. I know lots of people in our business who could make or break you. Now you have a decision to make in this moment that will change the rest of your working life. You can either work with me on this and I will make sure you have a career or you go for that cheap bit of skirt. But just think about it long and hard David because she may seem all you want now but how will she look in a few weeks when the honeymoon period wears off and you are stuck with someone who is too scared to leave this town, has no qualifications, no friends or family and is so clingy that even her own parents couldn't bare to be with her'?

Splythe was interrupted suddenly by David's fist which cracked onto his jaw as his body fell backwards like a tree being felled before bouncing on the ground. David looked down towering above his miserable opponent to the laughter of his brothers.

'Yes you laugh now', Splythe pulled himself to a sitting position shocked that his security stood uncertain behind him. 'But I think you have just give me the last laugh David'.

'Actually I want to just give you this'. Charlotte interrupted him as he turned to see that large bucket of elephant dung come crashing down onto his face and suit below it. 'That is what I think of you'.

'Get them away from me and off our land'! Splythe demanded his security to remove the brothers and Charlotte as he stood up trying to shake the dung of his suit and pointing his finger at Charlotte. 'You may be laughing now dear but least I am somebody. He is going back to London and you are going to be all alone'.

'Actually', Ziggy interrupted and looked at David. 'You left your phone at the flat and your boss called. Accepting your resignation and confirming you could use the holiday owed up but would then have to go back and finish your current project. It looks like he is staying all along with her'.

'Yes and even when he does go back to pack up his life in London. She has us to look after her', Joe nodded smiling at Charlotte.

The brief moment of solidarity was broken as David saw the police officers approaching through the gate towards them much to Splythe's delight.

'About time too, this man has physically assaulted me officers and this women has attacked me, sullying my good name and image with elephant excrement'.

'Now that is something you don't hear everyday'. Ziggy commented to a humored Joe.

'These thugs have attacked me and are trespassing on my land. I demand you arrest them'. Splythe smiled feeling he had won the battle.

'I will follow that up as soon as possible sir but we will have to get witness statements sorted after we are finished with yourself', the tall police officer stood looking at Herman's stained profile.

'What do you mean, finished with me'? Splythe looked puzzled.

'Herman Splythe, we require you to come to the station to help us with our inquires regarding alleged planning fraud and political intimidation allegations which have been made against you'.

'What do you mean'? Splythe's smile drained from his face.

'It looks like we are not the only ones who think you are full of it. You nasty little bully', Joe smiled as the officer insisted that Splythe went to the police car with them closely followed by his security team who were quickly making phone calls.

'Hot Chocolate David'? Ziggy smiled looking at David who was having his knuckles nursed by Charlotte.

CHAPTER THIRTY THREE

The whole story played in his head as he traveled through Dovey Junction and until he reached Aberystwyth. Feeling so real still he found it hard to believe it actually happened. He soon found himself walking down the platform and along the quiet evening streets. Ziggy's Coffee Shop was lit up like a beacon in the creeping darkness of the cold September night with its lights reflecting off the puddles that revealed to David what the weather had been like earlier in the day. Turning off his mobile phone he stood for a while looking inside to this hub of activity where everything had happened. Lifting his backpack from his shoulders and entering through the door as the aroma of coffee beans accompanied by the sound of relaxed conversation greeted him with a welcoming feeling long before anybody looked towards him. Busy with her back towards him he watch her using the shiny caffeine dispenser as he referred to it like an expert. Her shapely body being heightened by the Ziggy's personalised apron which she now proudly wore as an employee. Her hair tied back and with her new glasses on she turned to serve him as he placed his backpack down by the bookshelf. Within moments her regular customer smile turned in elation as Charlotte saw the man she loved standing in front of her for the first time in weeks. Not speaking she quickly skipped around the side of the counter and grabbed him by his hands pausing for a moment as she took him in before pulling for a warm loving kiss, gripping him tightly.

'I like the glasses'. David said looking at her as she pulled away to look at him.

'It is a benefit of legally existing, I can have a bank card and I can get some glasses. Seeing is brilliant, did you know when you wear these you can actually see individual blades of grass'. She stopped and leapt forward kissing him again.

'How blind were you? Did you actually recognise me when I walked in'?

'Well I have got to say it was a big let down', she smiled before leading him to a table. 'Hot chocolate sir'? Charlotte headed back to the counter and went towards the back of the shop to let Ziggy know before emerging again and making David a drink. Within a few moments Ziggy and Paul appeared looking happier than ever and went over to join them, embracing him. The three sat as Charlotte finished up her shift with David unable to take his eyes off the woman he loved.

'Good to be back is it David'? Paul smiled. 'You aren't interested in us are you'?

'Sorry, she just looks so happy and confident. She is beautiful'.

'You look all you want brother, you haven't seen her in three weeks'. Ziggy turned to look at Charlotte before looking back lowering his voice slightly. 'She is doing really well, she should be fully trained by the time Lynne packs up to go and live in Aberdyfith with Trevor'.

'She is a pain to live with though mate', Paul laughed. 'She has tidied our flat up and organised all our films. I don't envy you going flat hunting with her. Going to be a hard fight if you don't agree'.

'She can have which ever one she wants', David smiled looking across at her.

'Good method. I wish you luck'.

'How was she after I left'? David asked.

'A bit quiet for a while. I think after Gladys' funeral and then with you leaving she just felt alone for a bit but then as I increased her hours she kept herself busy and you know it just gets easier doesn't it. Noah was a good distraction for her, he really likes her. You may have some competition there'! Ziggy laughed. 'I mean don't get me wrong you can see it on her face sometimes and she has gone on a few long walks to clear her head but I think she is coping. It has been hard this last day or so. I think she was missing someone but I can't think who it was'.

'Well I missed her'. David smiled 'I can't believe I am here, I can't believe we are going on this trip together'.

'No, I must admit your first romantic get away is a strange choice but again I am guessing her choice'? Paul questioned.

'Yeah I am not quite sure what she is expecting'. David answered.

'I think she is expecting Disneyland the way she has been going on about it this last week', laughed Paul.

'It doesn't matter does it. The fact is you are back for good now to start a new life with her. You can't stop smiling and I don't know when the last time I saw you looking like that was'.

'How are things with Joe and Heather? He said they were good when I text him but they are going away this weekend'?

'Yes, they have gone to face her parents together for the first time since they got back together. Do you know they put an offer in to buy a new place together'? Ziggy asked.

'Yeah he said. Good old Herman Splythe hey. That money has come in useful after all'. David sat back relaxing more into the chair. 'How is old Herman anyway'?

'Office is packed up and the company seems to have pulled out of the area completely. Our land, the flats and even from what I understand Charlotte's old place. Don't know about Herman but his name is no longer on the councilor pages of the website. From what Joe found out we just opened a can of worms. He had been taking liberties and bending rules and paying people off for years'.

'And what about the land'? David looked at the recreation of the elephants bathing taken only two months earlier on the wall. 'What have they done with it now'?

'Just took it all down and cleaned it up once they moved them to the zoo'.

'Yeah I am pleased it was a safari park where they can roam a bit more freely, lots of land and stuff'.

'Not going to lie to you bro, she found that day the hardest

I think as her past was packed up and moved away'. Ziggy explained. 'But you know we are all moving forward now aren't we? You are going off on a trip of adventure and we are venue shopping this weekend'.

'I am really happy for you guys, I am'. David smiled.

'We were wondering about that actually'. Paul interrupted. 'We would really like Joe and you to both be our best men. What do you think'?

'Of course I will, I would be honored'.

'Well you did give us the magical moment with the elephants on the beach for me to ask him so I think it is only right'. Paul smiled at David.

'Charlotte', Ziggy called her over to the table where she sat next to David squeezing his hand. 'This city slicker here has packed his things into a removal van and then sat for five hours on a train to get here to see you and it wasn't just for your hot chocolate and his fondness of clean fresh sea air. You finish off early tonight and you two have the flat for a few hours. We will close up later and go and have some food. I imagine you probably want to spend some time alone without worrying about being quiet because of us'.

'Are you sure'? Charlotte asked shyly somewhat embarrassed by her want to take him up on the offer as he nodded. 'I will get my stuff'.

The two headed back to the flat via the local Chinese takeaway on the seafront not wanting to lose their empty flat time to eating out. Walking along the promenade Charlotte stopped looking out to sea as they reached the point where they had watched the elephants enjoying their mixed bathing. David held her hand tightly as she looked into the water.

'Are you alright'? He asked her unsure of the response.

'Yes', she nodded looking at him and quickly kissing him. 'I am. It is still hard you know. I miss her but you know the more I think about it the more I am convinced she was there that night with us. She was happy David, she was as happy as she ever was thanks to what we did that last day of her life. She is here for me if it gets too much'.

'Good, so am I don't forget'. David smiled as she turned and hugged him.

'I know, I have missed you. I don't think long distance relationships are much fun'.

'No especially when you have never traveled further than Dovey Junction', he smiled. 'But look at least we have talked through everything and really got to know each other'.

'Yes but there are somethings you can't do long distance' smiling she kissed him slowly looking into his eyes longingly.

'I think this food is going to get cold, we have got better things to be doing'. David started walking.

'We will need something to eat though, we have a long journey tomorrow'. Charlotte confirmed.

CHAPTER THIRTY FOUR

Standing in the empty kitchen where Gladys had cooked for her was harder for Charlotte than she realised it was going to be. David stood back as she walked running her hand along the old kitchen units which showed their age now the other furniture was removed. Taking it all in she asked David to wait outside for a few minutes with Lynne and Trevor as she said goodbye to the home she had her whole life in. Leaving the cottage she placed a copy of the local paper from the weekend which captured the event on the front page with a headline of *Mixed Bathing Open Again* on the fire place as she stood alone in the room.

'Nanna, we are off to find the gift you left me. I am going to take a shovel because I think I know where it is. Anyway I just wanted to say goodbye to the old place with you. Goodbye Nanna'. Gently closing the living room door she left the house for the final time.

❖ ❖ ❖

Walking out of the village where Lynne and Trevor left them the two headed up the hill side away from the coast. Walking up a narrow footpath Charlotte led David into woodland and along a semi trodden muddy pathway climbing steeply. After about three quarters of an hour the two emerged on a clearing where Charlotte stopped. Turning as he caught his breath David was able to see miles down the hillside out to the coastline on this clear morning in one of the most breathtaking views he had ever seen.

'We used to come camping here as a child. I had my first kiss here'. Charlotte smiled. 'Nanna walked up here with me even until last year. Took ages but I could sit here for hours. I did when I was in trouble. Not many people know about it, only a few we brought up here'.

'So what do you want to do'? David smiled.

'Well I think knowing Nanna she will have got Trevor to bury it for her. So I am guessing it wont be hard to find. Maybe beneath the fire stones'.

Picking the black tinged stones up within a minute of digging the two uncovered a large metal petty cash tin. Deciding not to open it until they were at their hotel that evening she pushed it into her bag and the two headed off.

CHAPTER THIRTY FIVE

An hour later they arrived at the platform of Dovey Junction. The sun now warm as they waited in the very place they first met each other. Charlotte placed her bag next to a bench and looked out across the wetlands.

'You okay'? David checked on her finding his own need for confirmation irritating.

'Yes, just feels strange. Knowing I am not going back there, that's all'.

'Look we could look at putting an offer in if that is what would make you happy. We could modernize it and make it a bit more suitable for a family'.

'No, no. I don't want it. Honestly, I needed to go back and say goodbye to the place but I want to find somewhere new now with you and enjoy our new life together. Going on adventures like this one, discovering new things and experiences. Visiting exotic places'. Charlotte stopped and walked to the end of the platform where the track forked into its two separate routes where she looked up the single track before it split.

'What is it'? David asked grabbing her hand weary of her proximity to the edge of the track.

'It's just that I have been at this station hundreds of times over the years and have never gone in that direction passed this point. This is the first time I am going to do the same rail trip that my real parents must have done when they left me here. In fact this is the first time I have even looked up that way since they left me here. It was safe not to look into the unknown. I don't even know what is around that corner'.

'That is no different from any of us, nobody knows what is

around the corner'.

'Scary isn't it'? Charlotte put her arm around David's waist as they headed to their bags hearing the oncoming train.

'Not when you are traveling together'. David smiled.

'I am scared about this journey. My hands are sweating. I am happy you are here with me. I love you'.

David wiped Charlotte's hair from her face and kissed her gently.

'I love you too. Now shall we go on our trip'?

'Okay then'. A beaming Charlotte smiled turning and stepping onto the train. 'I could get used to this high life'.

'Yes a weekend break to sunny Wolverhampton. Life doesn't get any better'. David smiled at her innocence to the world shaking his head with disbelief as he stepped on the train and sat with her. The only two people getting onto the train.

The loud beeps signaled the doors closing and the train gracefully pulled away from the platform and into the unknown world around the corner leaving the station quiet and empty once more.

A Short Story by Eleanor Phil-
lips (aged 6)....

Once upon a time there was a mouse in a mouse hole and the mouse came out of the mouse hole. The was a cat there and the mouse wanted to get some cheese so she tip-toed. When the mouse got there she was tied because she tip-toed a long way and she heard something!

The cat got the mouse and the mouse saw something. It was a cage! So the moust squeezed out of his hand and the cat ran as fast as he could. But the cat accidentally ran into the cage and the mouse shut the cage door and she locked the cage door with a key and got the cheese.

The mouse got back in the mouse hole and then ate the cheese. She got back in bed and went to sleep.

The end.

Printed in Great
Britain
by Amazon